Also by Tina Folsom

Samson's Lovely Mortal (Scanguards Vampires, Book 1)
Amaury's Hellion (Scanguards Vampires, Book 2)
Gabriel's Mate (Scanguards Vampires, Book 3)
Yvette's Haven (Scanguards Vampires, Book 4)
Zane's Redemption (Scanguards Vampires, Book 5)
Quinn's Undying Rose (Scanguards Vampires, Book 6)
Oliver's Hunger (Scanguards Vampires, Book 7)
Thomas's Choice (Scanguards Vampires, Book 8)
Silent Bite (Scanguards Vampires, Book 8 1/2)
Cain's Identity (Scanguards Vampires, Book 9)
Luther's Return (Scanguards Vampires – Book 10)
Blake's Pursuit (Scanguards Vampires – Book 11)

Lover Uncloaked (Stealth Guardians, Book 1)

A Touch of Greek (Out of Olympus, Book 1)
A Scent of Greek (Out of Olympus, Book 2)
A Taste of Greek (Out of Olympus, Book 3)

Lawful Escort
Lawful Lover
Lawful Wife
One Foolish Night
One Long Embrace
One Sizzling Touch

Venice Vampyr

Oliver's Hunger

(Scanguards Vampires – Book 7)

Tina Folsom

Oliver's Hunger is a work of fiction. Names, characters, places, and incidents are the products of the author's imagination and are used fictitiously. Any resemblance to actual events, locales, or persons, living or dead, is entirely coincidental.

Cover design: Elaina Lee
Cover photo: Dreamstime
Author Photo: © Marti Corn Photography

Printed in the United States of America

1

Hunger clawed at him. He fought the urge that controlled him, the need that made him shiver like an addict on withdrawal. He'd never imagined it being this painful, this difficult to resist, yet the thought of blood consumed every minute of his waking hours. Even during sleep, he only dreamt of pulsating veins, of warm blood that still contained a human's life force, of sinking his fangs into a living, breathing being. But worst of all, he dreamt of the power it gave him, the power over life and death.

With a violent shake, Oliver tried to rid himself of the thoughts. But just like most nights, he was unable to shake off his lust for blood, his insatiable appetite for it. Quinn, his sire, had told him it would wane with time, but even after two months as a vampire, he still felt as greedy for fresh blood as on his first night after his rebirth.

As he slipped into his long dark coat and shoved a clean handkerchief into his pocket, he cast a look back over his shoulder. He'd never lived as comfortably as he did now, thanks to his sire. Quinn and his wife Rose had asked him to move in with them after they'd bought a large house in Russian Hill, a neighborhood in San Francisco that reeked of old money.

If he'd had a say in it, he would have chosen the vibrant and young area south of Market Street. It had become his hunting ground over the last two months. When he wanted to feed, he looked for a convenient victim among the partygoers there or in the Mission, but often he didn't even make it that far.

On those occasions when he allowed his thirst for blood to grow too severe, when he delayed feeding to prove that he was stronger than the invisible foe inside him, he barely made it a few steps from his front door before he attacked an unsuspecting resident.

He'd been hiding his affliction as well as he could from everybody around him, but they knew. Whenever one of his friends or colleagues looked at him, he could see it in their eyes: they thought he wasn't even trying to resist the urge to take a human's blood. They believed he was taking the easy route, when in truth, he was fighting with his inner self every night. Nobody saw the turbulent storm that raged in him, the ferocious battles he fought with himself.

Nobody observed him losing those battles and caving in to the relentless demand of the devil inside him. When it happened, he was alone. Lost. Without guidance.

Knowing he couldn't delay his hunt any longer, Oliver strode down the stairs of the old Edwardian home. Despite the age of the home, it didn't feel stuffy. Quinn and Rose had taken great pains to furnish the house with a mix of period and contemporary furniture and turned it into a place of welcoming warmth. A true home. Something he'd never had before.

He felt ungrateful now, just thinking that he was going against his sire's wishes. Quinn had given him everything he could possibly want: a secure home, emotional support, a family. His job at Scanguards, where he'd worked as the owner's personal assistant for several years, had changed after his turning. And for the better: while he'd loved working directly for Samson, the powerful and ethical vampire who had built Scanguards into a nationwide security company, he preferred his new title—bodyguard.

Even though he'd already been undergoing bodyguard training at Scanguards while he was still human, he'd had to start nearly all over again, because as a vampire, he was thrown into an entirely different division, one that took on the most dangerous jobs. He thrived on it, loved every second of it. Which made the guilt even harder to bear. How could he ever become as good a bodyguard as his colleagues, when he couldn't even control his own urges? How could he defeat an enemy when he couldn't even overpower the demon that controlled him?

Disgusted with himself, Oliver turned at the foot of the stairs and cast a long look down the corridor that led to the kitchen. There, a larder full of bottled blood waited for him. Every conceivable blood type was stored there, even the one that was highest priced among their kind, because of its extraordinary sweetness: *0 negative*. It would be so easy to walk into the kitchen, open the pantry and take one of the bottles of donated blood which Scanguards procured via a fake medical supply company Samson had set up years ago. So easy to simply unscrew the cap and take a swig. But even the prospect of gorging himself on the tastiest blood type around did nothing to quell the urge to hunt.

He'd rather sink his fangs into the neck of a homeless person, drink blood that tasted as putrid as the man smelled, because it wasn't about the taste of the blood, it was all about what it did to him. It made him stronger, more powerful, invincible. He'd never felt better in his entire life than after feeding from a living human. Because blood coming straight from a vein still carried a human's life force, making it ultimately more potent. It was like a drug to him, giving him an incredible high that he'd never experienced before, not even when he'd been human and had experimented with drugs. Blood coming straight from a breathing human was his drug now. A dangerous drug he should stay away from.

He knew the dangers of drugs too well: as a human, he'd been down that road, but thanks to Samson, he'd turned around and made his way out of the hellhole it was leading him toward. He had conquered the demons once. And he was determined to do it again. But it seemed more difficult this time.

Giving up the sensations that went through his body when he fed from a human seemed like an impossible feat. Wasn't this what it meant to be a vampire? After all, he fed to survive. Generations of vampires before him had done the same. Had they too fought with themselves every night before they went out to hunt for fresh blood?

There were still plenty of vampires who fed off humans every night. Most of the men at Scanguards seemed to be an exception, but did that mean it was wrong that he wanted something different?

"God, why?" he cursed under his breath, knowing that for tonight he'd lost the battle.

He stalked to the entrance door when he heard footsteps coming from the living room.

"Going out?" Blake's voice cut through the silence in the home.

Oliver didn't turn to face him even when Blake stepped into the hallway, knowing his eyes had already turned red, indicating that he was about to lose control. He was in no mood to deal with his so-called half-brother.

"What's it to you?"

"Look at me!" Blake ordered.

"Don't think just because Quinn and Rose asked you to keep an eye on me, you're suddenly my keeper." The two lovebirds had left for a belated honeymoon and traveled to Quinn's old castle in England, but unfortunately, they had made sure Blake stayed put.

"I'm not blind, Oliver. I can see what's going on."

Oliver took another step toward the door. "Don't get involved in things that you don't understand!"

"You think I don't understand? Hell, I've been around vampires long enough to know what's happening."

He felt Blake approach and tensed. A second later, Blake put his hand on his shoulder, and Oliver whirled around, slamming Blake against the nearest wall in a split-second, then holding him there.

"You think two months with us makes you an expert?"

He had to hand it to him: Blake didn't flinch, even though he could crush the human with his bare hands if he wanted to.

"No, but we live here as a family. I would be totally dense if I didn't see what you're going through."

Oliver snarled. "I liked you better when you *were* dense and clueless. Before you found out who we are."

Blake huffed indignantly. "I was never dense and clueless! So, get your fucking paws off me, because I know you can't hurt me."

"Can't I?" he taunted, even though he knew Blake was right. Quinn would have his hide. It didn't mean he'd have to advertise that fact to Blake.

"Quinn will punish you."

"You think you're closer to him than I am? You think if push came to shove, he'd take your side?"

Truth be told, Oliver doubted that Quinn would take sides at all. During the short time the four had all lived together, Quinn had tried to be impartial and not interfere in the fights he and Blake seemed to have on a regular basis. Even Rose had shrugged it off, claiming there was just entirely too much testosterone in the house, and it was therefore inevitable that quarrels ensued.

Blake narrowed his eyes. "I'm his flesh and blood. As well as Rose's."

Oliver let out a bitter laugh. "You've barely got any of his blood left in you. You're his fucking fourth great-grandson! His blood is already so diluted, I can't even smell it on you anymore. But the blood that runs in my veins, the blood that made me into this, it's still strong. And he knows it. I'm his son—"

Blake suddenly chuckled. "Fuck, you're actually competing with me."

Oliver pulled back, loosening his grip. "It's no competition when it's pretty clear who'll win it."

"I wouldn't be so sure about that, little brother. You might be a vampire. But don't think you're stronger than me."

Oliver couldn't help himself, but he had to cut Blake down a bit before he got too self-confident. "You weren't talking like that when I bit you."

Instantly, Blake's face reddened like a ripe tomato and his chest puffed up. Yes, he could still push the punk's buttons whenever he wanted to.

With more force than he had expected, Blake pushed him off, freeing himself. Then he jabbed his index finger into Oliver's chest.

"I swear to you, one of these days, you're going to pay for that. Your fucking fangs are never gonna get anywhere close to me ever again, or you're a fucking dead man."

Blake's hand moved behind his back, but Oliver snatched it and grabbed what he'd hidden in the back of his waistband.

Inspecting the offending item, he shook his head, then waved pointedly with the stake that he'd taken from Blake. "And you still haven't learned that I'm faster than you."

Then he tucked the stake into his coat pocket and addressed him again, "You should be careful what you bring into this house. If Quinn and Rose ever find out that you're arming yourself, they'll be pissed."

"They have stakes in the house too! And other weapons that can kill vampires," Blake defended himself.

"Yes, but those weapons are locked up. As they should be."

"Hypocrite!"

Oliver let the word roll off his back, noticing that it didn't have any effect on him. "I suggest you go back to whatever you were doing, and let me be."

"Or what?" his half-brother challenged, raising his chin in defiance.

Stupid!

If only Blake knew how he was provoking him right now. If only he knew how close he was to snapping.

"I'm very hungry," Oliver answered between clenched teeth. "Very hungry. And if you give me any more lip, I'm going to forget what I promised Quinn and feed right here. And once I'm done with you, you won't even remember."

Blake backed away, his single step echoing in the empty hallway. "You wouldn't!" But despite the words, his eyes showed that he wasn't entirely sure about his statement. Doubts had crept into his mind.

"Wouldn't I?"

The way he felt right now, he'd sink his fangs into anything with a heartbeat. Blake's stupid attempt at trying to keep him from going out had pushed his need too far. Hunger surged. As it crested, Oliver felt his gums ache. He couldn't stop his fangs from descending, reaching their full length in the blink of an eye.

A snarl ripped from his throat.

His hands turned into claws, the fingertips now graced with sharp barbs that could rip a human's throat out in a heartbeat.

Blake retreated farther. "Fuck!"

"Run," Oliver whispered. But the word was meant for himself, not Blake. "Run!"

Finally, his body reacted. Oliver turned on his heels and charged for the door that led down to the garage. He more fell than ran down the stairs and reached his dark minivan just as another wave of hunger pain ripped through his body.

Shit!

He had to get away from here. Far away, or he would hurt Blake, and he knew he couldn't allow himself to sink that low. Despite the fact that he and Blake fought every occasion they got, they were family. And hurting Blake would mean disappointing Quinn. And despite what everybody thought of his inability to control his hunger, one thing he didn't want to do was to lose Quinn's support.

Oliver jumped into the car. When the engine howled, he shot out of the garage and raced down the street.

His knuckles clutched the steering wheel so tightly that they went white. Again he'd cut it too close. One of these nights, he would not be able to pull himself back from the brink and would do the inevitable: kill somebody.

2

Ursula heard the determined footsteps that echoed in the hallway and knew what this meant. The guard was coming to get her. Every time it happened, she dreaded it. After three long years in captivity, one would have thought she would be used to it, but with every time, the disgust for what they did to her grew. As did the fear, the fear that she would give up the fight, that she would finally succumb and lose herself, become a mindless vessel that only existed to serve their needs.

Twice a night, sometimes three times, they called upon her. She was growing weaker, she could feel it. Not only physically, but mentally too. And she wasn't the only one. The other girls were in the same situation. They were all Chinese like her. Some young, others older. It didn't seem to matter to them, because it wasn't the women's beauty they were after.

She'd been barely twenty-one when they'd captured her one night in New York after she'd left an evening lecture at NYU. It was her last semester, but she would never finish it. How she had dreaded the final exams—how eager she was to please her parents! If only she had those kind of simple problems now. They seemed so trivial now, so easy to solve.

Getting up from the bed, she grabbed the frame and pushed it closer to the wall, hiding what she'd carved into the exposed wooden beam behind: her parents' names and address and a message, telling them she was still alive. Every day she survived, she added a date to the list, her carvings now covering virtually the entire area hidden by the headboard.

She had only started the carving at this place, to which they had moved her three months earlier by her own count. At her previous prison, there had been no possibility to do the same—the walls had been made of concrete. Why they had moved her to this place, she didn't know. But one night, they'd simply packed everything and everybody onto several trucks and deserted the building from which they'd conducted their bloody business.

When the key turned in the lock, Ursula looked at the door. It swung open, revealing the guard who had come to lead her to a room where the next customer was already salivating for a taste. She recognized him as Dirk, and of all the guards, she hated him most. He took obvious pleasure in seeing her suffer, in seeing her be humiliated night after night.

There were always four guards on duty for the thirteen-or-so prisoners if she had counted correctly, even though there were more vampires on the premises. Whether her count of the girls was correct, she could never be sure; recently they had brought in two new girls, and it had been a while since she'd seen a girl called Lanfen. Had she died? Had they finally wrung too much from her fragile body? Ursula shuddered at the thought. No, she couldn't give up. She had to fight on, hope that she would somehow be saved.

"Your turn," Dirk ordered with a motion of his head.

She complied as she always did, setting one foot in front of the other, knowing that he would use whatever means necessary to make sure she executed his command. And means he had plenty. She had been at the receiving end of each and every one of them and could say with certainty that she liked none of his methods.

As she walked past him, her head held high, she felt his body shift. Then his mouth was at her ear.

"I like watching you the best. You've got more spirit than all the others together. Makes it so much more exciting. Have I ever told you what a turn-on that is for me?"

A cold shiver of disgust ran down her spine.

"Always have to jerk off right after it."

Ursula closed her eyes and pushed down the bile that rose as a result of his words. How dare he taunt her with something he knew was beyond her reach and the reach of every woman they had kidnapped?

When she turned and glared at him, he laughed.

"Oh, I forgot, that's right, you can't get off, can you? Despite the arousal that we allow you to sense, you'll never climax. Pity that."

Without thinking, she spit in his face. "Sick bastard."

Slowly he wiped the spit off his face, glaring at her with red flickering eyes. It took only a second for his fangs to descend. Then the back of his hand hit her right across the cheek, whipping her head to the side so forcefully that she feared it would rip her head off her shoulders.

Pain seared through her, a feeling she had learned to tolerate to a greater extent than she'd thought was possible. A defiant glare still in her eyes, she was aware that he would hurt her no further. She was too valuable to them. He couldn't kill the golden goose. His leader would stake him for it without giving it a second thought.

Dirk was holding onto his control with his last ounce of strength—she could see it in the glow of his red irises and the way the cords in his neck bulged. For an instant, she felt pride wash over her. She had gotten to him.

One nil for the human.

"Watch out, Ursula, one day you'll pay for this."

"Not tonight, vampire."

Because tonight, a customer was waiting for her. And he wanted his merchandise unblemished. After all, he was paying a high price for it.

Ursula had overheard the guards talking about the amounts of money that changed hands, and she'd been shocked. At the same time, it had made her aware of just how valuable each of the women they held was. And that they couldn't afford to lose one. It gave her some leverage.

Ursula turned and walked ahead of him, refraining from touching her cheek to soothe the pain. She wouldn't give him the satisfaction of letting him know that her flesh still stung from his violent slap. She had too much pride for that. Yes, even after three years, she hadn't let go of it yet. It was what kept her going, what fueled her defiance.

"The blue room," Dirk ordered behind her.

She turned the corner and headed for the room at the very end, passing a small window that would have provided light during the day, had it not been painted black from the inside. As she entered the familiar room, she allowed her eyes to roam. It was a corner room. There were two windows, one overlooking the main road, the other the side alley that culminated in a dead end. Both windows were small and hung with heavy velvet curtains.

In contrast to the sparse bedroom that Ursula lived in, this room was furnished rather lavishly. Two large sofas upholstered with the same velvet as the drapes dominated the room. A small washstand was tucked away in one corner, a supply of towels and soaps stacked next to it. A shelving unit occupied one interior wall, providing visual as well as audio entertainment should the customers wish this distraction. Many didn't.

When she heard the door shut behind her and the key turn in the lock, she reluctantly looked at the man who sat on one of the sofas.

"Sir," Dirk said behind her. "May I present your dinner and entertainment for tonight."

Then he gave her a shove into the other vampire's direction and hissed behind her, "Play nice, Ursula. You know I'm watching."

As if she could ever forget that.

The stranger patted the place next to him with his palm.

"Since this is your first time, I'd like to reiterate the rules," Dirk interrupted.

The customer raised an eyebrow, but said nothing and simply continued to run his eyes over her body. His fangs peeked from between his lips, and she knew they had extended fully. He was trying to act civil, when underneath that calm exterior, she could sense his impatience, his hunger for a special treat only few were privy to.

"You may choose where to drink from her. But you may not have sex with her."

"But—"

His protest was instantly cut off. "I said no sex. You're here for a taste of her blood, not her pussy." After giving him a stern look, Dirk continued, "You will stop when I tell you to. No exception. Her blood is potent. If you take too much, there's no telling what will happen."

The vampire narrowed his eyes. "What do you mean?"

Dirk took a step closer. "I mean that you'll become delirious if you take too much. Like an overdose. Understood?"

He nodded in response.

"Go ahead," Dirk ordered, tossing her a sideways glance.

Ursula steeled herself for what was to come as she took the few steps to the couch and stopped in front of the man. Leeches, she called them. Because that was what they came here for. To feed off the girls imprisoned in this godforsaken place.

Raising his eyelids, the strange vampire looked straight at her. There was a coldness in his look that chilled her. But she suppressed the shiver that ran down her spine. The goose bumps on her skin, however, she couldn't prevent. A lascivious smile curved his lips when he noticed them.

"I take the neck," he said.

Figured! Most of them did. They loved digging their dirty fangs into her neck while they pulled her against their vile bodies, pressing their hardening dicks against her like rutting animals. Few drank from her wrist, and those who did, eventually moved on to other areas of her body, losing control over their actions as her blood drugged them.

It was the reason why a guard was in the room at all times, forcing the leech to dislodge his fangs should it become evident that things were getting out of control. The guards were there for the girls' safety, but in Dirk's case, Ursula knew he took particular pleasure in the act of watching her.

A firm tug on her hand made her lose her balance and land on the sofa. Before she could straighten, the leech was already on her, his strong body holding her down as the sofa cushioned her back.

From the corner of her eye, she noticed that Dirk had taken a seat on the sofa opposite, his legs spread wide, one hand already resting on his crotch. The other unhooked the walkie-talkie from his belt and set it next to him on the couch. It appeared that he would already start fondling his dick during the show he'd come to watch, only to finish himself off afterwards.

Disgusted, she closed her eyes and clamped her jaw shut. She would get through this, just like all the other nights. She simply had to block everything around her out. Think of a better place, a safer place.

A rough hand brushed her long black hair away from her neck, then jerked her head to the side. The leech's hot breath invaded her senses as his head came closer and his mouth connected with her vulnerable skin. Instinctively, she shuddered. A grunt came over the vampire's lips just before he pierced her skin, sinking his fangs into her.

The pain was only momentary. The humiliation lasted longer. It was only the start. As he fed off her, greedily drinking her blood, gulping it down like a man who'd just run a marathon, she felt the ripples go through her body again. Slowly, they traveled from her neck down to her torso, crawling toward her breasts. Her nipples were already chafing against her T-shirt, and the zipper of the vampire's leather jacket pressed painfully against her sensitive flesh. When the tingling sensation reached her breasts, it combined with the pain and sent a hot flame shooting through her body.

She cried out, unable to keep her jaw clamped together any longer. A groan from the leech was the answer, before she felt his hand wander over her upper body, fondling, grabbing, squeezing. She knew Dirk wouldn't stop him as long as he didn't try to stick his dick inside her, because he enjoyed watching her discomfort, almost as if he could see the shame that flooded her.

Shame, because the vampire's actions aroused her.

She knew it wasn't natural, simply a byproduct of the feeding, and there was nothing she could do about it; nevertheless, she was ashamed at the way her body reacted. The way her pelvis tilted toward him, how her sex rubbed itself against his hardening dick, how her nipples sought the teeth of his jacket's zipper to find relief. Relief her captors had been denying her for three years.

With every pull on her vein, more sensations flooded her body, igniting a need in her that grew to monumental proportions. It was like this every time. It made her writhe underneath every leech she'd ever had, rub herself up against the strangers who violated her body in this way, who took from her what she was unwilling to give.

But as much as she struggled, just as she did now, her fists beating against him at the same time as the rest of her body pushed against him with an altogether different motive, she knew she wouldn't win tonight's battle. The vampires were always stronger, their bodies hard and heavy, their hold on her unbreakable, and their fangs lodged so deeply in her neck that she dared not turn her head for fear of having her throat ripped out.

Even as tears welled up in her eyes, she panted like a bitch in heat, her moans mixing with those of the vampire feeding off her.

Dear God, let it be over, she prayed.

But just like every night, nobody was coming to her rescue. Just as nobody was helping the other girls who shared her lot. Even now, she could hear similar noises coming from the room next door, only louder and as it appeared, more violent. She felt a kindred spirit to the other women, knew what they were going through, and her heart wept for them, because it was unable to weep for herself. No, she couldn't allow self-pity, or she would lose her resolve and her strength.

The leech's hands started to become less focused, veering off their aim, the way a drunk's movements eventually became uncoordinated. Soon, he'd let go of her. Soon, her ordeal would be over.

A crackling from the walkie-talkie suddenly broke through Ursula's consciousness. Then a voice came through.

"Red room, I need help. Now! The client is going apeshit on the girl! Reinforcements now!"

Dirk jumped from his couch, cursing. "Shit! On my way."

He ran toward the door and unlocked it, when a scream came from the other end of the hallway where the red room was located.

"Fuck!"

Then the door was slammed shut and Dirk was gone.

Ursula waited a couple of seconds, listening intently, but there was no other sound at the door; he hadn't locked the room on his way out.

Was this her chance?

3

Ursula tried to shift ever so carefully underneath the large vampire, testing at the same time, how responsive his movements were. She took one of his arms and lifted it, noticing how willingly he let himself be guided by her.

"Oh, yeah," she moaned, "more, take more."

He needed to drink more of her blood so she could overwhelm him. She'd seen the effects of her blood on several other leeches. When the guard hadn't intervened in time, or more often when the leech was new and unaccustomed to her blood, he'd passed out like a drunk. She hoped to make this particular leech succumb in the same way.

But it had to happen fast. Dirk wouldn't stay away forever, and whatever was going on in the red room would eventually be resolved. Then he'd return, and her chance of escape would vanish in a flash.

In an effort to urge the vampire on to take more of her blood, she pressed her pelvis against him and clamped her hand over his ass, squeezing hard. She knew enough about vampires by now to know that their sexual drive was intimately connected to their drive to feed. The more she turned him on, the harder he would suck on her vein, the more blood he'd take. And the more she could drug him.

Why her blood and that of the other girls did that to them, she didn't know. And at this moment, she didn't care. All she cared about right now was how fast she could drug him.

"That's good, more!" she encouraged him and heard him groan in response.

His hand came up as if he wanted to stroke her face, but it fell limply onto the sofa cushion instead.

Another scream from down the hall sent a shock through her body. Then she heard footsteps in the corridor. No!

Please let it not be Dirk!

She held her breath, but to her relief the footsteps went past the room and grew fainter again. It was now or never. Once another guard was helping in the red room, Dirk wouldn't be needed any longer and would return.

Suddenly, she felt the vampire go slack. As carefully as she could, she took hold of his head and eased it away from her, careful not to be injured by his fangs. But she wouldn't have had to worry: his fangs had already retracted. However, he'd passed out before he could lick her wound, which continued to bleed. Had he licked it, his saliva would have sealed it, stopping the bleeding.

Using all her remaining strength—and it wasn't much since she could already feel the effects of the blood loss—she rolled him to the side so she could slide out from underneath him. Breathing hard, she sat up, but she had no time to catch her breath. Dirk would be here any second.

Getting up, her knees nearly buckled, but with sheer willpower, she soldiered on, one hand pressed against the bleeding incisions of the vampire's fangs, the other stretched out in front of her to lend her more balance. Knowing that there was no escape through the two windows, because she would break her neck jumping from the fourth floor, she stumbled to the door and yanked it open.

The hallway was empty. Closing the door behind her, she ran back the way she'd walked earlier. There was only one way out from this floor, because she would never make it through the lower floors, which seemed to contain the reception area as well as living quarters for the vampires who ran this operation.

There was a fire escape. She'd noticed it one night when one of the vampires had opened the blackened window at the end of the corridor where it made a bend to the right. It was her only chance.

She ran for it, stumbling several times until she reached it. Frantically, she tried to push the lower portion of the old sash window up, but it didn't move. Panic surged through her. Had they nailed it shut? She jerked on it again, this time more violently. Her breath deserted her and she dropped her head.

Why? Why? she cursed inwardly and slammed her small fist against the frame.

Then her eyes fell on the metal mechanism on top of the frame. The window was latched. It was one of those old latches from decades ago that simply held the window shut with a small lever one pushed from one side to the other; no key was needed.

Throwing a look over her shoulder, she quickly unlatched the window, then pushed it up. Cool night air drifted into the sticky corridor, making her shiver instantly. Her gaze fell onto the metal platform that was built outside the small window. The fire escape hung from it.

With haste, she squeezed through the open window and set her feet onto the platform, testing whether it would hold her. It bent under her weight, making her glance at the bolts that secured it to the building. It was too dark to see much, but she would bet that the metal was rusty.

Grabbing the handrail, she took her first hesitant step, then another one. Then she set a foot on the metal ladder, descending one story, then another. At the second floor, she stopped. The ladder came to an end. Panicked she surveyed the platform, then discovered a stack of metal that appeared as if it was a ladder that had been gathered up. She kicked her foot against it, but it didn't move. Shouldn't it go all the way down to the ground?

Gingerly, she stepped on it, putting more weight onto what appeared to be the bottom step. Her hand grabbed the rail next to her, and underneath her fingers she felt a hook. She pulled on it.

All hell broke loose. The ladder released instantly, coming down with a loud thump, taking her with it as her feet continued resting on the last step. The freefall made adrenaline race through her veins, but seconds later she came to a dead stop, jerking her body forward. A metal rod snapped, slicing into her upper arm. Pain radiated through her, and she slammed her hand over the wound, trying to soothe the pain away.

But there was no time to lose now. The vampires would have heard the noise and would investigate.

Blindly, she ran out of the alley and into the next street. She didn't know where she was. When she and the other girls had been brought to this place it had been night, and they had been herded from a dark windowless truck into the building without getting a chance at seeing their surroundings. She didn't even know what city she was in.

Passing by a sign for an import/export company, she dashed into the next street, running as fast as she could. The streets were deserted, as if the area wasn't frequented by humans. Somewhere in the distance she heard cars, but still she saw nobody.

As she ran, she tried to take in her surroundings and make mental notes of street signs and buildings she passed.

Her lungs burned from exhaustion, her arm hurt from its encounter with the metal rod, and she could still feel blood trickling down her neck. If she couldn't close those wounds soon, she'd bleed out. She had to find help. At the same time she had to get away as far as possible from her captors, because they were like bloodhounds. They would smell her blood and be able to track her down.

Turning into the next street, she didn't slow her furious sprint. She was running on empty, and she knew it. But she wouldn't give up. She'd come this far, and freedom was just around the next corner. She couldn't let it slip through her fingers. Not when she was so close.

Before her eyes, everything became blurred, and she realized instantly that the blood loss was robbing her of her remaining strength. She stumbled, then caught herself. Her hands got hold of something soft. Thick fabric. Her fingers clawed at it, then hands pulled her up.

"What the fuck?" a male voice cursed.

"Help me," she begged. "They're after me. They're hunting me."

"Leave me alone," the stranger ordered and held her away at arm's length.

She lifted her head and looked at him for the first time. He was young, barely older than herself. Attractive too, if she could even make that kind of judgment in her foggy state of mind. His hair was dark and somewhat ruffled, his eyes piercing, his lips full and red.

Despite his words, he hadn't let go of her arms, supporting her weight which would have made her knees buckle otherwise.

Looking straight into his stunning blue eyes, she pleaded again, "Help me, please, I'll give you anything you want. Just get me out of here. To the next police station. Please!"

She needed help. Not just for herself, but also for the other girls. They had promised each other that whoever managed to escape would send help for the others.

His eyes narrowed a fraction as his forehead creased. His nostrils flared. "What's going on?"

"They're hunting me. You have to help me."

Suddenly his hands clamped tighter around her upper arms, and the pain in her wound intensified.

"Who's hunting you?" he hissed.

She couldn't tell him the truth, because the truth was too fantastic. He wouldn't believe her, he'd think she was some crazy junkie if she told him about the vampires. Still, she needed his assistance. "Please help me! I'll do anything."

He looked at her intensely, his eyes boring into her, almost as if he was trying to determine whether she was drunk or crazy, or both.

"Please. Do you have a car?"

She noticed his eyes briefly wander to a dark minivan parked at the side of the road. "Why?"

"Because I've got to get away from here. Or they'll find me." She darted nervous looks over her shoulder. So far, the vampires hadn't caught up with her, but they couldn't be far behind. But she also noticed that this man was still the only one in the vicinity. If he didn't help her, she wouldn't make it. She couldn't run any longer.

"Listen, I'm not interested in whatever trouble you're in. I've got my own." He released her arms, and she would have fallen, had she not quickly gripped the lapels of his coat.

He glared at her. "I said—"

Desperation made her say words she thought she'd never utter. "I'll sleep with you if you help me."

He stopped dead in his movements, his eyes suddenly traveling over her, his nostrils flaring once more. Afraid that he would find something he didn't like, she slung her arms around his neck and pulled his head to her. Her lips found his an instant later.

4

Oliver felt the warm lips of the strange Asian girl on his mouth, kissing him, while the scent of blood wrapped around him. Was he delirious? He had to be. Nothing else made sense. Why else would a beautiful young woman just throw herself at him and offer him sex in exchange for a ride out of this seedy area? And why would she smell so enticingly of blood when he knew he was sated after feeding only minutes earlier?

Without another thought, he wrapped his arms around her and pulled her closer. Her lips tasted sweet and clean. It told him that she didn't live on the streets. Her body smelled fresh, despite the scent of blood that clung to her. Had she been in a physical fight or were his senses so sharp tonight that he could smell her blood as if it were oozing from her body?

When he swept his tongue against her lips, they parted instantly, allowing him inside to explore her. Despite the fact that he was a stranger to her, she invited him to play with her, to tangle with her tongue, to lick her teeth, to kiss her more passionately that he'd kissed a woman in a long time. Was this a preview of how she would be in bed? Passionate, sensual, wild? Had she really offered him sex?

At the thought, his cock began to swell.

Fired on by the way she pressed herself against him and kissed him with abandon, he intensified his kiss, telling her that he was accepting her offer, that he would give her a ride out of this area, and then, he'd give her the ride of her life. Once they'd left the Bayview area behind, he would park the van and take her on the back bench.

Getting hotter by the second, he slid his hand down her back, palming her jeans-encased backside. A moan released from her lips, and he drew her closer, but his thick coat prevented him from rubbing his hardening cock against her.

Before he had a chance to open his coat, so he could feel her body more closely, the girl went slack in his arms. Her movements ceased.

Shocked, Oliver let go of her lips and stared at her. She was unconscious.

Fuck, what had he done now?

Her head fell back, causing her long black hair to expose her neck. That's when he saw them: the two small puncture wounds that could only have been caused by one kind of weapon. A vampire's fangs.

Blood still trickled from them. Instinctively he pressed his fingers over them and put pressure on them to stop the flow of blood. No wonder he'd smelled blood. Two things became instantly clear: there was a vampire in the area, and he hadn't erased the girl's memory after feeding from her, nor had he finished, because he hadn't licked her wounds. No wonder she had told him somebody was hunting her.

Shit!

Oliver's eyes quickly roamed the area. In the distance, he heard hasty footsteps, somebody running, but he couldn't yet see anybody. No matter who it was, he couldn't just stand here with the girl in his arms. Be it human or vampire approaching, neither was allowed to find him here. A human in this neighborhood was most likely a criminal and Oliver wasn't in the mood for a fight right now, and if the vampire who'd been feeding off her was approaching, he'd be utterly pissed off that she had escaped him. And he fancied a fight with a pissed off vampire even less.

Without further ado, he lifted the girl into his arms and unlocked the car, placing her on the back bench before he slid into the driver's seat. A moment later, he gunned the engine and raced out of the neighborhood as if a pack of wolves were chasing him.

The girl's blood smelled more intense now, and he was glad that he'd just only fed, otherwise he would not be able to resist the temptation she represented and continue where the other vampire had left off.

At the thought of his earlier feeding, he shivered in disgust. He'd been so greedy and already so far gone that he'd attacked the juvenile delinquent without finesse, without care whether the kid saw what he was. Only afterwards had he had the presence of mind to wipe the kid's memory of the horrific event. He'd felt so bad about what he'd done, about how much blood he'd taken, that he'd shoved a hand full of twenty-dollar-bills into his victim's jacket pocket. But still it hadn't erased his guilt.

He still felt disgusted with himself that he'd succumbed to his hunger again, that he hadn't been strong enough to resist and fight the demon inside him. Would he one day end up like one of those junkies living in the streets when Quinn and Scanguards had given up on him? When they'd decided that he was too much of a liability for them? He couldn't allow it. He had to prove to them and to himself that he was stronger, that he could be trusted, that he could be responsible.

Gripping the steering wheel tighter, he veered around another corner, finally leaving the Bayview behind him and entering the South of Market area. Normally, this was where he fed, but for some inexplicable reason, he'd been drawn to the seediest of neighborhoods tonight. Was somebody trying to tell him something? Was his subconscious mind trying to show him how he would end up if he didn't get a grip on himself?

Oliver pushed the thought aside to make way for a more pressing issue: the girl on his back seat. First, he had to make sure that she was all right, then he needed to find out what had happened, and eventually he would have to erase her memory, particularly if she was aware who'd been hunting her: a vampire. It didn't matter who the guy was, whether Oliver knew him or not, because it was an unwritten rule to guard a vampire's identity at all times. Humans weren't allowed to find out about the immortal creatures living in their midst.

Oliver threw a look over his shoulder, but the girl didn't stir. He recalled the way she'd looked at him with her beautiful almond shaped eyes that were as dark as the night itself, how she had pleaded with him to help her. He had already decided not to get involved in whatever her problem was, but then she'd surprised him with her offer.

Had she really meant it? She must have been scared out of her wits to offer a stranger sex, just so he'd save her. And by God, he would have taken it, but now? He shook his head. He couldn't take the offer now. It would be unethical.

Unethical? the little devil sitting on his shoulder asked. *What's unethical about having sex with a hot chick?*

And she was hot. Long, black hair, a slender, delicate figure, small, but well-formed boobs, and then those eyes: tilted upwards, yet large, their irises dark as night, yet brilliant in their reflection. She was

Chinese, he guessed, but he'd barely heard an accent when she'd spoken, so she was probably a second generation immigrant and belonged to the large Chinese community of San Francisco. And she was more beautiful than any other woman he'd ever encountered. When she'd made her offer of sex, his heart had stopped for a moment, because he couldn't believe his luck. This beautiful girl was willing to have sex with him?

Oliver gritted his teeth. Everything was wrong about taking advantage of a frightened woman, even though his cock didn't seem to care about that fact. No, that particular appendage was more than willing to hold her to her promise as soon as she awoke.

"Ah, crap," he hissed under his breath.

For once, he should have listened to Blake and stayed at home and drunk the bottled blood in the pantry instead. Then there would be two fewer things he had to worry about right now: one, he wouldn't feel so damn guilty about having fed from an innocent, and two, he wouldn't have an unconscious young woman in the back of his van, whose brains he wanted to fuck out as soon as she came to.

Oliver turned onto his street and glanced at the mansion he called home. Only the lights over the entrance were illuminated, otherwise the house was dark. It appeared that Blake had gone out, since it was too early for him to be in bed already. Ever since Blake had joined them after finding out that Quinn and Rose were his fourth great-grandparents, he kept more or less the same hours the vampires kept. He slept until early afternoon and stayed up into the early hours of the morning. Soon, he'd most likely have adjusted completely and remain awake all night.

Oliver operated the garage door opener and drove inside, parking the car in its usual spot next to the stairs that led up into the house. When he switched off the engine, quiet suddenly descended around him. He opened the car door and stepped out. No sound came from upstairs. Just as well. He didn't want to have to explain to Blake what had happened, when he didn't even know himself what he'd gotten into. With some luck, everything would be back to normal by the time Blake returned, and his nosy half-brother wouldn't be the wiser.

Walking to the van's sliding door, he opened it and looked at his passenger. She still lay there without moving. He bent down to her, verifying that she was breathing—she was—then he scooped her up in his arms and carried her upstairs.

With his elbow he switched on the lights in the hallway, then headed for the living room, where he did the same. Gently he laid her onto the large sectional, snatching the woolen blanket that lay over the armrest, and covered her with it.

Then he stood there, looking down at her. When he'd been human, he'd taken care of injured colleagues often enough, but his help had mostly constituted of feeding them his blood so their vampire bodies could heal. While he knew that vampire blood too had healing properties, he was unsure what to do right now. Not knowing what the woman suffered from, he didn't want to take such drastic steps as feeding her his blood. What if she woke while he did so? It would only make things worse.

As he shoved a shaking hand through his hair, he noticed the girl move. Instantly he bent down to her and realized that she was shaking. It was clear that she had the chills.

"Fuck!" he cursed.

He could only imagine that the other vampire had taken too much blood and weakened her. When another chill went through her body, Oliver lowered himself onto the couch, took her into his arms and held her close to him, but her shivers didn't cease.

He needed help. Professional help.

Quickly he pulled out his cell phone and dialed.

When the call connected, he made his request. "Maya, you need to come to the house. I need a doctor."

"Oliver?" she asked in surprise. "Are you hurt?"

"Not I. A human. Come quickly."

5

Cain glanced back at Blake who stood next to Cain's car. He'd been just about to leave for his patrol when the human had shown up, asking for help. "I have no idea where he is," Cain said to his human colleague.

Blake frowned. "Damn it, damn it, damn it!" Then he shoved a shaky hand through his thick dark hair. "What now?"

Cain had been witness to more than one argument between Blake and Oliver, and this wasn't the first time in the last couple of weeks that Blake had asked him for help tracking down his out-of-control half-brother.

"You worry about him. I didn't think you guys got on."

"I care about what he does to those humans. Next time he'll kill somebody. You should have seen him tonight. He was like a junkie about to lose it." He let out an angry huff. "Quinn and Rose should have never left for England. How do they expect me to keep him in check? I'm only human!"

"Way I see it, it's not for you to keep Oliver in check, nor for Quinn or Rose. Oliver has to conquer this all by himself."

"Then why did they ask me to take care of him in the first place?"

Cain shrugged. "Beats me."

"How did you do it?"

"Do what?"

"Get that lust for blood under control?"

Cain closed his eyes for a moment, searching the darkness for an answer, but found none. "I don't know. When I woke one night, I just *was*. There was no overwhelming urge for blood, which makes me think that I'd been a vampire for a long time already before I lost my memory. So, I can't give you any insight there."

He kept his tone light, belying the fact that every time he thought of his past and came up against a wall of nothing, of impenetrable emptiness, his gut clenched. Something was just beyond that darkness, too far to reach for it, yet close enough to sense its existence.

"Sorry, didn't mean to pry," Blake said then let his eyes survey the area.

Cain waved him off. "So what do you want me to do?" Cain asked, leaving it up to Blake to make a decision. This was not his fight.

"Can you help me find him? You know better where a vampire would go."

Involuntarily, Cain chuckled. "If I knew that, I'd be able to find all the crazies that roam this city."

"What do you mean?"

He contemplated his response but considering that Blake was a family member of one of Scanguards' directors, Cain didn't think he was speaking out of turn by letting him in on some news. "We have some problems right now. There have been incidents of vampires going berserk. As if they were on drugs or something. Total whack jobs."

Blake squared his shoulders. "I haven't heard anything about that. Drugged how? I thought drugs don't have any effect on vampires."

Cain nodded. "They don't. That's why this is so odd. Scanguards got the first reports about seven or eight weeks ago. The mayor hired us to keep an eye on it."

Shocked, Blake stared at him. "The mayor? You mean the humans know about vampires? Fuck!"

"No, of course not! The mayor is a hybrid. I'm surprised you don't know that. He's like Portia, Zane's wife, half-vampire, half-human. Guess that's why he's even able to be a mayor, otherwise he wouldn't be able to perform his duties during the day."

"I had no idea. What does he want us to do?"

"Us?" Cain grinned, secretly pleased at the human's eagerness to get some action. "Only vampires are assigned to this job. Humans are barred for obvious reasons. So don't get your hopes up. Dealing with those stoned-out-of-their-skull vampires isn't an easy job. So far, we've always gotten there too late, and could only clean up after them."

"Shit. What else do you know?"

"Not much. We haven't been able to catch one and question him, but from what other vampires tell us . . . "

"What other vampires?"

"Civilians, informants; vampires who alert us to what's going on. They say that those crazies babble on about some blood that's like a drug. Total bullshit if you ask me."

Blake hooked his thumbs into his belt. "What do you think it is then? What's driving them crazy?"

Cain looked past him into the dark. "Good old bloodlust. Nothing else. If they tell you anything else, it's just an excuse to cover up their own weaknesses."

"But how do you spot it? Can't you prevent it from happening?" Blake wanted to know.

"It's not easy to detect, unless it's already in an advanced stage. The affected vampire will get very erratic; his reasoning becomes illogical, his lies more daring. And his aggression toward others increases."

Blake swallowed hard. "You mean like Oliver? He's gotten very irrational. And aggressive."

"I don't know, Blake, maybe you're just projecting things on him. But I don't see it with Oliver. He's just trying to find his way. Give him a chance. Don't suffocate him. Nothing good will come of it."

"You didn't see him tonight. He wasn't himself. He was like a wild animal, ready to rip my throat out."

Cain lifted an eyebrow. Blake was probably exaggerating a bit. The human certainly had that tendency. "I've gotta go and do my job. I'll be late for my patrol."

"You don't believe me? Listen, Cain, what if Oliver flips and does something stupid? And what if you and I had the power to prevent it, but we didn't? How would you feel then?"

Cain sighed. He hated it when somebody tried to appeal to his conscience. He knew he had one, but for some reason it felt like an old unused muscle that had difficulty reacting. As if he had put that particular part of himself on ice for way too long. Almost as if he hadn't been allowed to have a conscience in his former life. But now, it reared its ugly head.

"Fine, we'll go look for him."

But he didn't have much hope of finding Oliver. A vampire who didn't want to be found was as good as invisible.

6

Oliver yanked the entrance door open before Maya had even reached the top of the stairs that led up to it. Wearing a white doctor's coat over her jeans and T-shirt and carrying a small black bag, she rushed inside, barely glancing at him. Surprised at her outfit, he let his eyes wander over her. Maybe this was exactly what Maya wore when she performed her medical duties. Not that he would know. He'd never visited the little medical office she ran from the basement of her home.

"Where?"

He motioned to the living room. "In there."

Oliver followed her as she walked inside. When she reached the sofa and dropped down next to the girl, Maya turned her head to him.

"A girl? Figures! What did you do this time?"

She didn't wait for an answer and opened her bag, pulling out her blood pressure kit.

"I didn't do anything to her. She was like that when I found her." Well, not exactly. She *had* been conscious at first.

She tossed him a scolding look as she wrapped the sleeve of the blood pressure kit around the girl's upper arm and pumped air into it. "Don't lie to me. I'm not blind."

Maya pointed to the girl's neck where two puncture wounds were still clearly visible. Blood had crusted over them after he'd put pressure on them earlier.

"I didn't do that!" He huffed angrily. "You don't think I did that, do you?"

Her eyes narrowed before she turned back to her patient and placed the stethoscope at the bend of her elbow. "I don't want to hear any of it now. Not in front of her. You and I will talk afterwards."

"But I didn't—"

"Another word out of you now and I'll call Gabriel and have him deal with you. You want that?"

Shit! Not only did Maya not believe him, she was going to rat him out to Gabriel—for something he hadn't even done! But he knew better than to argue with her now. He needed her to stabilize the girl. And once she was awake, she could confirm his story and tell Maya that she'd been running from another vampire, not from him.

"I thought Gabriel was in New York."

"He is, but it won't take long for him to come back."

Oliver clamped his jaw together. "When she wakes up, she'll tell you it wasn't me."

"*If* she wakes up." Maya removed the stethoscope from her ears and unwrapped the blood pressure device. "Her blood pressure is dangerously low. What did you do to her? Drain her?"

Had the other vampire taken too much of her blood? "What if somebody took too much blood? What would you do?"

Maya glared at him, clearly not liking the way he'd framed his question. But he'd be damned if he admitted something he hadn't done.

"Maya, damn it, what would you do?"

"A blood transfusion. What's her blood type?"

Oliver shrugged. "How should I know?"

"After two months you still can't tell what a human's blood type is after feeding from one?"

"I didn't . . . " *Feed from her*, he wanted to say, but thought of it otherwise. Maya wouldn't believe him anyway. "I couldn't tell."

"Fine. Then we'll have to give her *O-Neg*. Every human, no matter the blood type, tolerates it. Is there any left in the pantry?"

Oliver nodded. He sure hadn't taken it, and since Quinn and Rose had been gone for a week already, nobody would have touched the supplies since they had been restocked just before their departure. "I'll get it."

"Two bottles," Maya called after him.

Oliver ran into the kitchen and jerked the door to the pantry open where a large refrigerator stood in one corner. Inside, bottles of *AB-Pos* lined up with bottles of *A-Neg* and other varietals. Every conceivable blood type was represented. Quinn had thought that maybe if Oliver found his preferred blood type, he would be better able to curb his hunger and resist the urge to hunt for blood. Oliver had humored him and said he would try, but in the end, even after tasting all eight blood types, he had no particular preference for either. Blood coming straight from a human's vein was still his preference.

Oliver snatched two bottles of *O-Neg* from the shelf and let the refrigerator door fall shut.

By the time he was back in the living room, Maya had pulled more supplies from her black bag: needles, a long elastic tube, alcohol, and some ties. She was already preparing the girl's arm by swabbing the inside of her elbow with rubbing alcohol.

"Here."

Maya gave him a sideways glance. "Swab the lid with alcohol, then push this through it." She handed him a needle that was already attached to a tube. "Hold the bottle upright for now."

He did as he was told while watching Maya binding the girl's upper arm with the plastic tie, then inserting a different needle into her vein. At the end of it, a plastic contraption made sure that no blood flowing back from the vein would escape.

"Are you done?" she asked.

Oliver nodded. "Yes, what now?"

"Turn the bottle upside down and hold it up. Give me the end of the tube."

He watched as the red liquid from the bottle started making its way down inside the long tube. Before it reached the end, Maya squeezed the end of it, so no blood could escape. Then she connected it to the needle in the girl's arm. Turning the plastic valve at the side of it, Maya released the pressure on the tube, allowing some of the blood to escape and with it the remaining air. Then she turned the valve fully. The blood ran to the needle, then disappeared inside the girl's arm.

Turning the valve a little more, Maya looked at the bottle, regulating the speed with which the blood flowed into her patient. With bated breath, Oliver watched as the level of blood sank with each minute. It was a slow process, but he stood there almost frozen, not daring to move the bottle in case it disrupted the flow. He only let his eyes stray.

The girl still looked pale, and her breathing was shallow, the rise and fall of her chest barely noticeable. At the same time, her beauty was undeniable, her lips seeming redder than any human's—maybe an optical illusion because of the fact that she was so pale. Her eyes were closed, but he still remembered how she'd looked at him: with desperation and fear in them. She remembered clearly what the other vampire had done to her. For some odd reason, he wished it wasn't so. Rather, he wished that she had no memories of what had been done to her, when he knew instinctively that her memories would clear him of any wrongdoing. Yet the frightened look in her eyes had cut right through his chest.

"You've done this before, right?" he asked Maya, keeping his voice low, not wanting to disturb the quiet in the room.

"During residency, sure." She shrugged. "A long time ago."

Oliver shifted nervously. Did Maya know what she was doing? "But once you've learned it, you never forget it, right?"

"Hardly." She glanced up at him. "I was a Urologist, not an Emergency physician."

Before she'd been turned—that's what Maya meant, but she didn't need to say it. Even he knew that much about her past. She'd been attacked by one of their own, one of Scanguards, and turned against her will. In the end, everything had worked out for her, and she had bonded with the second-in-command at Scanguards, Gabriel.

Maya pointed to the injury on the girl's other arm. "That aside, I'm sure I can fix this."

"Should I lick her wound?" It would make sure the injury healed quickly, probably within minutes.

"Did you wipe her memory?"

Surprised at her question, Oliver shook his head. "No, I didn't. I wasn't the one who did this!"

"Stop it, Oliver! I'm not discussing this now."

"But I am!" He sucked in a breath of air. "I didn't do it. I didn't bite her; I didn't drain her; I didn't wipe her memory. She practically fell into my arms, running from another vampire. She begged me to help her escape. So I did. And she'll tell you that when she wakes up."

"Give it up. Why do you still have to pretend? It's me, Maya, I'm a doctor; I can help you."

"No you can't!"

"Obviously not." She looked back at the girl, picked up her stethoscope again and listened to her heart. When she tucked it away again, she continued, "Since we don't know what she remembers, I'm not interested in having to explain to her why her arm healed miraculously, so I'm going to bandage her the regular way. No licking.

And certainly not by you. You've had enough of her blood already, don't you think?"

Oliver let out a curse. "Ah, screw it! You've obviously decided not to believe me, so why do I even bother? Once she's awake—"

"Yes, yes, I know. She'll tell us it was some other big bad vampire," Maya mocked.

"Before the night is over, you're going to have to apologize to me," Oliver prophesized.

"Don't count on it." Then she pointed at the bottle. "Time for the next one."

Again Maya turned the valve, cutting off the blood supply to the needle in the girl's arm. Oliver helped her exchange the bottles. Within a minute, the second bottle of *O-Neg* was being transfused into the beautiful Asian girl he couldn't keep his eyes off.

Had she really offered him sex for his help?

He stretched his hand toward her face, stroking tenderly over her cheek when Maya loudly cleared her throat. Immediately he pulled his hand back.

"Just wanted to see if she feels warmer than earlier," he lied. "She was shaking with the chills when I called you." Well, at least that part was the truth, even though his reason for touching her wasn't. He'd simply wanted to feel her soft skin and be reminded of the kiss they had shared for such a brief moment.

"A side effect of the blood loss," Maya commented and went about cleaning her patient's arm wound. It wasn't deep; rather it appeared to be only a superficial cut. She cleaned it out with rubbing alcohol, then placed Steri-strips over it before covering up the area with gauze and affixing it with tape.

When the second bottle was fully drained a short while later, Maya removed the needle and put pressure on the puncture wound, until the small opening stopped bleeding, then put a band-aid over it.

Oliver felt impatience grow in him. "And now?"

"Let's see if she responds."

Maya placed her hand on the girl's good arm and shook her gently. "Wake up. Come, I know you can hear me. Wake up."

The strange girl stirred, her head falling to the side, prominently exposing the puncture wounds on her neck once more. Oliver pointed to them, giving Maya a questioning look.

She quickly took a piece of gauze and saturated it with rubbing alcohol, then swabbed the area with it.

"Ouch!"

It was the first word from the girl since she'd collapsed in his arms. Relief washed through him. She would be all right.

Her hand reached for her neck as she opened her eyes at the same time.

7

Ursula felt a stinging pain as something wet brushed over her neck and raised her hand to slap it over the source of the pain: the puncture wounds. Darn, why did they sting? They'd never stung before when a vampire had licked them to close them.

Her eyes shot open in the same instant, and within a second everything came rushing back to her. She wasn't reclined on the couch in the blue room of her prison anymore, even though she lay on a soft surface. She had escaped the blue room and the vampire on top of her. She'd outsmarted Dirk. That thought almost made her smile. Almost.

If only she knew where she was and who the two people standing over her were. She tried to focus her eyes, but it took her a few seconds to truly be able to see the two in front of her clearly. The woman's white coat became less fuzzy and she read the stitching over the breast pocket. *Dr. Maya Giles* it said. Long dark hair cascaded over her shoulders.

Thank God, she'd made it to a hospital! Somehow, she'd escaped and managed to reach a safe place. Now everything would be good, and she would be going home to see her parents again.

As she shifted, her arm slid against a cushion, sending another wave of pain through her body—not strong, but nevertheless noticeable. She bit back a curse. It was all worth it. Her wounds would heal quickly, much quicker than the ones she carried inside her.

Her gaze drifted away from the white doctor's coat to the man who stood next to the doctor. She instantly realized that she'd seen him before. Out there somewhere. On the streets. Taking a deep breath, she collected her thoughts. It finally came to her. He was the young man she'd asked for help. Seeing him together with the doctor confirmed that he'd helped her in the end. He looked at her, apprehension in his eyes.

"You're awake," the female voice said, making Ursula turn her gaze away from him.

She tried to nod, but the action caused her discomfort as if she had a migraine. "What happened?" she asked instead.

"I took care of your injuries. What's your name?" Dr. Giles asked.

"Ursula. Am I in the hospital?" She scooted up, bringing herself into a half-sitting position, for the first time allowing herself to take in her surroundings. But what she saw wasn't what she was expecting.

This wasn't a hospital, but a private residence. By the looks of it she was in someone's living room. Why hadn't her rescuer brought her to the emergency room? Slowly she turned toward him, her forehead working itself into a frown. She noticed how he shifted from one foot to the other.

"I thought it would be better to get you to my personal physician. It was quicker. And Maya is the best," he explained. His gaze flickered toward the doctor who nodded in agreement.

"And you are?" Ursula pressed out.

"Oliver, my name is Oliver. You remember me, don't you? You asked me for help."

Ursula sucked in a breath. Her memory was fully intact, but at the same time, the experience she'd gained over the last three years had taught her to be cautious about what she admitted. Besides, she still remembered offering him sex for helping her. Was that why he'd brought her here, rather than driven her to a hospital? Was he going to cash in on her promise as soon as she felt well enough? And why shouldn't he? After all, she'd made a promise, and not only that, she'd kissed him to show him that she meant business. What virile guy would turn down such an offer?

She allowed her eyes to travel over his body. He was well built, muscular, yet lean at the same time. His jeans fit him like a second skin, making her aware of his masculinity. After the display of testosterone she'd been exposed to in her prison, she expected that the sight of such maleness would turn her off, but the opposite was true. The same feeling that had spread through her when she'd kissed him filled her even now. And this time she couldn't write it off as a side effect of the fear she'd experienced during her escape.

"I'm . . . uh," she murmured, wondering how to answer. Was it wise to admit that she remembered only too clearly what had happened?

The doctor dropped down on her haunches, bringing her to eyelevel. "You suffered from massive blood loss. Do you remember what happened to you?"

The blood loss! Her hand instinctively came up, wanting to touch the puncture wounds the leech had left, but in the last second, she grabbed the pillow instead, pulling it onto her lap. She couldn't tell these strangers about the vampires. If she did, who knew what they would do with her? First, they wouldn't believe her anyway. And then? Would they have her evaluated by a psychiatrist? Bring her to a closed institution? No, she couldn't afford this delay. She had to get to her parents and make sure they knew she was alive and safe. And then she had to send help to the other girls—she had made that promise, and she would not renege on it.

"Blood loss?" she mouthed, hoping she sounded surprised. "What happened?"

Oliver dropped down as well, bringing his face closer so she could look into his eyes. "When I found you, you were injured and suffering from blood loss. Somebody attacked you. You were running away from somebody."

Ursula shook her head slowly, pretending she was trying to remember the events. "I don't know. I don't remember being attacked."

"But you must, you told me," Oliver insisted, his voice strained, his forehead creased.

Maya put a hand on his arm, interrupting him, then looked back at her. "You were in very bad shape when I got to you. Your blood pressure was dangerously low and your heart was close to giving in. I gave you a blood transfusion."

Ursula's heartbeat instantly doubled. She knew it had been close. She knew she'd let the leech take more than other vampires had before him, but it had been the only way to drug him. However, she couldn't tell these two any of this.

"Thank you for saving my life, Dr. Giles."

"I'm glad I wasn't far. Now tell me, what do you remember?"

Ursula threw a cautious look in Oliver's direction, noticing how he parted his lips, as if wanting to say something. For effect, she pressed her palm against her temple. "I don't know. I was walking home after an evening class . . . "

"In the Bayview? There are no classes out there," Oliver protested. He leaned in.

"What Bayview?" she interrupted.

"The Bayview district of San Francisco. It's a bad area."

So that was where she was, in San Francisco. So many miles from home. At the other side of the continent.

"I don't remember how I got there." She allowed the tears that she'd suppressed for three years to well up in her eyes, lending credibility to her lies. "I can't remember anything, don't you understand?"

She caught how Dr. Giles shot Oliver a displeased look.

"But, that's impossible!" he objected once more. This time he reached for her, putting his hand on her forearm. "You must remember. You asked me to help you." His eyes bored into her, their blue brilliant in its intensity.

For a moment she wanted to move toward him, assure him that he was right, that she remembered every second of their encounter: the way his arms had held her, the way his lips had pressed against hers. Their kiss. The fleeting feeling of safety and the desire that lay beneath.

"Let her be, Oliver. Can't you see that she's in shock?" the doctor scolded him and tore his hand from her arm.

Oddly enough the spot now felt cold in comparison, his body heat having left her. Not wanting him to say anything else on the subject, Ursula asked a question of her own, "Who are you? Why didn't you bring me to a hospital?"

Oliver and the doctor exchanged an odd look. She noticed how his Adam's apple bobbed, before he turned his face back to her.

"As I said, I thought it better if . . . " His voice trailed off.

"I was closer than the nearest hospital," the doctor continued in his stead. "And time was of the essence."

While Ursula believed that time had indeed been of the essence, she wasn't convinced that it had been easier to bring her to a private home. "So this is your house?"

Dr. Giles shook her head. "No, it's Oliver's."

"Yours?"

"Actually, my, uh . . . parents' house." He looked almost embarrassed about his admission.

"I live only a few blocks away," the doctor continued. "Oliver did the right thing to bring you here."

Ursula looked at her arm and noticed the bandage that was wrapped around it where her skin had met with a metal rod from the fire escape and lost the uneven battle. It was true; the doctor had patched her up. She also felt better, not as woozy, and stronger too. In a hospital they couldn't have done any better either. She was well enough to leave.

"I thank you very much for helping me."

She swung her legs off the couch and pushed the pillow and the blanket off her lap, then pulled herself up. Instantly she swayed. Oliver jumped up from his crouching position and caught her just as her knees buckled.

"Got you."

His muscular arms reached around her, holding her up, reminding her of their earlier embrace. Heat suffused her cheeks, because a desire to rub herself against him to find release overwhelmed her even now in the weakened state she found herself in.

"Woah, woah," Maya called out. "I said I took care of your injuries, but that doesn't mean you're fit to get up yet. You're still too weak."

"I'm fine, I just need a moment." She pushed against Oliver, but he didn't release her. Instead he held her even tighter. Their gazes collided.

"Don't you remember what you said to me?" he whispered. "Not even what you did then?"

She knew he was alluding to her offer and her kiss, but as much as she wanted to admit the truth, she couldn't, because it would also mean admitting that she was running from somebody, and to explain why she had two puncture wounds on her neck. Anybody who'd ever watched a Dracula movie would know what this meant. All she could do was to deny she knew anything about it, so she could leave and return home. Home. See her parents. Feel safe again.

"I need to call my parents. I need to talk to them."

The doctor moved closer and addressed Oliver, "Let her sit down again." Then the doctor smiled at her. "You'll need to rest a bit first. You can talk to your parents a little later. First, I'd like to ask you a few more things."

Somewhat reluctantly, Oliver helped her sit down on the sofa. When she felt the soft cushions support her back, she let out a breath of relief. One more second in his arms, and she would have started panting. It was clear that the sexual arousal the vampire's bite had caused in her, had still not left her body. Even after what must have been an hour or even two after being bitten by the leech, she still felt the need to touch and be touched.

"You said you were walking home from a class. Where was the class?" Maya asked.

Frantically, Ursula scrambled for an answer. She knew nothing about San Francisco. But every large city had to have a college. Holding her breath, she answered, "The community college."

"Out in Sunnyside? That's far from the Bayview."

Ursula shrugged.

"Do you know how you got there?"

"I told you, I don't remember. It's like my memory was wiped clean." She looked away, wanting to avoid her scrutinizing look.

"Fine, I believe you. It must be the shock. It's not uncommon."

Relieved Ursula lifted her head and caught how the doctor's eyes narrowed as she looked at Oliver. His jaw set as if he was clamping it down tightly, and he glared back at Maya. It appeared as if a silent battle was raging between them.

Then the doctor turned her head back to her and pasted on a smile. "Why don't you rest for a little while?" She snatched the blanket from where Ursula had dropped it earlier. "Here. You'll probably be a little cold, but that's normal after the blood loss."

To her surprise Oliver took the blanket from Dr. Giles' hand and spread it over Ursula's legs. Then he gave her a sad smile almost as if he had a difficult chore ahead of him.

"Oliver, a word," Dr. Giles said.

He looked up at the doctor, then back at her. "You'll be safe here."

She quickly lowered her lashes. Had he realized that she hadn't really lost her memory? Did he know she was lying and wanted to tell her that the people who were chasing her would never find her here? Or were his words of reassurance simply a casually thrown away sentence?

8

Deep in thought, Oliver stepped into the library across the hall. Why was the girl lying? Why didn't she admit what had happened? Was she too embarrassed about her wanton behavior that she'd decided to pretend it had never happened? As if she were afraid that he would collect on her promise of a night of sex if she admitted that she'd made it. Was that why she pretended not to remember a thing? It was the only thing that made sense. Maybe he could somehow explain to her that he wouldn't force her to do anything she didn't want to do, if only she would tell the truth.

When Maya entered the room behind him, he knew she was pissed. If the glare on her face weren't an indication for it, then the way she now stood, her legs in a wide stance, her hands placed at her hips, left no doubt.

"Of all the despicable things you could do, you had to attack a young girl and leave her at death's door?" The words spewed from her mouth like a fountain of poison. "You really think I'm stupid?"

Oliver took a step toward her, squaring his shoulders. "That's not true! I didn't do it!"

"Bullshit! Your handwriting is all over it."

He narrowed his eyes, getting angrier by the second. He'd done awful things in the two months since he'd been a vampire, but he hadn't done anything to that girl. "I never touched her! I saved her from another vampire!"

"Give it up, Oliver! Why do you continue lying when we both know what the truth is? You nearly drained her and then you wiped her memory so she wouldn't remember you."

"I didn't wipe her memory! She's lying. She remembers what happened!"

Maya shook her head, disbelief in her gaze. "She doesn't remember anything! You made sure of it to cover your tracks!"

He balled his hands into fists. "If I really wanted to cover my tracks, why the hell would I bring her here then? Tell me that, huh, why? And why would I call you for help?"

She contemplated his question only for a split-second. "Because you felt remorse afterwards. It's always like that with you. Haven't you noticed that? You go on a binge, and afterwards you feel like crap because of what you've done. It's not any different now."

"You have no idea how I feel! You've never been through what I'm going through."

Maya narrowed her eyes and went toe-to-toe with him. "What are you insinuating?"

"You know exactly what I mean."

"No, tell me," she challenged.

"You never craved human blood. You have no idea what it's like. All you wanted was Gabriel's blood."

"And that makes you think I never went through what you're going through now? That I never had those cravings? Grow up! We all have the same cravings, no matter whose blood it is we want. Your cravings aren't any worse than anybody else's. But *you* choose to act on them. You choose to show no restraint!"

At the accusation, Oliver pressed his lips together. His chest heaved, and he felt the cords in his neck bulge. "How dare you accuse me of willfully acting the way I do?"

"Oh, I dare a lot more!" She pointed her finger toward the door. "I also dare accuse you of attacking this girl and leaving her half dead! Is that how you want to live? Always a step away from killing an innocent?"

Her words chilled him to the bone. Often enough he'd been close to doing just that, but tonight, Maya was wrong. Tonight, he'd rescued an innocent. "I didn't bite her! Do you want to know what happened? Do you? Or will that shake your preconceived opinion of me?"

"Go ahead! Dish up some more lies if it makes you feel better."

"They're not lies! I don't know why the girl isn't telling you what happened, but I can venture a guess. She hasn't lost her memory. She just doesn't want to admit what happened."

Maya raised her eyebrows, then crossed her arms over her chest. "Admit what?"

He had to say it, as much as he wanted to keep this piece of information to himself. "That she offered me sex in exchange for helping her. She—"

Maya's laughter interrupted him. "Oh my god! I can't believe you couldn't come up with a better excuse. What is it? Has the blood gone to your head and made you dizzy? No girl like her would offer you sex in exchange for help. She's not a prostitute. Have you lost your mind?"

"She did! She offered me sex if I helped her and then she kissed me. And when she collapsed in my arms, I saw the bite marks of the other vampire. That's when I brought her here."

"She kissed you? Stop Oliver, you're just digging yourself deeper and deeper into a hole."

"But it's true! You must believe me! She was running from somebody. She begged me to help her."

Maya let out a sigh, seemingly exhausted. "It's me, Maya. You don't have to continue making stuff up. Just tell me what really happened and I'll try to put a good word in with Gabriel and Samson."

"I'm not lying! It's the truth. I didn't bite her!"

She scowled at him. "Fine. Play it your way. Continue lying, but it'll make it only worse. If you at least showed remorse for your actions, I could convince Gabriel and Samson to be lenient with you, but since you've decided to be a hard-ass about it, don't expect to be treated with kid gloves."

In disbelief Oliver shook his head. This couldn't be happening. He would be taken to task for something he hadn't done. "That's not fair! I'm innocent!"

Maya rolled her eyes. "Innocent? There's nothing innocent about you. The only innocent in this house is that girl in the next room. And you've robbed her of that innocence. You should at least have the decency to admit your guilt like a man."

Oliver closed his eyes. He knew it had been a mistake to help the girl. He should have followed his first instinct and turned around the minute she'd approached him. But no, knight in shining armor that he fancied himself, he'd wanted to help her.

Liar.

He cringed. Okay, so he'd only decided to help her *after* she'd made her outrageous offer of sex. Not that he would have ever held her to it anyway! It didn't matter: he'd gotten involved, and now he was in a hell lot of trouble and as long as the girl didn't admit the truth, it was his word against hers.

The evidence was damning: bite marks on the girl's neck and massive blood loss. Maybe if he could talk to the girl and assure her that he wouldn't collect on her promise, maybe then she would tell Maya what really happened.

He had to try it.

"I'll talk to her again. Alone." He made a step toward the door.

"Not a chance," Maya objected instantly and blocked the door. "Do you think I don't know what you're trying to do?"

"Do what?" he ground out and ran his hand through his hair.

"You're going to try and influence her, using mind control."

Oliver narrowed his eyes. "Maybe you wanna get your facts straight for a change: as Thomas will be able to confirm, I haven't quite mastered the art of mind control yet."

In fact, he was having problems with it and assumed that his problems with being able to control his hunger for blood had something to do with it. They robbed him of the energy necessary to exercise mind control and being able to plant fake memories into his victims' minds. He was, however, fully capable of erasing a person's memory. It was a skill that required less finesse and was more instinctual than the art of mind control, even though the two skills were related.

Thomas, Scanguards' IT genius and master of mind control, was tutoring him to help him over his issues. He was making progress, but he was nowhere near mastering the skill. At best, he succeeded only fifty percent of the time.

"Still, you're not—"

"Damn it, Maya!" he flared up. "What do you want from me? You've already made up your mind about my guilt, and now you won't even allow me to talk to the only witness who can confirm my innocence. Even in a court of law I'd have a better chance than with you!"

And he'd seen the inside of more than one courtroom. In his days as a human, before Samson, the owner of Scanguards, had taken him under his wing, he'd been in and out of jail for possession of drugs and other offenses. He'd never committed any violent crimes, but he knew if Samson hadn't come along and taken pity on him, he would have gone down that road. The crowd he was running with was on that path already.

"We have our own rules," Maya insisted.

Before he could reply, he heard the front door opening. Was the girl leaving? Panicked, Oliver fairly jumped at the door and ripped it open, peering out into the hallway.

Relief and dread collided instantly. The person who'd opened the entrance door was Blake, and behind him, Cain entered. Their gazes immediately landed on him.

"We've been looking for you," Blake said, his tone accusatory.

"Fuck you!" Oliver replied. He wasn't in the mood to have another confrontation. The one with Maya was enough for one night. He turned away.

A moment later, he felt a hand on his shoulder. He swiveled and faced Blake, shaking off his hand in the process.

"I'm not done talking. Cain and I searched the entire city for you."

"You've found me. Now leave me alone."

"Not so fast, little brother. I wanna know where you went tonight."

"I don't owe you any explanations." And if Blake annoyed him any longer, he'd instead get a beating.

Cain suddenly looked past his shoulder. "Hey Maya, what are you doing here?"

Oliver turned quickly, tossing her a warning look. "It's none of their business."

"What's none of our business?" It figured that Blake wouldn't let go. Once he had gotten something into his head, he held onto it like a dog to a bone.

"Nothing!" Oliver bit out. "Now get out of my house, all of you and leave me alone!"

"Not gonna happen," Maya insisted.

"I live here, so you have no right to throw me out!" Blake interrupted.

"Guess, I'm not wanted here," Cain added and turned toward the door.

But Maya stopped him. "Don't leave, Cain, we might need you."

By now, Oliver was fuming. "The fuck we do! I'll handle this! There's no need for all of Scanguards to get involved."

Cain stopped in his tracks, his eyes suddenly narrowing as if he perceived a threat. "What happened?"

Oliver thrust his chin up. "Nothing happened! Would you all stop meddling in my affairs and leave me alone!"

He caught Cain exchanging a glance with Maya.

"I want you to keep an eye on Oliver while I confer with Gabriel and Samson," she said to Cain.

Disgusted at her treachery, Oliver glared at her. "I can't believe you're doing this! I trusted you. That's why I called you!"

"It's for your own good."

He raised his voice. "The fuck it is! I'm telling the truth! But you don't want to see that. You don't believe there's any good left in me. You've given up on me, just like everybody else!"

Maya put her hand on his forearm, but he shook it off. "That's not true. You'll see that when you've calmed down."

"I am calm!" But the tightness in his jaw belied his words. His gums itched, and he could feel the tips of his fangs extending.

"Yeah, I can see that!" Blake mocked.

Oliver pounced on Blake, before his last word had even left his lips.

"Stop it now!" Maya warned, but Oliver ignored her.

Instead, he slammed Blake against the wall and held him there, his body suspended in the air. "You little jerk! You wanna know what it's like to be a vampire, do you? Maybe I should just turn you and see how you cope with it, huh? Is that what you want? Is that why you're constantly provoking me?"

"Get off me, you fucking bastard!" Blake ordered, aiming his fists at him.

"You want a fight?" Oliver challenged.

"Damn it, Oliver!" Maya cursed and grabbed his arm. "Cain!"

A moment later, Cain attacked him from the other side. Furious, Oliver let go of Blake and spun on his heels. He felt his fangs extend to full length and caught sight of his hands: they had turned into claws. Yes, he was spoiling for a fight.

Raising his head, he looked at his two attackers, whose fangs had also extended, when he caught a movement in the corner of his eye. His head whipped in its direction.

Shit!

Ursula, the girl he'd rescued from an unknown vampire, stood in the door to the living room, her eyes wide in shock, her hands gripping the door frame for support.

"Oh God," she said breathlessly. "You're one of them. You're all like them!"

9

With disbelief and horror, Ursula looked at the scene in the entrance hall. How could this have happened? She'd stepped from the frying pan into the fire. Nothing had changed. Her entire daring escape had been for nothing. She was still in the hands of vampires, only different ones this time. Despair spread inside her, pushing tears into her eyes.

There was no use in running: all four of them blocked the entrance door. Besides, she was aware of a vampire's speed and knew that if she tried to make it to the French doors in the living room that led outside to a terrace, they would catch her in no time. Particularly since she was still weakened from the recent blood loss.

Gathering all her remaining strength, she stared at Oliver, the man who'd rescued her. Well, maybe *rescue* wasn't the right word after all. He'd captured her. His eyes were red now, his fangs extended, and his fingertips were topped with razor-sharp claws. His mouth stood open, and his lips looked red and plump. And still inviting.

God, no! Her stomach twisted as she remembered the kiss they'd shared. She'd kissed a monster, the very creature she hated most in this world. And she had liked it; even now, there was no denying it. Her body had burned with desire, and she could only hope that it was solely an aftereffect of the feeding she'd been subjected to a short time earlier. Because she could never desire a vampire.

Before her eyes, the red in Oliver's eyes dissipated, and the tips of his fangs pulled back, disappearing in his mouth. Even his claws vanished as if she had simply been imagining them.

"You're vampires," she repeated, her voice flat.

Oliver shook off the hands of Dr. Giles and the dark haired vampire, who had been holding his arms. Dr. Giles? She probably wasn't even a doctor.

"I'm sorry you had to see this." He took a tentative step closer.

She flinched. Immediately, he stopped in his approach, his eyes looking at her full of regret. Regret? No, she had to be mistaken. She'd never seen any vampire exhibit such a feeling. Their feelings were limited to greed, hate, and lust.

"I won't hurt you."

She listened to Oliver's words and suppressed the urge to laugh hysterically. Of course he would hurt her, just like the other vampires had. So why pretend? Why lie to her? Why torture her? Maybe he was more cruel than even Dirk was. More cruel because he came in a package that had almost made her trust him, almost made her feel safe. Only to dash her hopes later.

The tears that she'd held back until now escaped from her eyes, making their way down her cheeks, burning hotly. She didn't dare take a breath.

"Please don't cry."

His voice was soothing, and when she closed her eyes, she could imagine surrendering to it. Maybe it was time to give up, to stop struggling and accept her fate. She would always be a blood whore to them. They would never let her go.

She would never see her parents again. And she wouldn't be able to help rescue the other girls. With her next breath, a sob tore from her chest.

"I want to go home."

Her knees buckled, her vision blurred. She saw them move all at once, coming toward her. Would they drain her tonight? Would this finally be the end?

"I've got her," Oliver said to his friends, his voice sharp and unyielding.

Then she felt him lift her into his arms and carry her back into the living room. The gentleness with which he placed her on the couch surprised her, but maybe she was delirious. As soon as she sat, he pulled the blanket over her lower body and stepped back.

"You're safe here," he claimed.

The other three had entered the room behind him and stood close.

"Who is she?" one of the men asked.

The doctor turned to him. "Oliver brought her here."

He walked past her and stretched his hand out to her, giving her a charming smile. "I'm Blake."

She stared at his hand and pressed herself deeper into the sofa cushions.

"She's scared, can't you see that?" Oliver admonished him and pushed him aside.

"Well, that's probably because you scared her!" Blake countered.

"Stay out of it!"

"I live here too, so I have a right to know what's going on!"

Oliver glared at him, then looked back at her. "I think I have to explain a few things to you now that you've seen what we are." He cleared his throat. "You've already met Maya. She's a doctor, but she's also a vampire. And this—" He pointed to the dark haired vampire who hadn't said anything yet. "—is Cain. He works for Scanguards. He's one of our vampire bodyguards."

So they called their prison guards bodyguards instead. Same difference!

Then he pointed to Blake. "That's Blake. He's my half-brother."

Blake squared his shoulders. "I'm human."

His claim stunned her. They had a human living in their midst? What for? As a constant source for blood? Her mouth gaped open as she stared at him. He was handsome, tall and a little broader than Oliver. And oddly, it didn't appear as if he was restrained in any way. He seemed under no duress. On the contrary, it appeared that he was self-confident and ready to pick a fight with Oliver at the drop of a hat. The hostile glares between the two hadn't escaped her notice.

"Human?" she echoed.

"Yes," Blake answered and smiled at her. "It's complicated. But let's just keep it simple. For all intents and purposes, this dude here is my half-brother. As annoying as he can be."

Oliver pressed his lips into a thin line as if trying not to contest Blake's comment.

"How are you feeling?" the doctor suddenly asked.

Ursula looked up at her, clearing her throat. "Dr. Giles, I really don't know why you care." Why were they still pretending to be concerned about her wellbeing? What difference did it make?

Maya raised an eyebrow. "First, please call me Maya, everybody does. And second, I do care, because Oliver put you into this situation."

Ursula's gaze drifted to Oliver, wondering what Maya meant with her comment. She noticed how his facial features tightened as he glared back at Maya.

"As I said before, I didn't do it!"

"Didn't do what?" Blake interrupted.

Oliver swiveled on his heels to face his half-brother. "Bite her."

"Nearly drained her," Maya added.

"You fucking asshole!" Blake yelled. "How could you? Look at her! How could you do that to a nice girl like her?"

Blake's hands balled into fists and he swung. Oliver blocked his hit, but before he could land his own fist in Blake's face, Ursula interrupted them. "He didn't bite me."

Instantly everyone went quiet and turned to look at her.

"It wasn't him who bit me," she repeated, unsure why she even bothered defending him.

"You remember!" Oliver's voice was full of relief. Suddenly his face split into a huge smile and before she knew what he wanted to do, he approached her and reached for her hands. He squeezed them hard.

"Thank you, thank you, thank you!" he said exuberantly, before he let go of her hands and turned to Maya, giving her a pointed look. "Well, Maya?"

Maya shrugged. "Well, the circumstances were . . . " Then she stopped herself. "I'm glad I was wrong. I apologize for judging you wrongly."

Ursula listened to the conversation, but nothing made sense. Why did it matter to any of them whether Oliver had bitten her or not? Why did they care?

"Since you remember, please tell us what happened." Maya pointed to her neck. "I know you were bitten by a vampire. Who was it? We need to know so we can stop the bastard from doing it again. Obviously whoever did this was out of control, leaving you half-dead."

Slowly Ursula shook her head, unable to trust her ears. Maya wanted to stop who'd done this to her? She must have heard wrong.

"You want to do what?"

Maya gave her a strange look. "Rein that bastard in. He can't endanger humans like that. We'll have to make sure of it."

"But . . . " Ursula swept her gaze to the others in the room, who seemed as concerned about the situation as Maya. "Why would you do that? You're vampires too. You do the same."

Oliver moved closer, crouching down before her so he was eyelevel with her and she wouldn't have to crane her neck anymore. The gesture was kind, she realized, and wondered why he did it.

"We're civilized. We're all part of the same group. We work for a company called Scanguards. Most of us are bodyguards or security guards, and we're sworn to protect humans. Even against our own race."

She shook her head in disbelief. It was impossible. No, she had to be delirious to be hearing something so incredible. "No, that can't be."

"It's true," Blake chimed in. "As much as some have difficulty keeping their lust for blood under control—" He tossed a pointed look at Oliver. "—Scanguards' men live by a strict code of ethics. Believe me, if that weren't the case, I wouldn't be alive today, nor be living among them without fear for my life."

She shifted her gaze back to Oliver. "You mean you don't bite people?"

A flash of guilt flared in his eyes before he dropped his lids to avoid her scrutiny. "Most of us drink blood from a bottle. It's donated. We purchase it through a medical supply company."

His careful phrasing hadn't escaped her notice. "Most of you?"

His eyelids swung open fully, his long dark lashes almost touching his brows. The intense blue of his eyes mesmerized her, just like it had when she'd first met him in the dark street.

"Not all. Some of us still struggle to . . . adjust. But it's not easy. The temptation is always there."

She noticed his gaze drift to her neck and felt a tingling sensation race through her body. Fear clamped down her vocal cords, making her unable to speak. At the same time she was unable to tear her eyes away from his.

Fear and desire collided as he inched closer, reminding her of their kiss. He had been so warm, so tender. And now she knew also how deadly his kiss could be. He could have bitten her then and finished what the other vampire had started. Still, she couldn't move, could only watch as he approached.

"Oliver!" Cain's sharp voice made him jerk back and jump to his feet.

Oliver ran a hand through his hair. "Sorry. As I was saying, we won't hurt you."

Ursula nodded as if on autopilot, while her brain tried to understand what this development meant for her immediate future. Was she truly safe? It was too good to be true, and when something was too good to be true, it wasn't true. Everybody who'd ever seen a commercial for a miracle weight loss pill knew that.

"This company you mention, Scanguards, what do they do?" Were they just another front for the blood trade that did the same nefarious things her captors had done to her and the other girls?

"Scanguards is a security company. We protect individuals: dignitaries, politicians, or celebrities. Anybody really who can afford us. We have both human and vampire employees. Humans work all daytime jobs, but the rest of us, we take on the nightshift if you will. Our assignments are generally more dangerous. But we're trained for that."

Ursula couldn't help but notice the pride in his voice when Oliver spoke, nor the sheen of excitement that sparkled in his eyes now. Yet his words sounded so foreign, so impossible to believe. "Vampires who protect humans?"

Oliver smiled. "We're the good guys."

She couldn't help but shake her head. There were no good guys.

Next to Oliver, Blake grinned at her too. "They are. When I was kidnapped by a bunch of bad vampires, all of Scanguards came to my aid to rescue me. They risked their lives for mine."

Oliver tossed him a mischievous sideways glance. "Only because you're Quinn's grandson. If I'd had a say in it, I would have let them keep your sorry ass."

Ursula watched the exchange with interest. Scanguards had fought other vampires to save a human? Could she hope that they would come to the rescue of those girls that were still imprisoned as blood whores? Or would Scanguards only lift a finger for their own family members?

"Admit it, bro, you love having me around."

Oliver rolled his eyes. "Right." Then he turned back to her. "Don't mind him. But what he said is true: we come to the rescue when we're needed or when one of our own, human or vampire, is in danger. I've been involved in a lot of rescue missions myself."

Again, pride shone through his words. He clearly loved what he was doing. Had she stumbled upon the only group of people who could help her and the other girls? Could she trust them? Were they what they claimed to be, or were they no better than the vampires who'd held her in captivity for three years?

"And what do you do?" she asked before she could stop herself.

"Me? I'm a bodyguard."

"Enough of talking about us," Cain suddenly interrupted, his eyes narrowing somewhat, as if he was suspicious of her. "Why don't you tell us what happened to you, so we can determine what to do?"

Ursula swallowed hard. Cain's mouth was set in a hard line, which made him look determined and unyielding. Instinctively she realized that he wouldn't allow the others to give her any more information than they had already.

Oliver exchanged a look with Cain, then nodded before looking back at her. "No offense, Ursula, but we've already told you more about us than we would tell any human under normal circumstances. You have to understand we need to protect our secrets."

Secrets? Of course they had secrets. All vampires did. And they would not show her the skeletons that were in their closets.

"Tell us," Maya insisted, her voice softer than Cain's, but not any less urging. "What happened to you?"

Ursula hesitated. How much could she tell them? What if they were connected to the other vampires after all and returned her to them once they found out where she had escaped from?

When Oliver crouched down in front of her again and encapsulated her hand in his large palm, she shifted her gaze to look into his eyes.

His lips moved and expelled two whispered words. "Tell me."

As if under a spell, she opened her mouth. The words were out before she could stop them. "I was imprisoned by vampires."

10

Shocked, Oliver sucked in a breath. Had he heard right, or was the fact that he was so close to this beautiful girl screwing with his senses?

"Imprisoned?"

He briefly glanced at his friends, but they looked as stunned as he, clearly having heard the same words from Ursula's mouth.

Her big brown eyes were wide like saucers, and she appeared as surprised by the revelation as he was. Had she not wanted to reveal this or was she making up lies? Or was she simply a very good actress?

Maybe Cain had been right to cut off her questions, so he wouldn't reveal too much about Scanguards. After all, she was a stranger, and even though she'd been bitten by a vampire, it could have all been a setup to get close to them, to infiltrate Scanguards. What if some group of vampires was using her as bait? Even now, she could be under their control. Despite his physical attraction to her, he had to be careful. If he got involved, it would only end badly when it turned out that she was working for the enemy. He would never go against Scanguards, not even for the hottest woman he'd met in a long time. His eyes involuntarily dropped to her chest where her small breasts moved up and down as she breathed. At the same time he noticed how clammy her hand was and how fast her heart beat.

When he raised his gaze to look into her eyes again, he realized that what he was seeing were signs of fear. Did she fear him and his friends, or did she fear the vampire who had bitten her?

"Please," he urged her. "Tell me what happened."

Slowly, she pulled her hand from his. Reluctantly he allowed it.

"They held me for three years."

The words choked out from her throat as if she had trouble speaking.

Stunned by her words, he remained silent and waited for her to continue. She took several breaths, looking at his friends then turned her head to the side, avoiding eye contact with him.

"I was a student at NYU when they captured me one night after I left an evening lecture. I couldn't believe what was happening. Vampires didn't exist! They couldn't exist. They were just myth, folklore. They only existed in movies. I never thought . . . " Her voice broke.

Oliver wanted to say so much, but his throat felt parched all of a sudden.

"They took me to a building where they kept me locked up. I wasn't the only one. There were other girls like me." She looked up and met his gaze. Her eyes were moist, but she wasn't crying.

Of its own volition, his hand came up, wanting to stroke her cheek to comfort her, but in the last minute, he pulled it back, not wanting to expose his feelings to her or his friends. He had to stay impartial. It was the hallmark of a good bodyguard. Cain had been trying to teach him that very fact, and Gabriel had reinforced it countless times.

However, it didn't change the fact that he was affected by her words. He felt compassion.

"What did they do to you?"

Ursula thrust her chin up, her mouth setting into a hard line. "They pimped us out as blood whores."

"Blood whores?" Maya gasped in disbelief.

His own reaction wasn't any different. "I've never heard of blood whores." He turned to Cain to ask for reassurance.

His colleague shook his head. "There's no such thing. There's no need for that."

Ursula pulled her shoulders up and straightened, her lips trembling as she continued, "They used me and the other girls as blood whores. Two, sometimes three times a night they would bring vampires in to drink from us; leeches we called them." She choked. "Some of the girls didn't make it. But they always found new ones to replace the ones who died."

Cain took a step closer. "That's impossible. There's no need to keep humans imprisoned for their blood. Even those vampires who don't drink bottled blood wouldn't have any need for this. They'll simply go out and h—"

"Find somebody to drink from," Oliver interrupted him quickly. *Hunt*, Cain had wanted to say, and somehow Oliver didn't think it was the right word to use in Ursula's presence. "No vampire would go through the trouble of keeping a human imprisoned just to have blood at hand at all times."

If that were the case, why not drink it from a bottle? At least that's how he felt: he loved the hunt. The thrill of it was what drove him out there night after night. And he could only imagine that it was the same for those vampires who hadn't taken to bottled blood. They were in it for the chase. They wouldn't want the bother of keeping a human in a prison to feed from him like from a caged animal.

"They ran a business," Ursula insisted. "They charged a high price for our blood. And the leeches paid it without flinching."

"Why pay for something they can get for free on the street?" Maya threw in, her voice just as skeptical as Cain's comment had been.

Oliver searched Ursula's face for any tells that she was lying. Thomas was trying to teach him this skill, but he hadn't mastered it yet. However, from what he could tell, she wasn't lying. Unless, she didn't know she was lying: it was possible that a vampire had wiped her memories and planted fresh ones in her mind. She would never know that she was lying. The only question was, why would another vampire do this? Why concoct such a story? Was somebody trying to lead Scanguards into a trap by appealing to their sense of honor and duty, knowing they would help those in need?

Suspicious of her story, Oliver applied what he'd learned from Thomas: ask questions to see if the person could keep their story straight. Liars had a way of forgetting the small details of their carefully constructed stories and eventually made mistakes.

"You said you went to NYU. Did they bring you to San Francisco upon your kidnapping?"

She shook her head. "We stayed somewhere in New York for a long time. One night they suddenly packed everything up, and we were put in the back of a large truck and driven cross country. I arrived in San Francisco only about three months ago. I didn't even know what city I was in until tonight."

"Where did they keep you?"

She shrugged. "A large building, maybe an old apartment building or an old hotel. I'm not sure. It was dark when we arrived and I was never let outside. They kept us locked up, and even when we were led into the rooms where the vampires fed from us, there was always a guard to watch us."

"Where is the building located?"

Her eyes filled with tears. "I don't know. Not far from where you found me. I'm not sure about the exact location. I was only concerned with getting away from them."

Cain cleared his throat. "Yeah, about that. How *did* you get away, given that there was a guard?"

Ursula shut her eyes for a moment, and when she opened them again, she looked away. "The guard wasn't careful. He was called to another room when there was an altercation with one of the leeches. He forgot to lock the door. I was able to get out through a fire escape."

"Was there only one guard?" Cain continued.

She shook her head. "There were many of them. But they were all busy watching the other girls," she hastened to add.

Oliver gave her a wary glance. Her heartbeat had accelerated and he could sense her glands producing more sweat. Not an unpleasant odor by any stretch, but nevertheless, she was sweating, and this meant she was nervous. Nervous because she was lying? Or simply agitated because she was recalling her ordeal?

If only he knew.

When her face turned fully to him, their gazes collided. Oliver sucked in a breath of air and with it her scent. Hunger instantly surged through him, even though he'd fed only a few short hours earlier. He shouldn't feel hungry; he shouldn't lust for blood again so soon. He'd taken plenty from the juvenile he'd met in the Bayview district. More than enough. It should last him for twenty-four hours. Yet a strange craving came over him, and he wasn't sure whether he wanted to bite or kiss her. Either possibility seemed equally enticing. And equally wrong for the situation.

"Please, you have to believe me," she begged.

He felt Maya approach from behind. "You must admit, it's a fantastic story."

"And it doesn't make sense," Cain added.

"But couldn't it be possible?" Blake asked. "There are some bad guys out there as we all know."

Oliver turned, looking at Maya and Cain. "Blake is right. We can't just dismiss this. If she's telling the truth, then we have a problem on our hands."

Ursula jumped to her feet, drawing his attention back to her. "You think I'm lying?"

Oliver got up and instinctively reached for her, but she sidestepped him. "That's not what I'm saying."

Tears brimming at her eyes, she glared at him. "Then what *are* you saying?"

Nervously he shifted his weight, glancing at Cain who shrugged. "Want me to tell her?"

Clearly his colleague had the same suspicion as he did. And he seemed to have no qualms about voicing it. But Oliver was man enough to do his own dirty work. And accusing her of something she might be innocent of wasn't pretty. But it was a possibility he couldn't simply dismiss.

When Ursula nailed him with her questioning look, he sighed. "It's possible that the vampire who bit you planted these memories in your mind so you'd tell us about it and lead us into a trap. You wouldn't even know that you're lying."

She jolted, taking another step away from him. "What? You think this isn't true? You think it's made up? No! No! I lived through this. For three years, I endured their cruelty, the humiliation, the pain. I know what I saw and what I felt. It's real."

Her chest heaved from the effort it must have taken her to raise her voice to him and make her impassioned plea.

"For three years my parents have been looking for me."

"How do you know that?" Cain asked.

She whipped her head in his direction. "Because they love me. They would never give up on me." She withstood Cain's scrutinizing look until Cain was the one who broke it. When he did, she turned and looked back at Oliver. "I need to tell them I'm alive."

He recognized the pain that sat deep in her eyes and felt his heart clench in response. Maybe she was telling the truth, as outrageous as it sounded. But for the sake of Scanguards and their own safety, they had to take precautions before they could proceed.

"Later, but we'll have to verify a few facts first." His years of training with Scanguards kicked in. It was vital that he didn't make a mistake now: Gabriel was already keeping an eye on everything he did because of his uncontrollable hunger for blood. If he now jeopardized Scanguards by not verifying Ursula's story first, then his boss would have his hide.

"We need to know about your background so we can confirm who you are," he said, feeling just a little bit guilty for not believing her.

The disappointed look she shot him cut through him like a knife. Yep, there was no way in hell she would ever sleep with him—not now, not after he'd disappointed her. It shouldn't matter, but it did. Because the kiss she'd given him had held such promise and made him hungry for more. Was he doomed to fight yet another hunger he had no way of satisfying?

Her voice sounded resigned when she finally addressed him again. "What do you want to know?"

"Your name, name of your parents, where you lived. When you were abducted and where." Then he nodded to Cain. "Cain, make notes. I want you to search for anything you can find. There would be police reports and possibly newspaper articles of Ursula's kidnapping."

He hoped so, because he didn't like the idea that she was a liar and trying to trick them. However, he liked the idea even less that she had lived in captivity for three years, subjected to a group of vampires who fed from her whenever they pleased, and probably even worse.

He knew what went along with a feeding, the sexual arousal it produced in both the host and the vampire. If her story was true, they would have raped her countless times. Violently.

But he couldn't bring himself to ask her. For his own sake: because knowing that somebody might have used her that way, violated her body not just by taking her blood, but by sexually assaulting her, made his blood boil. He would have to kill somebody then.

11

After Ursula had given them the details Oliver had asked for, Cain nodded and headed for the door. "I'll get back to you with my findings as soon as I can."

"Thanks, I appreciate it," Oliver answered.

The entrance door fell shut behind Cain, and Oliver's gaze fell on Maya who picked up her black doctor's bag.

"Blake, Oliver, a word." She motioned them into the foyer, but turned before they reached it to look back at Ursula. "Everything will turn out all right. One way or another."

Oliver noticed Ursula's doubting look, then followed Maya, pulling the door halfway shut after Blake had joined them.

"Yes?" Oliver asked tightly.

"I'll be speaking with Gabriel about this."

"Why bother him? He's busy in New York right now." He'd rather not have Gabriel find out about this when there were so many things that weren't clear yet.

"Just because he's gone for a few days doesn't mean anybody is going to keep anything from him. You should know that." She gave him a stern look. "You're both responsible for the girl's wellbeing. Keep a close eye on her, and don't allow her to leave. It's for her own safety. Do we understand each other?"

Blake nodded.

Oliver grunted. As if he needed to be told. He knew what the drill was. "I've got it covered. This is my case."

Maya raised a surprised eyebrow. "Gabriel will decide that. In the meantime, do as I say." Then she put her hand on the door handle. "And Oliver, I'm really sorry I accused you earlier. But if you bite her now, Gabriel will have your ass."

Oliver huffed angrily. "I have no intention of biting her!"

"I've seen the way you looked at her."

Blake put a reassuring hand on her shoulder and opened the door in her stead. "Don't worry, I'll make sure he doesn't touch her."

"Thanks, Blake."

When the door closed behind her, Blake grinned at him. "Well, let's see how we can make our charge a little more comfortable."

Before he could reach the door to the living room, Oliver pulled him back. "Oh, I know what you're doing."

His half-brother glanced over his shoulder. "Just saving a pretty girl from the big bad vampire."

Oliver clenched his teeth. "You're not saving her from anything! I saw her first."

"What's that got to do with it? She clearly doesn't like vampires, and since I'm the only human around at the moment, don't mind if I try my luck."

"You're not gonna try anything, do you understand me?"

"How are you gonna stop me?" Blake challenged.

Many things came to mind as an answer: to rip his throat out was one of them. Shocked by his violent thoughts, Oliver dropped his hand and simply glared at him. Blake knew full well that he wouldn't hurt him and thus draw Quinn's wrath upon him. But it didn't mean, he'd allow Blake to make a pass at the girl.

"Why would she go for you? You really think you're that charming?" he mocked.

Blake grinned and pulled his stomach in, puffing his chest out like a peacock. "Oh, I am. Much more charming than you can ever be. Plus I have an advantage: I'm human. I'm afraid, for once, you've encountered a woman who isn't gonna drop her panties for the mighty vampire."

Fuming at his claim, Oliver opened his mouth and let out words he wanted to take back a second later. "She's already offered me sex!"

A gasp from the door made him cringe.

Shit, shit, shit!

He shouldn't have allowed Blake to provoke him. In slow motion, Oliver turned toward where Ursula stood in the door frame, staring at him in horror. Clearly, she hadn't wanted anybody to know what she'd said to him in that dark street. Neither had he. Not only had he told Maya about it, which Ursula thankfully didn't know, but now he was even bragging to Blake about it. Stupid move!

"Guess my chances just went up," Blake murmured.

"Shut up!" Oliver hissed.

Ursula glared at both of them. "If you think that I'll spread my legs for either one of you, think again!"

"But I'm human," Blake said.

"So are millions of other men in this country, and I won't sleep with them either."

"But you don't even know me yet."

Oliver couldn't suppress a grin at Blake's pathetic attempt to win her favor. At least it took the heat off him.

"I've seen enough!" Then her eyes shifted and she stared at Oliver. "And what are you grinning at?"

Instantly, he put on a serious face. "Just a facial tick. Don't take any notice of it."

By the indignant look she tossed him, he realized she knew he was lying. But was she at least giving him points for originality?

She huffed, obviously lost for words, and turned, slamming the door behind her.

One nil for the vampire. At least he still had a chance.

"No way did she offer you sex." Blake's incredulous words made him turn his head.

He wouldn't be goaded into giving any more secrets away than he already had, such as that Ursula had kissed him—quite passionately at that. This time, his half-brother would not provoke him into saying something he didn't want to divulge. Therefore Oliver simply shrugged.

"Think what you want."

It was bad enough that Maya knew about it. He could only hope that she didn't pass this piece of information on to Gabriel. Knowing his sense of propriety, he'd pull him off this case instantly and have somebody else watch her. Not that it was a real case yet. At the moment it was nothing more than Oliver helping a girl in trouble. Whether this had anything to do with Scanguards would unfold soon, he hoped.

In the meantime, he should mend what he'd screwed up.

When he put his hand on the doorknob, he felt Blake's hand on his shoulder. "Hey, what are you doing?"

Oliver gave him a pointed look. "What's it look like? I'm going into the living room." He shook off his hand. "So if you wouldn't mind . . . "

"Not alone, you're not."

"Don't you have anything better to do than spy on me?"

Blake's eyes narrowed. "I wouldn't have to spy on you if you knew how to behave."

"That's rich, coming from you! If I remember well, you just tried to make a pass at her. And you're telling me I can't behave?"

Without another glance, Oliver opened the door and entered the living room. Behind him, Blake crowded into the room. Figured that his halfwit half-brother couldn't take a hint.

Ursula stood at the window, peering out into the dark, even though he knew she couldn't see anything out there with the light from the living room reflecting in the glass pane. She spun around when she heard his footsteps.

"I didn't mean to startle you." Oliver pointed to the window. "You should come away from there. Somebody might see you. I can't be sure that nobody followed us."

She quickly walked away from the window and approached the fireplace. Even though Oliver hadn't noticed anybody following them, he had to admit that he had been too preoccupied to pay proper attention.

Ursula raised her chin and looked straight at him. "I want to call my parents."

For a moment, he contemplated her request, but he already knew what his answer would be. He couldn't allow her to contact anybody. Not until Cain had verified her story. "Later."

Her eyes blazed with anger and hurt. "You're not any better than the vampires who kept me captive."

"That's not fair. I haven't done anything to you to hurt you."

"But you're locking me up just like they did. You don't allow me to talk to my parents. And how long until you're going to attack me for my blood? How long?"

Right now, he wanted to scream, but clenched his jaw. "Never! I'm not a savage. I'll prove it to you." What was he saying?

"How?" she challenged.

Without taking his eyes off her, he issued an order. "Blake, get me a bottle of blood from the pantry."

"What?" his half-brother asked. "You serious?"

"You heard me."

He heard Blake's boots scratch against the wooden floorboards as he left the room.

Ursula gave him a doubtful look. "What are you trying to do?"

"I'll prove to you that I'm civilized, that I don't want your blood." He knew he was lying, but he had to convince her otherwise. Or he would never get the other thing he wanted: her body, underneath him, panting in ecstasy.

"By drinking blood from a bottle? That's not going to prove anything!"

She was probably right, but it would establish something else. "At least for the next twenty-four hours you'll know that I'm sated and that you're safe from me. If you've really spent the last three years with vampires, you know their habits, their urges, their needs. You know that a vampire has no urge to attack you for your blood if he's fed sufficiently."

There was an almost unperceivable nod. Still, the doubt in her eyes didn't disappear. "Doesn't mean I'm safe from you."

He met her eyes and had to silently agree with her. No, she was not safe from him. He could maybe stave off the hunger he felt for her blood by feeding more than he normally did, but how could he suppress the desire that was growing inside his belly? Could he really watch over her without giving into the temptation to touch her, kiss her, press his body against hers? Or would the fire that she had ignited with her kiss get out of control and demand he take her and strip her naked? And once she was naked and panting beneath him, would he find the strength to resist biting her? He doubted it.

How could he even have such thoughts, knowing what she'd been through? The last thing she probably wanted was a man lusting after her, let alone touching her.

Unable to rebut her statement, he looked away. He was glad that he was saved from answering when Blake reentered the room and pressed a bottle of blood into his hand.

"Thanks."

Oliver didn't waste a second unscrewing the top and putting the bottle to his lips. It was awful: lifeless, bland, and cold. But it wasn't the temperature that bothered him: it was the fact that he couldn't sink his fangs into human flesh as he drank. It was different and didn't give him the same thrill he felt when hunting a human and feeding from him. It left him with a feeling of emptiness. But he swallowed the blood nevertheless. His body would be sated, and just like he'd told her, he wouldn't lust after Ursula's blood for many hours. It didn't mean his mind would be sated—that part of him still hungered for the hunt, to feel the thrill of sinking his fangs into a living, breathing mortal.

From under his half closed eyelids, he noticed her watching him. She showed no disgust at his action. Maybe she had been desensitized by what she'd seen in captivity, or maybe she had learned to hide her feelings well.

When he set the empty bottle down, he addressed her again, "Maybe you want to rest. I'll show you to the guest room."

"The guest room is a mess," Blake claimed. "It's full with boxes of Rose's clothes while the closet in the master is being redone."

Oliver glanced back at Blake. "I forgot. My room then."

"I'm not sleeping in your—"

He raised his hand to stop her. "I won't be using it. Besides, it has an en-suite bathroom with a tub, in case you want to . . . " He allowed his voice to trail off. Imagining her in his bathtub, surrounded by hot water and foam suddenly robbed him of his ability to speak.

"Does it have a lock?"

"The bathroom does, the door to my room doesn't. But I promise you, nobody will walk in there while you're in it."

She hesitated for a short moment. "Fine."

12

No lock on the bedroom door: at least it meant they couldn't lock her in. And since the bathroom locked, she could even get a few minutes of privacy.

Ursula sighed with relief.

"I'll show you to my room," Oliver offered.

Blake instantly cut in, a pointed look directed at him. "We both will."

She refrained from rolling her eyes at their show of excess testosterone.

Oliver's room was on the third floor of the massive mansion. A large oak staircase led to the upper floors. Ursula made note of her surroundings. When Oliver opened the door to his room and stepped inside, she followed him. Blake entered behind her.

For an Edwardian, the room was large. And a little messy.

Oliver rushed to snatch a pair of boxer briefs from the floor and hid it behind his back. "Sorry," he apologized softly. He motioned to one corner of the room. "That's the bathroom. Fresh towels are in the closet, and if you want to change your shirt, there are plenty of T-shirts in there if you want to borrow one."

She looked down at her top and noticed the blood stains on it. But did she really want to wear one of his T-shirts? Why was he trying to be so nice to her? To give her a false sense of security? She swore not to fall for it.

Nodding, she looked around. She slowly walked to the window and peered outside. There was no fire escape in front of the window. She turned slowly.

"It's a nice room. Is it just the two of you living here?"

If they thought she was making polite conversation, they would be mistaken. All she wanted to know was whether somebody else could show up at the house later, messing up her plans.

Oliver smiled. "Our parents own the house, Quinn and Rose. But they're on their honeymoon in England."

England? Far enough away for them not to return suddenly. But something else in his answer didn't make sense. "Honeymoon?" If they had two adult sons, why were they just now going on their honeymoon?

"Yes, it's a little complicated," Oliver offered.

Blake chuckled. "I'll explain it to you if you want."

She shrugged. The more she found out what and who she was dealing with, the better. Other than that, she wasn't in the least bit interested in what their family circumstances were. *Right.*

Clearly excited that he had something to talk about, Blake launched into his explanation. "I'm actually their only blood relative and—"

"If you must tell the story," Oliver interrupted, "then please keep your facts straight. I carry Quinn's blood, so I'm as much a blood relative as you are."

Ursula gazed at him, finding it odd that he seemed slightly upset at Blake's words. As if he wanted to make sure not to be left out.

"Well, okay, so I used the wrong words, big deal! Anyway." Blake turned back to look at her. "Quinn and Rose are my fourth great-grandparents. They had a falling out two hundred years ago and only reunited a couple of months ago."

That explained one thing: Rose and Quinn were vampires. However, something else of Blake's story couldn't be true then. "Vampires can't have children. I overheard the guards talk about it."

The knowledge had somehow filled her with satisfaction: at least it meant that vampires couldn't procreate the way humans did, and therefore one way of replenishing their ranks was closed to them.

"Not entirely true," Oliver threw in. "Vampire males can father children with their human mates. But in Quinn's and Rose's case it was different: they were both human when they had a child."

Blake nodded eagerly. "Yes, and that's the line I come from." Then he pointed to Oliver. "Oliver is only related to Quinn, not to Rose."

Oliver glared at him. "Which doesn't make me any less family." Then he relaxed his facial muscles. "Quinn is my sire. I've been working for Scanguards for over three years. I was human then, but I knew what they were, but Samson, the owner, he took me under his wing. I was his right hand, his eyes and ears during the day when he was vulnerable."

Ursula couldn't help but notice the proud sheen in his eyes when he spoke of his boss.

"I was with them out of my own free will. Until . . . " He hesitated and stared at his shoes.

She didn't say anything, simply waited anxiously for him to continue. How had he become a vampire? Had he chosen it? Or had they finally forced it on him?

"Anyway, I'm sure you'll be comfortable here."

Then his look darted past her toward the bed. Whatever he saw there made him approach. She held her breath, wondering if he'd suddenly attack her. However, he walked past her, making her turn.

Reaching for something on the nightstand, he mumbled, "Just a precaution."

That's when she saw what he was doing: he unplugged the small black telephone that had blended in with the dark color of the furniture. Darn! She hadn't instantly noticed it upon entering the room, but she would have seen it once she made a more careful assessment of her surroundings when she was alone. Too late. Her chances of calling her parents had just decreased.

She swallowed away her disappointment and met Oliver's gaze. His blue eyes shimmered with what looked like regret. She shook off the thought. No, vampires didn't feel regret. Maybe she was simply too exhausted to think clearly.

As if he sensed her frustration, he said, "I'm really sorry, but we can't risk you calling anybody. It might not only put us in danger, but you too. I know you want to talk to your parents, but what if whoever captured you watches them now that you escaped? They must know that you'll try to contact them. It would give your hiding place away."

Grudgingly, she had to admit that he was right. Her blood was too valuable for them to lose her. They would try to recapture her and use any means to do that. But Oliver didn't know that.

Without thinking, her next words left her lips. "So you believe me?"

He seemed to contemplate his answer while he swept a long look over her body, one that strangely enough made her feel hot and tingly.

"My gut feeling tells me that you told us the truth, but I can't always trust my gut. I need proof, because too many things don't make sense."

"Like what?" she countered.

"Why they would keep you captive for your blood when it's freely available on the streets."

Her blood wasn't freely available on the streets as he put it, but she couldn't tell him that. Once he knew what her blood did, he would want it too. He too would see the potential to make a lot of money by pimping her out to other vampires, just like her captors had done. No, she couldn't divulge that kind of information.

"It happened, but I don't know why," she lied, trying not to blink when their eyes locked. Could he tell she was lying?

"Let's just say there was a compelling reason, just for argument's sake," he conceded. "Then I find it very strange that you were able to escape at all. You said they had guards to watch you."

Ursula pushed her shoulders back. "Yes they did. But the guard was called away to another room when there was trouble. I used the opportunity to escape."

Oliver shook his head. "And the other vampire? The one who fed from you? Where was he? See how that doesn't make sense? Surely he didn't leave the room too."

"Of course he didn't."

"Don't tell me you overpowered a vampire by yourself."

The mocking look in Oliver's eyes got her dander up. How dare he make fun of her?

"And what makes you think I can't do that?"

"Look at you! You're what, five three, five four? And how heavy? A hundred and twenty pounds? You couldn't even overpower a human male, let alone a vampire. Somebody must have helped you escape."

Angrily, she fisted her hands at her hips and glared at him. But she kept her tongue in check. "The jerk didn't care! Okay? He had gotten what he'd come for and let me walk out of the room! He didn't know I was escaping. He probably assumed that I was going back to my room."

When Oliver stared at her with suspicion in his eyes, she withstood his gaze without blinking.

"I don't believe it."

"Can't you leave her alone?" Blake griped behind him. "What's so important about it now? She escaped. End of story."

"What are you not telling me?" Oliver insisted, ignoring his half-brother.

"There's nothing."

He didn't believe her; that much was clear. She couldn't even blame him.

Slowly, he stepped back. "Fine. We'll talk tomorrow. You're tired and you've been through a lot. Make yourself at home. There's a TV, music, books. If you're hungry, Blake will bring you some food."

Then he turned and left the room. She heard his footsteps fade as he walked down the hall.

"Are you hungry?" Blake asked.

"No."

Blake nodded and turned away, leaving her alone.

For now, she had dodged a bullet, but how much longer could she keep the truth from Oliver?

13

Ursula sank into the warm water, allowing it to caress her tired body, taking pains to keep her injured arm out of the water so that the bandage didn't get wet.

She had not only locked the bathroom door but also wedged the clothes hamper underneath the door handle as an extra precaution. She wouldn't put it past Oliver—or Blake—to barge in so they could look at her naked. Both of them had stared at her with lusting eyes. With Blake, she knew for sure he wasn't lusting after her blood, but with Oliver she had her doubts. Maybe he wanted both: her body and her blood. After all, she'd offered him her body before. Perhaps he wanted to collect on her promise, now that she was out of immediate danger.

But she hadn't made this promise to a vampire—not knowingly anyway. She'd made it to a handsome young man, a man she'd believed to be human, and she'd made her promise out of desperation. Things had changed since. He had turned out to be the enemy.

That thought sobered her. How could she not have seen the signs? After three years living with vampires, she'd developed a sense for recognizing what features gave them away: their fluid, graceful movements, the alertness in their eyes, their seemingly perfect and flawless skin. And then of course their speed. But Oliver had simply stood there, not moving when she'd met him, eliminating the possibility of recognizing him as a vampire by his movements.

His blue eyes had mesmerized her, blinded her so that she hadn't seen anything else.

She jerked her thoughts away from him. There was no use crying over spilled milk. What was more important now was to work on a plan of action—just as soon as she finished her bath. However, feeling how the warm water relaxed her aching muscles, how it soothed her tired body, made her want to simply close her eyes and allow sleep to take her away to a safe place. Maybe if she could just take a moment and rest, everything would look less desperate, less hopeless.

But no, she couldn't allow herself to weaken. Determined to remain strong and alert, she reached for the shower gel and lathered her body, ridding herself of the last traces of blood and dirt that had accumulated during her escape from her prison. She scrubbed harder and harder as if by doing so, she could scrub away the scars of the last three years.

Yet she still felt dirty, sullied by the vampires who'd used her. It was a stain she feared would never disappear, no matter how much soap she used to wash it away.

Realizing the futility of her efforts, her eyes welled up. And in the privacy of a stranger's bathroom, she allowed the tears to come. How long she cried, she couldn't tell, but when she finally stopped, the water was tepid.

Numb from her show of weakness, she reached for the towel she'd pulled from a closet earlier and dried herself off. She pulled on her pants without her panties—those were currently hanging over the towel rack to dry—, but when she looked at her blood- and dirt-stained T-shirt, she considered Oliver's offer of fresh clothes.

It cost her a good deal of pride to admit to herself that she wanted to feel a clean shirt on her skin. Tossing her own T-shirt on the floor, she removed the barricade in front of the door and unlocked it.

The bedroom was empty—nobody had entered it. It was a relief.

Scrutinizing Oliver's closet, Ursula found nothing out of the ordinary: his taste in clothes was very … *human.* Jeans in varying shades of blue and black, T-shirts in a variety of colors, several business suits—which surprised her, since he didn't look like he wore formalwear—and shoes, belts, and ties.

She opened a drawer: socks. The one next to it revealed a stack of underwear. A wave of heat shot through her. Red-faced, she shut the drawer quickly. Of course she knew that even vampires wore boxers or briefs. But she wasn't interested which category Oliver belonged to. She already knew that: he'd picked up a pair of boxer briefs off the floor earlier.

Blindly jerking a T-shirt from one of the stacks, she closed the closet door. She quickly pulled the shirt over her head and tucked its ends into her pants. It was too large for her, which was to be expected, but it did its job.

Ursula glanced at the clock on the bedside table. At least four if not five more hours till sunrise. It was time to make a decision: stay here with the vampires and hope she could convince them to help her and the other girls who were still imprisoned, or make a run for it, hoping the police would believe her story and help her.

Which scenario had the higher likelihood of succeeding?

As always when facing a monumental decision that could change her life for either the better or the worse, she contemplated each side on its own merits. First her option of escaping and running to the police: it seemed relatively simple. Only two men were in the house, one of them a human whose senses weren't any sharper than hers. While Blake looked strong, she had the feeling she could outsmart him. Not so Oliver. But knowing that vampires were nocturnal creatures, it was highly likely that he was sleeping deeply during daylight hours, making a daytime escape her only viable option. Besides, even if he woke, once she'd fled from the house, he couldn't follow her if he didn't want to be burned to a crisp by the sun.

Finding a police station shouldn't be too difficult. She could ask any passerby for directions. But once there, what would she tell them? That a group of vampires had kidnapped her and were still holding a dozen other girls captive? No. They would think she was crazy. What if she told them that some illegal prostitution ring was imprisoning girls? It was a more likely scenario, and the police would surely investigate. She was sure that once she went to the Bayview district, where Oliver said he'd found her, she would find her way back to her former prison. She'd made sure to remember street names and memorable buildings.

But once the police were there, raiding the building, what would happen then? She knew that the mortal weapons the police had would never kill a vampire. What they needed were stakes and guns with silver bullets, a fact she'd learned during her captivity. The police would be slaughtered by the vampires. She herself would be far enough away to escape and be able to return home. But could she live with the guilt of having sent so many men to their deaths? And what about the other girls? Could she live with the knowledge that they were still imprisoned as blood whores?

Ursula shook her head.

But was her other option any better? Could she convince the vampires from Scanguards to help her and go after her captors to save the other girls and make sure this didn't happen to anybody else? The more she thought about it, the more she knew she had no choice. If anybody could fight those vampires, it would be other vampires. They would know what to expect and be prepared to fight them. It would at least be a fair fight. But if they succeeded, could she keep it a secret what her blood and the blood of the other girls meant to a vampire? Or would they find out that their blood acted like a potent drug on a vampire? Would they too want it for themselves?

Over and over she thought about the consequences of staying rather than trying to escape to take her chances with the police. In her gut, she knew the answer to her dilemma, but was afraid of admitting it to herself. As minute after minute passed, she couldn't delay her decision any longer. She would stay.

However, there was one thing she had to do first: she needed to call her parents to tell them she was all right and that she would be home soon. One short phone call, only for a few seconds, that's all she needed. Short enough that nobody could trace it back to Oliver's house.

But since Oliver had removed the phone from her room, she had to find another one. Maybe he kept a spare one somewhere. If not, she would have to venture downstairs once he was asleep and try the library or the kitchen. Didn't everybody have a phone in the kitchen?

Ursula reached for the remote and switched on the TV, turning up the volume so the sound masked her own actions. She was fully aware that vampires had excellent hearing, sharper than that of any human. Let him think she was watching TV.

While a dull infomercial about the latest weight loss drug droned from the monitor, she explored the bedroom.

Thoroughly, she went about her search, not leaving a single corner untouched. However, her hopes were quickly dashed: no computer with internet access, no old cell phone, no spare phone she could plug into the wall jack. What he had in abundance were music CDs and a large collection of movies on DVD.

If she didn't know any better, she would have imagined this room belonged to a perfectly normal man, a *human* man, not a vampire. Everything looked so decidedly . . . normal.

Not that she had ever been in a vampire's bedroom before. Even though she knew that most of the vampire guards lived in the same building that she'd been imprisoned in, she had never been to the lower floors where their quarters were located.

Disappointed that she had found nothing useful, she plopped onto the bed, propping the two pillows behind her back, and started flicking through the channels. When she turned her head, she inhaled a heady scent: masculine, strong, appealing. She recognized that smell: it was the same way Oliver had smelled when she'd kissed him. It did something to her. It made her want to touch herself to find release. Damn it, but she wouldn't do it. She wouldn't touch herself, because she was turned on by the scent of a vampire!

Shame coursed through her at the mere thought of it. No, she would not sink that low, no matter how long she'd not felt any sexual satisfaction. Even though she wasn't shackled any longer, she would not give into her desires now. Soon she would be truly free. Then she could begin to live again.

Ursula closed her eyes and breathed deeply, trying to think of other things. Of going back to college to finish her education, of finally seeing her parents again. Of going out to movies with friends, of family gatherings, of trips to the beach. Things any normal young woman wanted. Things that had been stolen from her.

With a sigh, she relaxed into the pillows and pulled one corner of the blanket over her lower body to ward off the chill she suddenly felt. Tiredness crept up her legs and settled in her belly. Maybe she would just nap for a few minutes. Only to gain her strength back.

Ursula jerked up to a sitting position. For a second she didn't know where she was, but then it all came back to her. It hadn't been a dream.

"Good morning," a male voice said, making her heart stop and her head spin in the direction it came from.

Relief took two more seconds to set in when she realized that a news caster on TV had spoken the words, greeting his viewers as he started one of the local morning shows.

Jumping up from bed, she ran to the window, pushing the heavy drapes aside. When she looked outside, she realized that even though it was already daylight, not much of it penetrated the window pane. She focused her eyes on the glass and noticed that a thin colored film was over it, which appeared to limit the amount of sunlight entering the room. She wondered whether this film worked like a sun block, even though it wasn't dark enough to block out all rays like a black cover would have done. Was it maybe reflective on the other side, thus diverting sunlight like a mirror?

Well, it didn't matter to her. It was time to get ready. She had to stalk downstairs and find a phone.

Nervousness made her mouth feel parched. To find relief, she marched into the bathroom and gulped down a mouth full of water from the faucet, then stared at herself in the mirror. The puffiness around her eyes had waned and nobody would ever know that she'd cried. Why that made her feel better, she didn't know. It wasn't like she cared about a vampire's opinion of her.

Leaving the TV on to provide cover for any noise she made, she carefully turned the door knob and eased the door to the hallway open. The light was dim. Only one small wall sconce provided light at the opposite end. The floor below seemed to be dark.

Having assured herself that nobody guarded her door, she snuck outside and silently shut the bedroom door behind her. Taking caution to tread lightly, she walked toward the staircase. The plush rug underneath her shoes provided sufficient cushioning to absorb the sound of her footsteps.

When she reached the head of the stairs, she gripped the railing then eased one foot lower, then the next, careful not to trip. As she descended, leaving the third floor behind her, it got darker. As she had guessed, no lights were turned on on this floor. She could only see a faint shimmer of light coming up from the first floor, most likely from the light in the entrance hall.

When she set her foot on the last step, reaching the second floor, she continued to use the handrail for guidance. *Halfway there*, she encouraged herself.

The house was quiet. Oliver was probably sleeping. And Blake, even if he was awake, didn't have the kind of hearing a vampire possessed. If she remained quiet and breathed only shallow breaths, he would never hear her.

A few more steps and she would reach the top of the last flight of stairs.

"Leaving us so soon?"

Her breath hitched, and her heart skipped a couple of beats. Then Oliver's hands were on her, forcing her away from the stairs. Within a fraction of a second, she found herself pressed against the wall, his body and arms forming a cage around her she couldn't escape from.

Seconds passed with nobody speaking.

"Speechless?" he mocked.

"I . . . " She hated that he was right. No words came from her throat as her brain still dealt with the shock of being caught. Or maybe it was the shock of feeling his body so close to hers.

"Ursula, Ursula . . . " He shook his head as his hand moved to her face to brush a strand of her black hair out of her face. "What an unusual name for a Chinese girl. Is it even your name?"

Defiantly she thrust her chin up. "My father was a big fan of Ursula Andress. And there's no law saying I have to have a Chinese name because I'm Chinese." Even though she did, of course. Her middle name was Chinese, and all her relatives called her by her Chinese, not her western name.

"I see your father has great taste in women."

"I'm surprised you know who she is."

"She was a Bond girl."

Ursula had seen the many DVDs Oliver owned, but she hadn't bothered looking through them to find out what he was interested in. Apparently he liked 007.

"Now let me go." She pushed against him, but he didn't give an inch.

"No."

Angry at his refusal, she pressed her lips together.

He laughed softly. "You really thought you could sneak out of the house without me noticing?"

She decided not to correct him. There was no need for him to find out she was trying to call her parents.

"I thought you'd lived with vampires for the last few years. Didn't that teach you anything about us? Our skills?"

His head came closer. "Our desires?"

She swallowed hard at his insinuation, but at the same time she was unable to break eye contact. His blue eyes looked at her with such intensity that she felt paralyzed.

"Yes," he said even more softly, "especially our desires."

His gaze dropped to her lips, and just by doing so, he made them tremble.

"Do you remember our kiss?" He didn't wait for an answer, not that she had the strength to give one. "When I close my eyes, I can still feel your lips on mine."

She sucked in a breath, and the subsequent expansion of her chest caused her nipples to brush against his hard chest. His eyes instantly widened before he responded by pressing his body harder against hers.

"And I remember what you offered me."

Finally she found her voice again. "I'll never sleep with a vampire!"

He lowered his lids so quickly, she couldn't see his reaction to her words. "I figured that much. But tell me, if I were human, would you have slept with me?"

She gasped at his bold question. "That's not a—"

"Just answer the question," he interrupted. "If we had met under other circumstances, and if I were still human, would you have done more than just kiss me? Would you have gone to bed with me?"

She turned her head away to escape his penetrating eyes, but his hand on her chin forced her head back to look at him.

Would she have slept with him? Ursula studied his handsome features, his stubborn chin, his large nose, and strong eyebrows. She tried not to look at his lips, but they were hard to avoid. Yes, had they met on a university campus or been introduced at a party, she would have dated him, taken him back to her dorm room and stripped him naked. But this was not how it had happened.

She shook her head. "No!"

"Liar," he whispered without malice. "My pretty little liar. How much I wish right now to still be human."

Frozen in place, she watched his lips approach. When they touched hers, it seemed without haste, almost as if he was giving her time to pull back. Yet she couldn't escape the growing need inside her, even though she didn't want to admit it to herself. She wanted to feel his lips again.

When his mouth pressed more firmly against hers, she tilted her head and parted her lips. A low groan came from Oliver's throat and bounced against her. Then his tongue stroked over her lips before dipping inside her.

She'd never felt anything so soft and . . . gentle, almost as if he was afraid of scaring or hurting her. But the only thing that scared her more than his kiss was her reaction to it. If he asked her now whether she would have slept with him, her answer would be a resounding *yes*. Luckily, he was too busy kissing her to ask any more questions.

14

For the second time in less than twenty-four hours, he was kissing Ursula. But this time, he enjoyed it even more than the first time. Taking his time, Oliver coaxed her into the kiss with gentle, teasing strokes. The last thing he wanted to do was to scare her off. It would be challenging enough to get her to trust him and look past the fact that he was the very creature she hated. Therefore, he would play against type: be gentle instead of demanding, tender instead of aggressive, and soft instead of hard.

Well, maybe not the latter: it was physically impossible as he could already feel. Because he was hard, rock hard. The moment he'd seen her contemplate his question whether she would sleep with him if he were human, blood had shot into his cock and made it swell.

Despite his resolution not to come across as demanding and aggressive, Oliver ground his hips against her belly, pressing her harder against the wall. Everything male in him wanted to make her aware of his need. When she acknowledged the fact that she felt his erection with a low moan, he wanted to howl. But instead of intensifying his kiss, he held onto his control with every fiber of his being.

Easy, he cautioned himself.

His hand combed through her silken hair, the texture of it soft yet strong and perfectly straight. As he continued to delve into the warm cavern of her mouth and dance seductively with her, his thumb stroked along the plump vein on her neck. It pulsed under his caress, calling to him. He ignored that particular need, knowing that he couldn't go there: if he bit her, she would never sleep with him, and right now, his need to feel his body joined with hers was stronger than his craving for blood. Much stronger.

In fact, his desire to have sex with her nearly completely drowned out his need for blood. Nothing had ever managed to do that. Ever since he'd become a vampire two months earlier, he hadn't even felt the need for sex, because his craving for blood had overshadowed everything.

His few trips to Vera's brothel had—contrary to common belief—not been for the purpose of sex. Rather he'd gone there for the company.

When he felt Ursula shove one hand into his hair and caress his nape with the other, a shiver raced down his spine. He ripped his lips from hers, taking a much needed breath of air.

"Oh God, baby!"

Then he sank his lips onto her neck and planted open-mouthed kisses onto her hot skin.

"So beautiful," he murmured, and slid one hand down her torso.

When he encountered her braless breast and cupped it, Ursula let out a sigh. Then a breathless word came from her lips. "Yes."

Both man and vampire in him howled triumphantly. He nibbled his way to her earlobe, while continuing to tease her breast, his fingers capturing her hardened nipple through the fabric. With every moment, her breathing became more erratic, her heartbeat faster. Her scent changed: the sweet smell of arousal now teased his nostrils, awakening the vampire inside him. But he couldn't allow the beast to come to the surface. Too much depended on how she perceived him, and unleashing his untamed side would only destroy what progress he'd made so far.

After all, Ursula was responding to him, clearly forgetting that she was kissing a vampire and allowing him to touch her intimately. Allowing him to arouse her. Just like she aroused him. He didn't want to destroy this feeling by reminding her of what he was: a predator.

Her body felt pliable in his arms, precious even. Maybe knowing what she'd been through in her short life was the reason why he felt protective toward her. There could be no other reason for it. As for the lust she roused in him, the reason for it was undeniable: Ursula was the most enticing woman he'd ever met. Beautiful and exotic, strong and determined, and so passionate. Her sexual energy was impossible to overlook. It seemed to radiate from every pore of her tantalizing body. How a man could ever look at her and not be instantly tempted to haul her off to his bed was unfathomable to him.

At the thought, he felt a sharp stab in his chest, as if somebody were poking him with a blade. Reminded of how Blake had looked at her earlier, how he'd tried to use his—admittedly considerable—charm on her, drove Oliver to press his lips back onto hers to sear them with a kiss that he hoped would make her forget that his half-brother even existed.

Yes, he had to make sure Ursula only looked at him, only offered her sinful body to him. Tangling with her tongue, he captured more of her sweet taste, inhaled more of her scent. Like a cocoon, it wrapped around him, just like her arms embraced him, holding him close to her.

Releasing her lips, he issued his demand, "Touch me."

Without missing a beat, her eyes still closed, her hands slid down to his ass.

"My cock, touch my cock."

He pulled one of her hands from his backside and drew back just enough for her to slide her hand between them. When her warm palm cupped his straining hard-on a second later, he groaned loudly and sank his lips back on her neck, kissing her heated flesh.

"Yes, baby!" he encouraged her.

A bolt of electricity shot through him when she squeezed him. Instinctively, he pressed himself harder into her hand, asking her for more, demanding she repeat her action.

She did.

The pleasure she gave him with her touch was building with every stroke and every caress of her hand. Like an experienced temptress, Ursula traced the length of his erection with her fingernails, chasing every sane thought from his mind.

"Like that?" she whispered, her voice as breathless as his own.

"Just like that," he mumbled against her skin, not wanting to remove his lips from her neck. He licked and nibbled, kissed and caressed purposely playful so as to keep himself from losing control. But he knew it was in vain. If she continued touching him like she did, he would have her naked underneath him in a short while. But was she ready for this? For him?

Or would she curse him when she came to her senses? Because he wasn't any better than the vampires who'd taken her blood and . . . Oh God, he couldn't even finish the thought of how else they had used her body. How could he, Oliver, dare to do the same?

Before he could answer the question for himself, he felt hands on his shoulders, ripping him away from Ursula. He stumbled backwards, crashing against the banister before he caught himself.

"What the—?"

His last word was shoved back into his throat by Blake's fist landing in his face.

"Fucking asshole! You're biting her? Jerk!" Blake cursed and swung again.

But Oliver had already recovered and caught the fist flying toward him once more. With a practiced blow, he catapulted his interfering half-brother against the wall, then pinned him there.

"I didn't bite her, you idiot!" He tossed a sideways glance at Ursula, whose eyes had widened.

She shrunk back from him now, her hands nervously smoothing over her T-shirt. Her lips were swollen, her neck red from where he'd kissed her. Only now Oliver noticed that the overhead light in the corridor was on. Blake must have switched it on, and in his addled state, Oliver hadn't even noticed. His vampire senses had deserted him while kissing Ursula.

Blake followed his look, his eyes traveling over Ursula's body. "Then what . . . " He stopped himself. "Oh! Jesus, Oliver! You're still a jerk! After all she's been through?"

Sobering, Oliver let go of him. Blake was right, but he would never admit it to him. He sought eye contact with Ursula, but she avoided his gaze.

"I'm sorry, Ursula. I don't know what got into me." It was a lie. Yes, he was sorry, but he knew what had gotten into him: Ursula. She'd gotten under his skin. She'd awakened desires in him that he hadn't paid much attention to in his short life as a vampire. Was that why they were overwhelming him now, because he'd not stilled those desires in a while?

Ursula didn't answer.

Christ, he felt like an ass. He'd seduced her, and by the looks of it now, she regretted having let herself go. And what added to her obvious embarrassment was that Blake had caught them in the act.

He glared back at his half-brother. "What do you want up here anyway? Weren't you supposed to guard the doors?"

"Cain's calling. He has some information for you," Blake answered.

"Is he still on the phone?"

"He's waiting on Scanguards' internal system for you."

"Excuse me." With an apologetic glance at Ursula Oliver turned and went downstairs, leaving Blake with her.

At least he could be sure of one thing: Ursula wouldn't allow Blake to touch her now, not after what had just happened. And Blake was smart enough not to try anything, if only not to be thrown into the same pot as Oliver.

Oliver marched into the study and dropped into the chair behind the desk. The screen showed Cain, also sitting at a desk. They were connected via Scanguards' secure communication system, a video conferencing program similar to Skype. However, it was encrypted and, thanks to Thomas's programming skills, hacker-proof.

"There you are."

"What's up? What did you find?"

Cain looked serious. "Quite a bit, but I'm not sure you'll like it."

Oliver squeezed shut his eyes for a moment. He was in so deep already, he could only hope that the news wasn't all bad. If Ursula was lying to them and turned out to be a plant by a rival vampire group, he wasn't sure how he'd extricate himself from the situation he was in. He wanted Ursula, and with every kiss his need grew stronger.

"Go on, don't make me pull it out of your nose."

Cain nodded. "I've found newspaper articles about her disappearance, and Thomas was able to get me the corresponding police reports. The photo is definitely her. Her name is Ursula Wei Ling Tseng. Daughter of a Chinese diplomat stationed at the Chinese embassy in Washington DC. An only child. She went to NYU before she disappeared."

Oliver relaxed, dropping his shoulders to release the tension in his neck. "So far it checks out then. So, what am I not gonna like?"

Cain grimaced. "She told us she was abducted." He shook his head. "More like she ran away."

A gasp from the door made Oliver look away from the screen. Ursula stood there, her mouth gaping open. Blake was behind her.

"That's not true!" She rushed into the room and rounded the desk, then repeated her words when she stared at Cain on the screen. "It's a lie."

Oliver sensed her distress, but didn't dare put a soothing hand on her arm. "Are you sure, Cain?" he asked instead, forcing his voice to remain calm, despite the storm raging inside him.

"Sorry, but yes." He held up a few sheets of paper. "It's in the police report. Apparently they found a note written by Ursula."

Shock rolling off her in spades, Ursula leaned toward the computer. "I never wrote a note! There was no note!"

"That's not all," Cain continued. "The report says that you and your parents had a big fight days before your disappearance."

Ursula jerked back, and Oliver noticed how she flinched. "But . . . " She hesitated, looking down to him, tears welling up in her eyes. "I . . . it was all a big misunderstanding. I was stressed out about my exams. I didn't mean to quarrel with them."

Her eyes begged him for understanding, and his heart broke for her.

The clearing of a throat came from the speakers. "The evidence the police found, the note, a piece of your clothing on a pier in Manhattan . . . they concluded that you cracked, that you couldn't take it. It was ruled a suicide."

A sob tore from Ursula's chest. Oliver noticed her grip the edge of the desk for support and jumped up, catching her before her knees buckled.

"My parents think I'm dead?" she sobbed. "No. No, please, no."

Oliver looked back toward the screen. "Thanks, Cain. I'll call you back later."

Then he led Ursula to the Chesterfield sofa that stood below the window and lowered her down, taking a seat next to her without releasing her from his arms.

Her tears were only interrupted by frantic gulps for air, which resulted in even louder sobs. He'd never seen a woman cry like this.

"They think I'm dead," she repeated over and over again.

Oliver stroked his palm over her hair and pressed her head against his chest. "I'm so sorry, baby."

"Please believe me," she whispered barely audible.

"I do. I believe you."

His doubts about her story had evaporated the moment she'd cried out after finding out that everybody believed her dead. Her reaction had been instantaneous and pure. She hadn't faked her death and run away. Whoever had kidnapped her, had done that to stop her parents and the police from looking for her. He had no doubts about that now.

"My parents," she sniffed. "I have to let them know I'm alive."

He nodded. "I'll take care of it. But you'll need to give me some time. If your kidnappers took such pains to make you disappear, I wouldn't put it past them to watch your parents now that you escaped. They must anticipate that your parents will be the first people you'll contact. I want to make sure nobody is tapping their phone or intercepting any communications to them."

"But, you don't understand! They must be hurting. I have to tell them I'm still alive." She stared at him with a look that could squeeze blood from a stone.

"Oliver is right," Blake said from the door. "Not just for your safety, but also for theirs. What if they threaten your parents if they have reason to believe they know where you are?"

The words seemed to sink in, because finally Ursula nodded. But it didn't diminish the pain that was etched on her face.

"I'll arrange for our office in New York to send somebody to Washington and check out the situation. If everything is clear, we'll arrange for you to speak to them. I promise you," Oliver said.

It was a promise he was determined to keep.

15

"You'd better be right about this," Zane warned.

Oliver squared his shoulders and lifted his chin slightly. They stood next to Zane's Hummer which was parked outside of Oliver's house. The sun had set only a half hour earlier.

"She's telling the truth. You have to believe her."

"I don't *have* to do anything. The only reason I'm even authorizing this is because the whole story intrigues me."

"If Gabriel were here, he would—"

"But he isn't here," Zane cut him off. "I'm in charge right now. And I expect my orders to be followed."

Oliver bit back his next remark. Zane could be such an asshole sometimes. And now that he was subbing for Gabriel, who was visiting Scanguards' New York headquarters to assure himself that everything was running smoothly, Zane was downright unbearable.

"Understood."

A black Porsche careened around the corner, barreling toward them. Neither he nor Zane flinched. When the car came to a stop only inches from them, Oliver shook his head.

"He loves to make an entrance," Oliver said and watched as the car door opened and Amaury emerged.

A wide grin spread over his colleague's face, and the light evening breeze blew through his long dark hair. His piercing blue eyes were even more brilliant at night than during daytime.

"Right on time," Zane acknowledged and raised his hand in greeting.

Oliver took a step toward him. "Hey Amaury, thanks for coming."

"Didn't want to miss the action." Amaury's gravelly voice echoed in the quiet side street.

"We'll see if there's any action to be had," Zane cautioned. "Amaury, you'll ride with me. Oliver, you're taking Cain and the girl."

"She has a name."

Zane cocked an eyebrow. "Ursula then. We'll follow you, Oliver. And she'd better not be leading us on a wild goose chase. Call me when you're in the car, and keep the line open. I want to hear everything that's going on."

With a tight nod, Oliver turned and walked back up the stairs leading to the entrance door. After Cain had given him all the information pertaining to Ursula's background, he'd contacted Zane to ask him for help, knowing that if he did anything without Scanguards' support, he would put not only himself, but most likely others in danger. That by *others* he was primarily thinking of Ursula was something he kept to himself.

When he entered the living room, Ursula shot up from the couch, and both Cain and Blake looked at him expectantly.

"Zane's agreed to it."

Blake grinned. "Excellent! Some action!"

"You're not coming, Blake."

"What?"

"You heard me. Nobody is in the mood to save your ass tonight."

It wasn't exactly how Zane had put it, but since they didn't know what they would be facing, they had agreed to leave the human behind. It was bad enough that they had to take one human—Ursula. Two could distract them when they ran into trouble.

"That's totally unfair!" Blake complained.

"Life isn't fair. Get used to it." Then Oliver motioned to Cain and Ursula. "Let's go. We're taking the minivan. Zane and Amaury will follow in the Hummer."

As Ursula walked past him, their gazes collided. A silent thank you shimmered in her eyes. He hoped that he wasn't wrong about her, and that she wasn't leading them into a trap.

Moments later, they were in the van, Cain sitting on the back bench, Ursula in the passenger seat. Oliver gunned the engine and shot out into the street. As he passed the parked Hummer, he speed dialed Zane's cell phone. It was answered before it could ring even once.

"Lead."

In the back mirror Oliver saw Zane's Hummer follow him. "I'm heading down to the Bayview to where I ran into Ursula." He glanced at her from the side. "After that, she'll have to guide us."

Ursula nodded nervously. "I'll do my best."

"You'd better," Zane's voice came over the loudspeakers.

"She will," Oliver said with determination before concentrating on the heavy evening traffic downtown.

They rode in silence until he crossed the 3rd Street bridge behind the baseball park, passed a few swanky new housing developments, and then entered the less savory neighborhood of Bayview.

The area didn't have much going for itself. It was crime-ridden, and even the recent extension of the rail line—the MUNI as it was called—down 3rd Street did little to improve the area. If anything, it made it easier for the thugs to get around.

Oliver would know: he'd grown up here. And he didn't relish being back. It reminded him of the sins of his youth, the gang of thugs he'd consorted with, the crimes he'd committed. With every block that brought them farther into the heart of the neighborhood, he felt his shoulders and chest tighten.

Only a night earlier he'd been down here, feeding on a down-and-out youngster. He felt disgusted at the thought now. Why had he even come down here? He'd avoided the neighborhood ever since he'd started working for Scanguards, but ever since his turning two months earlier something had drawn him to it again. Had he sensed that somebody here needed his help?

He shook off the stupid thought. He wasn't psychic, nor had he any special gifts like Samson or Gabriel, or even Yvette. Perhaps he had simply considered the Bayview an easy hunting ground where he could still his lust for blood. Nothing more. Only tonight, he wasn't here for blood, even though he'd left the house on an empty stomach. He felt it growl now, but he pushed back the hunger. For a few hours, he would be all right. Then later, when this raid was over, he would feed. The memory of drinking the bottled blood the night before still haunted him: it had left him empty and unsatisfied. And he had no intention of repeating the experience.

Oliver slowed the car. "This is where I was when Ursula asked me for help."

"Okay. Which direction did she come from?" Zane asked over the open line of the cell phone.

"East," he answered and pointed toward the intersection.

"Yes, I think so." There was a hesitation in Ursula's voice.

When he looked at her, she nodded quickly. "I'm pretty sure."

Oliver turned into the next street and kept the car at low speed, giving Ursula a chance to find her bearings.

"Do you recognize anything?" he asked softly.

Her gaze darted around, first to the left then to the right, then straight out front. Her hands fisted at her thighs. "Yes, it looks familiar. But I was running. And afraid."

"Try harder!"

At Zane's harsh command, Oliver noticed her flinch.

She instantly pointed her finger to a target in the distance. "That way. I noticed that boarded up shop."

Yard by yard, they progressed through the area, slowly reaching the edge of the neighborhood where it bled into the worst of what San Francisco had to offer: Hunter's Point, a place no tourist ever saw, a place even most San Franciscans never ventured into. Few people lived here, and many of those who did lived in desolate public housing projects. Closer to the Bay, many of the plots of land lay bare; others were occupied by old warehouses and industrial complexes.

Not far from India Basin Park, Ursula's breathing suddenly changed. "Stop," she whispered.

Oliver brought the car to a stop and confirmed with a look in the mirror that Zane had done the same. "What is it?"

Her hand trembled when she pointed it toward something past the windshield. "There. The sign for the import/export company. I ran past it." She swallowed. "The building where they held me is just around the corner. Right on the next block."

Oliver put the car back in gear and inched forward.

"No. Don't go too close," she begged.

He glanced at her. "You'll have to point out the building to us, and since I doubt you want to get out of the car, I have to drive closer to it."

Oliver noticed her jaw tightening in concert with the rest of her body as if she was trying to steel herself against an invisible attacker.

"Don't worry, if anybody approaches us, we'll speed away." And then he and his colleagues would come back later without her. But he didn't tell her this.

"Which building is it?" Zane asked.

Oliver turned the corner, slowing to a crawl, then his eyes followed Ursula's outstretched hand.

"That one."

16

The four-story building was built of bricks, and it looked just as foreboding as it had the night she'd escaped its walls. A chill ran down Ursula's spine just looking at it. Fear tightened her throat, making her unable to say anything else.

"The brick building?" Zane asked over the loudspeaker.

"Yes," Oliver confirmed.

"Looks dark. There are no cars in the vicinity, no movement I can detect. Nothing. I say it's deserted. I wouldn't normally do this tonight, but let's not waste any time and check it out now."

"No! No, they'll catch you. You'll need more people," Ursula warned, overtaken by panic. If they went in there just the four of them, they could easily be overpowered. And then she wouldn't be any further than before: her kidnappers would recapture her.

"Cain, stay with the girl. The rest of us, let's go."

Before she could stop Oliver, he opened the car door and got out. She saw how the two other vampires, Zane and Amaury, left the Hummer.

Oliver had described Zane to her earlier while they'd been waiting for him and Amaury. But even his comment that Zane only looked tough because of his bald head, couldn't have prepared her for what she saw. He was tall and lean. When he briefly turned his head to look in her direction, his ice-cold gaze chilled her to the bone. His mouth was pressed into a thin line. His gait was determined, purposeful, and she knew instinctively that those long legs could chase down their prey in seconds. She never wanted to be caught on Zane's wrong side.

Amaury seemed different. Compared to Zane, he looked like a cuddly bear, but she wasn't fooled. He was just as deadly, and with more mass than his colleague, he could crush any human or vampire without effort. Those two were dangerous, deadly vampires.

She watched as they joined Oliver and marched toward the building. When they passed a streetlight, she noticed that all three of them carried guns. She pulled in a quick breath: she hadn't noticed that Oliver had been armed when he'd left the car.

"Don't worry, they know what they're doing," Cain said from the driver's seat.

She shrieked. She hadn't seen that he'd also exited the van and taken Oliver's spot while she'd watched the three vampires walk toward her former prison.

Cain shrugged. "Just in case we need to make a quick getaway."

Ursula wrapped her arms around her torso, feeling cold and scared. The vampire next to her wasn't like Oliver. Yes, he seemed friendly on the surface. He didn't carry his hostility on his sleeve like Zane—even seeing Zane only from the distance she'd felt that—but there was something unreadable about him. It made her feel uneasy around him. Oliver, on the other hand, unleashed an entirely different feeling in her. She felt drawn to him in the most primal way she had ever felt. Was it the fact that he was the first man who'd kissed her in over three years? Was it because she was so starved for physical intimacy that she had temporarily pushed aside her disgust for vampires when he'd pressed his lips onto hers?

Whatever it was, the intensity of it scared her. Because she knew that if it happened again, it would be as impossible for her to push him away as it had been to refuse his demand to touch him.

Wanting to silence her thoughts, she searched for a topic of conversation. "How long have you been working for Scanguards?"

Cain's eyes narrowed, suspicion rolling off him. "Why are you asking?"

"No reason."

She looked out the window. Oliver and his colleagues had disappeared. Had they entered the building or walked around it? "Where are they?"

"Inside."

At his nonchalant voice, she glared at him. "Aren't you worried?"

"They know what they're doing. Amaury and Zane are the best."

Her legs trembled. She pressed her palms onto her thighs to hide the fact that she was full of fear. "And Oliver?" Why hadn't Cain said that Oliver was one of the best too?

Cain hesitated. "He's still . . . young."

"But he can defend himself, right?"

"Of course he can. You worry about him?"

Ursula pressed herself back into the seat. "No."

Liar, liar, pants on fire.

"Then stop fidgeting. If what you say is true, and those vampires run some sort of blood brothel, my colleagues will pose as clients to get the lay of the land. They won't start a fight tonight."

Why hadn't Oliver told her that? Was he afraid she'd find a way of warning her kidnappers? Did he still not believe her?

"And the guns?"

"You've got good eyesight."

"That doesn't answer my question," she shot back.

"Maybe I'm not in the mood to answer questions." He looked at her, his eyes hard and unyielding. "I've read your file cover to cover. The police reports, the newspaper articles. Add to that what you told us yourself. The fact that you escaped from that place." He motioned his head toward the building. "Looks like a pretty hard thing to do, particularly if there are as many vampires on the premises as you claim. Something about your story stinks. And just because you managed to wrap Oliver around your little finger, doesn't mean you'll have as easy a time with the rest of us. I, for one, don't think with my dick!"

Ursula huffed angrily. She opened her mouth, but he cut her off.

"Save your breath!"

She folded her arms over her chest and looked out the window, watching the building intently. It was dark, but that didn't have to mean anything. All windows were either painted black from the inside or boarded up, or in some cases hung with heavy drapes, so that no light could penetrate. Likewise, no light could escape to the outside. She was certain her captors had done this on purpose so that nobody would be drawn to the building and start asking questions.

How they attracted clients, she could only guess. Word-of-Mouth most likely. They couldn't very well advertise that they had blood whores with special blood for hire.

Time seemed to stand still. Nervously, Ursula chewed on her fingernails, when she finally saw a movement at the door to the building. The entrance door opened, and one-by-one the three vampires stepped out, then walked straight toward the van.

Anxiously she waited. All three walked to her side of the van, but Zane was the first to reach it. He opened her door, lashing an angry glare at her.

"What that fuck was that about?" he asked.

Jolted by his harsh tone, she shrunk back from him. "What happened?"

"Nothing happened! Absolutely nothing!" Zane ground out. "Waste of my fucking time!"

Ursula's gaze darted past him, searching Oliver. When he met her eyes, she saw something akin to disappointment in them.

"Oliver," she begged.

Oliver hesitated a second before he spoke. "The place was empty."

Automatically she shook her head. "No, no, that's not possible." She pointed her hand toward the building. "That's the house. I'm absolutely sure. That's where they imprisoned me."

Oliver cast his eyes down as if trying to avoid her. Behind him, Amaury's face was set in stone.

"There's nothing in there," Amaury added. "No vampire, no human, no furniture."

In disbelief, she shook her head. "No, you're lying! They're in there. They have to be!"

"We have no reason to lie!" Zane snarled. "You, on the other hand, have been leading us on a wild goose chase. I don't know what your game is, but honestly, at this point I don't care. Because it ends here."

Equally shocked and frightened by Zane's words, she felt her hands tremble. What was he planning to do to her?

"Please, I can prove it! I'll show you where I carved my name into the wall of my cell. I can—"

Zane leaned in, his face half a foot from hers, interrupting her. "I don't care for your lies. Whatever your game is, I'm not playing it."

Then he turned toward Oliver.

"Wipe her memory, and then you and Cain will put her on a plane to Washington DC. Send an anonymous message to her parents to pick her up from the airport. If anything goes wrong, I'll make you responsible. Are we clear on that, Oliver?"

No! she wanted to scream, but fear of what Zane would do if she did clamped down her vocal cords.

Oliver stared at Zane. "Listen, there must be another way."

His bald-headed friend glared at him. "Do as I say!" He pointed back toward the building. "You've been in there. It was empty."

"Yes, too empty. And it smelled clean too, as if a cleaning crew had been through there just recently. Don't you think that's suspicious?"

"Doesn't have to mean anything."

"I think we should wait until Gabriel is back from New York."

Zane narrowed his eyes. "What for?"

Oliver motioned him farther away from the car and lowered his voice, not wanting Ursula to overhear his suggestion. "He could look into her memories and tell us what she's seen."

"That won't help if somebody planted false memories in her."

"I disagree. Gabriel was able to see in Maya's memories where they had been altered by a vampire. He would recognize it if somebody had tampered with her memories. I think we should wait."

Zane shook his head almost instantly. "Listen, Oliver. There was nothing in there. If she really escaped from that building last night, why didn't we find any traces of anything in there? I tell you why: because they were never there in the first place. My order stands. You can either take care of it together with Cain, or Cain will do it on his own!"

"No!" Oliver protested. He didn't want anybody manhandling her. "I'll do it." And he already hated himself for it. But he couldn't dispute their findings: the property was empty and there was no trace of any other vampires or of the girls Ursula had mentioned. She had lied to him again, and as much as he wished he were wrong, he couldn't simply set aside the evidence.

Zane nodded, but before he could walk away, his cell phone rang.

"Yes?" he answered it with a bark.

Oliver's sensitive hearing picked up the voice on the other end, Thomas's.

"A couple of crazy vamps were spotted in a nightclub downtown! I need all available men! Now!"

"Shit!" Zane cursed, waved Amaury toward the Hummer, then looked to Cain, who still sat in the minivan. "Change of plans: Cain, we need you. We have a lead on those vamps going berserk."

"Fuck!" Cain cursed as he jumped out of the van.

"If we hurry, I think we can get them this time!" Zane answered, tossing a look back at Oliver and pointing his finger at him. "You have your orders. I don't like sending you on your own. Don't make me regret it!"

Then he and his two colleagues jumped into the Hummer and sped off.

When Oliver looked back at Ursula, he noticed her pleading look. Her brown eyes looked like saucers, a rim of wetness around them. He shut the passenger door without a word and averted his gaze.

Oliver got into the driver's seat and pulled the door shut. Without looking at Ursula, he turned the key in the ignition and put the car in drive. Then he turned the van around and watched how the building disappeared from the rear-view mirror when he turned at the next intersection.

He headed toward the freeway that led to the airport which was located a half hour south of San Francisco. Traffic was light.

"Please don't do this," she pleaded, her voice sounding choked up.

He kept his eyes on the road, afraid that he would falter if he looked at her. "I have no choice."

Without Scanguards' backing, he couldn't do anything else for her. His trust in her was shaken. He'd actually believed her when she'd told him about her imprisonment, even more so when he'd seen her break after hearing the news that her parents believed her to be dead. What a fool he'd been to allow a pretty woman to cloud his judgment.

"You always have a choice," she claimed. "You just don't want to believe me."

He spun his head to stare at her. "I did believe you! But you lied to me and my colleagues. You led us around by our noses." *And me by my dick*, he should have added. "I'm afraid, I'm all done with believing in lies for tonight."

"They're not lies!" she cried out, glaring back at him.

God, how her cheeks flared with anger, and how beautiful it made her look. And her lips, so plump and inviting despite the lies that rolled over them.

Oliver trained his look back on the freeway. "I even gave you the benefit of the doubt when you didn't want to tell me how you really escaped. I did everything to convince my colleagues to check out your claims. I stuck my neck out for you!"

"Please, don't give up on me. There are other lives at stake. The other girls—"

"There are no other girls!" he cut her off, gripping the steering wheel more tightly. "You've made it all up. And I don't even want to know anymore why." Because he didn't want to hear any more lies. Not out of that pretty mouth she'd kissed him with. Oh damn, why could he not forget that? Would this image haunt him forever?

"You're the only one who can help us. I would have gone to the police if I believed that they had a chance to defeat those vampires. But they'll just be slaughtered. You and your colleagues, you're the only ones who can do this. I need you."

His heart clenched. *She needed him.* It was an admission that would have made him rejoice only hours earlier, but after seeing the empty building that she claimed had been her prison, the words made him almost nauseous.

"I don't care anymore," he replied, the words cutting deep into his own heart.

"What do I have to do for you to help me?"

He ran his hand through his hair. "You want me to help you?"

"Yes."

He tossed an angry glare at her. "Then give me something . . . just one piece of information that will help me believe you. Something, so I know you're telling me the truth." He kept his eyes on her and noticed her pull in a breath. Her eyelids lowered, and he saw the apprehension in her eyes, the hesitation that made her remain silent.

Disappointed, he tore his gaze away from her. "I knew it. You've never had any intention of telling me the truth." He shook his head and gave a bitter laugh. "How stupid I've been. To think that I actually liked you. And not just because I wanted to sleep with you."

"And now, you don't want that anymore?" Her voice was suddenly calm and sounded almost resigned.

"No," he lied. Because if he touched her now, he would never be able to wipe her memory and put her on that plane.

"Liar," she said softly.

"I don't care what you believe."

From the corner of his eye, he saw her nod. "Fine. I'll tell you everything. But only you. None of your colleagues can ever find out. If you don't believe me after that, then put me on a plane home. But if you believe me, then help me and those girls."

He glanced at her, trying to figure out what she was up to.

"Take the next exit and pull over, please, so we can talk."

He narrowed his eyes in suspicion. "If you think you can get your way by seducing me, think again. I'm not that gullible."

She gave him an unexpected smile. "No, you're not. Even though you're very cute—for a vampire."

He opened his mouth, but she cut him off before he could come back with an answer.

"What have you got to lose? Even if I were trying to seduce you, which I'm not, would it be such a hardship? It's a win-win situation for you. I'm the one who's risking everything."

Oliver instinctively let his eyes travel over her body, then lifted them back to her face. "What are you risking?"

"I risk you draining me once you know what my blood is capable of."

17

Oliver crossed three lanes to veer into the exit lane and get off the freeway. At the next intersection, he turned and found a small side street which led to a copse of trees next to a dilapidated house with a foreclosure sign in its front yard.

He killed the engine, before turning in his seat to face Ursula. Her words had made him more curious than he liked to admit.

"I'm all ears."

He watched her swallow before she spoke. "There were about a dozen girls. At first we didn't know why they had captured us. But there were similarities between us. All of the girls were Chinese, originally from mainland China. All of them had been captured in the US. Some were older, some pretty, others not. So we knew it wasn't beauty they were after. Or youth. It was our blood."

He nodded, still skeptical about where she was going with this. "Go on."

"They brought in vampires to feed from us. Two, sometimes three times a night. But during the feedings they kept a close eye on the vampires who fed from us. They made sure they didn't take too much. But we all noticed a change in them when they stopped drinking from us: they looked delirious, spaced out. As if they were stoned."

Oliver arched an eyebrow. "Stoned? I'm sorry, but vampires don't get stoned. We aren't susceptible to any human drugs. Not to alcohol, coke, or heroine. Nor to pot or anything else."

She nodded. "I learned that. But nevertheless, the vampires got high—on our blood."

"Impossible." Yet even as he said it, temptation made his gums itch, indicating that his body was longing for blood—preferably Ursula's. This was a bad time for his hunger to creep up on him.

"That's what we thought too, but we knew it was happening. And then there were other signs: the guards never drank our blood, even though they looked like they were tempted. And they talked about us:

how valuable we were, how much our blood sold for to their clients. The amount they charged seemed staggering. I have no idea what an ounce of cocaine costs, but the guards were saying that our blood sold for more. You questioned how I escaped. The guard was called to help in another room because one of the clients was going wild—probably as a result of the blood—and I used the time to make sure the vampire who was feeding off me took more than he should. I drugged him. He passed out and I was able to escape."

Oliver listened intently. Was it at all possible that it had happened exactly as she claimed? "Did nobody notice your escape?"

"I'm sure they did, but they were too late. I used the fire escape and ran until I bumped into you."

He remembered all too well. Was that why she'd been so close to death, because she'd made that vampire drink excessive amounts of her blood? As he thought back to the moment he'd met her, he remembered hearing footsteps in the distance. He hadn't waited to see who was approaching.

"They must have packed up when they realized that I escaped and couldn't find me. They must have feared that I would bring somebody back to their hiding place."

Oliver nodded slowly. "The building was looking a little too clean for that area. As if somebody had made sure to erase their tracks. Who was running the show?"

"I don't know. Whoever he was, he never came to the floor where we lived and . . . where they fed off us. In fact I don't think that even the guards knew who he was. I got the feeling that whoever was behind this was guarding his identity. And the guards were afraid of him."

Oliver had to continue questioning her, not only because he needed to find out as much as possible, but also because he had to distract himself from his hunger. And the more she talked about blood, the more he wanted to sink his fangs into her. "What did you hear?"

"That any guard would be severely punished if a girl in his care died because he didn't stop a leech from taking too much blood. The guards suspected that their boss had snitches in the building to make sure he knew what was going on at all times."

The whole story still sounded bizarre. But why would she make it up? "Why only Chinese girls? Did the vampires have a preference?"

"I think it had something to do with our blood. Why would they only have about a dozen girls, when they could surely capture more in any big city? It made me think that what we have is rare. Maybe something genetic, maybe only something that is found in the blood of Chinese women."

Blood. The word pulsed through his body. "Did they ever actually tell you that you had special blood?"

She shook her head. "Only indirectly."

Oliver pursed his lips. "I don't know, Ursula, your story is fantastic. But I have no way of verifying it." He sighed. "I've been ordered to buy you a plane ticket and give you enough money to get home. Give me a reason to defy my orders. One tiny proof."

Her breath suddenly hitched. "The money. Of course!" Then she put her hand on his arm, the contact sending a heat wave through his body, intensifying his hunger. "Oliver, wait, wait! I have proof!"

The way his name rolled off her lips made him hot all over.

"There's more. How could I have forgotten? I managed to steal a wallet from one of the leeches when he and the guard were distracted."

"Why didn't you tell Zane that earlier?"

"Zane scared the hell out of me! I tried, but I couldn't think straight with him glaring at me."

Oliver frowned. "He has that effect on people."

"So much happened in the last twenty-four hours. I just didn't think." When he gave her a questioning look, she continued, "I'd planned that if I ever managed to escape, I would use the money and credit cards in the wallet to get home. I hid it in my room. The name on the credit cards will lead us to one of the leeches. All you need to do is question him and you'll know I'm telling the truth."

He allowed the news to charge through his body, rejoicing silently, but then he sobered. "The building was completely empty. All the furniture is gone. So, wherever you hid it, the wallet is gone." And therefore another possibility of trying to verify her story had vanished with it.

She shook her head. "No. It's still there. I hid it underneath the floorboards. They wouldn't have found it."

"So you want me to drive you back there, is that it?" And damn it if he wasn't just a tad bit curious as to whether she was right. No, it was more than that: he wanted her to be right. He wanted the story to be true. Because then he could prove his colleagues wrong and investigate further. And he wouldn't have to wipe her memory and send her home. And then maybe, just maybe, whatever was brewing between them would have a chance to develop.

Ursula looked straight into his eyes, her gaze open and direct. "Yes. So I can prove to you that I'm not lying."

The drive back to her former prison seemed long. Maybe it felt that way to her, because she was anxious about going back inside the place that she considered hell. Or perhaps she was afraid that against all odds her captors had found her hiding place and removed the wallet, leaving her empty handed.

What would she do then? She had exhausted all means of convincing Oliver that he could trust her. Short of letting him taste her blood, she had nothing left. And she wouldn't allow him to drink her blood, too afraid that he wouldn't be able to handle it—and this time there would be no guard to watch out for her safety.

By the time they reached the building again and got out of the car, her hands were shaking uncontrollably. Oliver gave her a sideways glance, then took her hand in his. The warmth of his skin was instantly soothing.

"Easy," he said softly. "I promise you there's nobody inside."

She answered him with a hesitant half-smile and held onto his hand, knowing that he was the only ally she had, even though their alliance was shaky at best and could dissolve again as quickly as it had formed.

With tentative steps she walked next to him. When they reached the door to her former prison, Oliver pushed it open and gave her a gentle shove inside. He followed close behind her, his breathing the only thing she could hear.

Her hand searched his in the darkness, and she was glad when he didn't reject her touch.

"I can't see anything," she whispered.

"I don't want to switch on the light down here where it can be seen from the street. I can guide us through the dark if you tell me where you want to go."

"To the fourth floor."

As he led her up the stairs, she tried to block out the shivers that ran up her spine at the thought of what this place represented. She was surprised when she felt Oliver's hand rub over her arm in a soothing motion.

"Thank you," she murmured.

"Almost there."

When they reached the top of the last flight of stairs, she heard a light switch being flipped. A moment later, the dim lights in the hallway came on, helping her find her bearings. Instantly, she looked at him.

"Is it safe to have the light on now?"

He nodded. "There are only two windows in the corridor and both are blacked out."

Relieved, Ursula pointed toward the other end of the hallway. "That's where the fire escape is that I used." Then she turned in the other direction. "The room is that way."

Her pace slowed as she walked past the many doors that led to the rooms of the other girls. So many times, she'd heard sobs coming from them. But tonight, silence descended on the entire floor. Despite walking slowly, she finally reached the door to her former prison cell. She laid her hand on the door knob, but couldn't find the strength to push it open.

Frozen in place, she closed her eyes.

"We'll do it together," Oliver murmured behind her and put his hand over hers, turning the doorknob.

When the door opened inward, she took a hesitant step forward and reached for the light switch, flipping it. Then her eyes scanned the small room. It was empty, just like the rest of the house. How many hours had she spent in here, hoping and praying to be rescued?

"There was a bed here. They shackled me to it during the day so I couldn't move." She pointed to one corner where a wooden beam was exposed. The lower half of it had always been hidden by her headboard, but now it was visible.

She walked to it and heard Oliver's footsteps behind her as he followed. When she dropped down to the floor, she ran her fingers over the letters she had carved into the surface of the beam. "My name, my parents address, in case somebody found it, so that they could tell them I was here."

She turned to look at Oliver and noticed him staring at where her fingers were pointing. Then he too ran his hand over the surface of the wood. His eyes locked with hers.

"I'm so sorry."

If she hadn't seen his lips move, she would have missed his whispered words.

Surprised at the tenderness in his look, she was unable to move as his face came closer. His lips touched her cheek, pressing a soft kiss on her skin.

Swallowing away the lump in her throat she shifted and pointed to the floor. "It's down here."

Oliver backed away to give her space while she pressed on one side of the loose floorboard, thus tilting the other side up so she could grip it and pull it up.

She reached inside, her heart beating into her throat, praying that her captors hadn't discovered the compartment that held the stolen wallet. Her fingers touched something smooth, and she breathed a sigh of relief as she pulled out the leather wallet. She handed it to Oliver.

"This is it."

Oliver opened it, leafing through the cards inside. "Perfect."

Then he helped her up. "Let's get out of here. I can see that you feel uncomfortable in here." He motioned his head to the spot where her bed had once stood. "It must be terrible to return to the place where you've been raped."

She stared at him, her mouth dropping open. He thought she'd been raped?

"I apologize. I shouldn't have reminded you."

Before she could even think of how to respond, he ushered her out of the room and the building. When she sat in the van again and watched him put the key into the ignition, she put her hand on his arm, stopping him.

Surprised, he turned his head to her, but said nothing.

She didn't know why she felt compelled to correct his misconception, but she did. Perhaps his tenderness and the understanding that he had shown while in her former cell had done something to her. Or maybe she was just getting soft.

"We were never raped."

Surprise lit up his eyes. "But the vampires . . . the bite. You must have experienced the arousal. And with somebody as beautiful as you . . . "

He thought she was beautiful?

"I'm sorry to say, but I don't see what vampire could resist. I didn't mean to pry, and it doesn't matter that you don't want to tell me. I had no right to mention it. Just forget it."

He appeared embarrassed. And so utterly human.

"I know about the sexual arousal, I've been through it so many times, but the guards, they made sure the leeches never touched us that way. It would have reduced the potency of our blood, they said."

"What?" Confusion tainted his voice.

"They claimed that if a girl experienced sexual gratification, it would negate the drugging effect her blood had. That's why they never raped us. They weren't going to blemish the merchandise. That's also why we were shackled to our beds at daytime. So we couldn't touch ourselves."

Oliver's mouth dropped open as the news sank in.

Ursula nodded slowly, remembering the sleepless hours during which she'd fought her sexual urges. "And during nighttime, they used mind control on us so we wouldn't try to masturbate when we were alone."

"You mean . . . ?" He stopped himself.

She looked away, suddenly embarrassed that she'd been so frank. She didn't have to tell him about this part of her ordeal, but for some reason, she wanted him to understand what she'd been through. "I haven't had an orgasm since they captured me three years ago."

At her admission, she heard him exhale sharply. "Oh my god!"

She felt heat suffuse her cheeks.

"But you're so full of passion." He reached for her hand, making her look at him.

"I wish I could make it up to you." Instantly he seemed to realize what he'd said. "Oh God, no, that's not what I meant. I meant . . . "

She knew exactly what he meant. It should make her recoil, yet it didn't. Even though Oliver was a vampire, over the last few hours she'd seen another side of him. He cared. He'd listened and put his disbelief aside. He'd made an effort to help her. And the way he'd behaved when she'd been afraid to enter her former prison cell was downright sensitive. As if he could sense what she felt. Was it so wrong to want to lean against him for support? For some warmth?

"Maybe you can . . . " Her voice trembled slightly when she continued, "I crave to be touched." Touched by him. By the vampire who had rescued her.

Oliver reached for her, his hand cupping her cheek. "You want *me* to touch you?"

Ursula closed her eyes and leaned into his palm. "Would it be such a hardship?"

She felt him shake his head. "Do you really think I'm cute, I mean, for a vampire?"

She opened her eyes and smiled at him. Cute? It didn't even begin to describe what she felt. "Cute was maybe not the right word."

"What's the right word then?" he asked and inched closer.

Her gaze dropped to his parted lips. "What would you do if I said I found you . . . hot?"

Oliver groaned. "Are you playing with me, Ursula? Because if you are, you should stop, or I'll do something you might not want me to."

She scooted closer to him. "And what would that be?"

No, she wasn't playing with him. She wanted him. And she was sure now that it wasn't the residual arousal from the vampire's bite. Too many hours had passed since. No, what she felt right now was different. She wanted Oliver. And she wanted to forget.

"I thought you hated vampires," he deflected.

"I do." But she couldn't conjure up that same feeling for Oliver.

"Then why would you want to sleep with me?"

She brushed her index finger over his lower lip. "When you kissed me in your house, you made me want more." So much more than she'd hoped for in the last three years.

"That simple?"

Ursula gave a short shake of her head. "No. Nothing is simple. But I want to feel alive again. Can you do that for me? Can you help me feel alive?"

Oliver's face came closer, and his lips approached her mouth until they were only an inch from hers. "Anything you want, baby."

18

Oliver slanted his lips over hers and took her mouth in a kiss, first gently and softly in case she changed her mind, but when she didn't, he pulled her closer and deepened the kiss.

He couldn't believe this turn of events. From the moment Ursula had entered the abandoned building, he'd instinctively known that she was telling the truth. He'd sensed her fear. Finding the wallet from a client of the blood brothel—as he would call it—was confirmation enough for him that he could trust her.

But finding out that she hadn't been raped, that none of those despicable vampires had laid their dirty paws on her, made him rejoice. At the same time he cursed them for denying her any sort of carnal pleasure.

He severed the kiss and looked at her. "Let's go home." Then he would take her to his bed and make sure she got the release she needed.

To his surprise Ursula shook her head. "I can't wait. Please." She eyed the bench in the back of the van.

Oliver's heart skipped a beat. "Now? Here? In the van?"

More blood pumped into his cock, making him harder than a crow bar. At the same time hunger surged through him. He had to feed, and soon, or he wouldn't be master of his own actions anymore.

"Yes," she murmured and slid her hand onto his thigh, then moved it upwards.

When her fingers reached the outline of his hard-on, he groaned, his hunger instantly forgotten. "Get in the back."

He locked the doors, then followed her. When he saw her hand opening the top button of her jeans, he stopped her. She stared at him in surprise.

"If you think I'm going to rush this, you're wrong."

"But—"

He smiled. "No *but*. If you want to sleep with me, then we're going through all the motions: the kissing, the touching, the seduction. I'm not going to pass up an opportunity to make love to the most beautiful girl I've ever seen and just fuck her like an animal."

Her expression softened, and her cheeks colored in a pretty pink, while her eyelids fluttered. "You want to make love to me?"

Oliver moved closer and shelved her chin on his palm. "And I want to make you come so hard that you think the world is exploding around you. Isn't that what you want?"

Her lashes swung up, almost touching her eyebrows. Her eyes shimmered. "Oliver?"

"Hmm?"

"Why are you so good to me?"

"Because you need somebody who's good to you." And more than anything, he wanted to be that person.

"Are we gonna talk all night, or are you going to kiss me?"

He chuckled. Ah, how he loved an eager woman! "In my mind I've never stopped kissing you."

She moved closer, her mouth less than an inch from his now. "Make it a reality then."

When he took her mouth again, the world around him blended into the background. Soft lips pressed against him, her hands pulled him closer, urging him to drag her body against his. With one movement, he pulled her onto his lap, so she straddled him. His hand on her lower back, he pressed her to him.

"That's better," he murmured.

Oliver captured her lips again and delved into the warm caverns of her mouth. He stroked and licked, tasted and explored. Her response was just as eager: with strong strokes, she played with his tongue. Lust surged through him, sending hot bolts of fire through his core and into the tip of his cock.

He moaned into her mouth, an action she echoed a few seconds later. Slanting his head, he sought a deeper connection, a fiercer kiss. Her hands dug into his shoulders as if she was holding on for dear life, and her response to him became even more passionate.

Then he suddenly felt her lick along his teeth. Shock catapulted through him when he felt a corresponding itching in his gums. He knew what this meant: his fangs were about to descend.

Ursula licked again. He severed the kiss, holding her a few inches away from him, breathing hard.

"Don't!"

Startled, she stared at him, apprehension spreading over her face. "What's wrong?"

He dropped his lids. God, how could he explain this to her without reminding her of what he was and what she was potentially unleashing in him?

"Please, am I doing something wrong?" Her voice cracked.

No, he couldn't disappoint her, couldn't let her cry again. But he had to be honest with her. When he raised his eyes to meet hers, he swallowed hard.

"When you lick my teeth like that, I can feel my fangs descend."

Her breath hitched.

"Fangs are the most erogenous zones in a vampire. They want to feel you licking them. But I can't allow that, because if I do . . . " He hesitated, searching her face for signs of fear.

"What'll happen?"

Oliver's gaze dropped to the pulsing vein at her neck. "Once my fangs are out, it won't take long until I can't hold back my hunger for blood. I would bite you."

She sucked in a quick gulp of air.

Seeing that she was withdrawing from him, he quickly added, "But I won't. I promise you. I won't do that to you. You've been through enough. Please give me a chance. If we're careful . . . "

He hoped he wasn't lying. Could he truly hold back his hunger for the next hour so he could make love to her without subjecting her to the one thing she hated most: being bitten by a vampire?

"Careful, how?" she asked and approached slowly, her head dipping to the crook between his neck and shoulder. "Like this?" She pressed a gentle kiss on his skin, then another one.

Oliver closed his eyes, allowing the tender caress to sweep him away. "Perfect."

Her hands tugged on his T-shirt, pulling it from his jeans.

"Take it off," she whispered into his ear.

He did as she demanded, welcoming the cool air that touched his heated skin. But the relief didn't last, because a second later, her hands were on his chest, caressing him. His head fell back against the headrest.

Wasn't he supposed to be the one seducing her, not the other way around? Clearly, things weren't going exactly as planned, not that he was complaining.

However, he'd made her a promise: to give her sexual pleasure. And he would not break his promise. It was time to take back the reins.

Oliver reached for her T-shirt, pulling it from her jeans. "Lift your arms."

She didn't hesitate and let him strip her of her T-shirt, exposing her bare breasts to him.

"Beautiful."

Her breasts were small, but perfectly formed, round and firm. He cupped one and squeezed lightly, then dipped his head to suck her nipple into his mouth. The little rosebud was already hard when he swiped his tongue over it. Her skin tasted of citrus fruits, pure and young. Innocent. The thought suddenly threw up a question.

"Are you a virgin?"

She shook her head. "No."

"Good," he murmured against her soft skin. "Because I would hate for you to feel pain when I'm inside you." No matter how short-lived that pain would be.

He returned to teasing her nipple, then paid her other breast the same attention, all the while listening and watching for her reactions so he could figure out what she liked most. He worked his way down to her stomach then shifted her with one move, placing her with her back down on the bench, so he could bend over her.

While his lips were blazing a trail down to her navel, his hands were already opening her jeans and lowering the zipper. When he pulled on her pants and looked up, he noticed her watching him, her lips parted, her breaths uneven. Desire shone from her eyes, and her cheeks were as flushed as her entire torso.

"I haven't done this in so long," she said, her voice low and almost apologetic.

He chuckled softly. "It's like riding a bike." Only tonight she would ride him. The thought sent another wave of heat through his body, igniting him even further.

He freed her of her jeans and panties, pulling off her shoes in the process, then let the items fall to the floor. She lay in front of him in the nude. He was glad for his vampire vision which allowed him so see her in her full glory despite the dim light.

Stroking his hands up from her calves to her thighs, he spread her legs apart then lowered his head toward the apex of her thighs.

"You're going to—?" She stopped herself.

Oliver lifted his eyes to look at her face. "You didn't think I would pass this up?" Not a chance. "When I said, we're going through all the motions, I meant it. And that includes tasting your sweet pussy."

The moment his mouth connected with her nether lips, Ursula moaned. Oliver licked at the dew that was already covering her plump flesh and let the taste spread over his tongue. His body hardened. Fuck! She tasted amazing. Spreading her as wide as was possible in the confined space they were in, he licked over her wet folds, nibbled, and explored. And with every soft moan and sigh that came from Ursula, his determination to make her climax rose.

He'd always loved sucking a woman, but the beautiful Asian girl in his arms was even more of a treat. To know that he could give her something she'd longed for for three years spurred him on. Licking higher up, he headed for her clit. The small bundle of nerves was already swollen, a sign of her arousal. He gently caressed it with his tongue. Ursula almost lifted off the bench, her body tensing.

"Easy, baby," he appeased her. "I'll be gentle."

Yet that gentleness cost him: inside him, the beast wanted to be unleashed and exert its prowess on her. Holding back his wild side was a struggle he knew he would eventually lose. Still, he was determined to put up a fight. Because satisfying Ursula was more important right now than anything else. It would cement her trust in him; he was sure of it. And he wanted her to trust him.

With renewed determination, he continued to stroke his tongue over her tender organ, slowly putting more and more pressure on it. Ursula's breathing changed, becoming more uneven. Her heartbeat pulsed through her body in a rapid rhythm, the sound amplified by his vampire hearing. Her excitement fueled his own, and he was painfully aware of the hard-on that strained against the zipper of his jeans, which he was still wearing in order not to drive his aching cock into her before she had found her release. Once he was naked, there was no telling what he would do.

Like a cat, Ursula twisted underneath him, her moans getting louder, her sighs more pronounced. He doubled his efforts, realizing she was close.

"It's not working," she said. "I can't." Frustration and disappointment collided in her voice.

Fuck! He wasn't doing it right.

19

Ursula squeezed her eyes shut. She was so close, yet farther away from a climax than she'd ever been. Her body wasn't complying, but was still holding on to the tension it had felt the last three years. As if the shackles were still tying her to her bed and her captors' thoughts still invading her mind, preventing her from finding release.

"Baby, I'm sorry, I'm not doing it right," she heard Oliver say.

She opened her eyes and watched him sit up. He looked distressed.

"It's not your fault. I just can't."

His hand came up, tenderly stroking her cheek. "We'll try something else."

She shook her head. "It's no use. My body doesn't work that way anymore."

Oliver scooted closer and put his arms around her. "Nonsense, baby. You're just a little tense." She sensed him hesitating. "Is it because I'm a vampire? Are you afraid that I'll bite you?"

She met his eyes and noticed how he dreaded her answer. With a shake of her head, she tried to wipe away his concerns, but inside, she knew she carried a tiny speck of worry that he might lose control and bite her after all. She didn't allow it to rise to the surface, not wanting to disappoint him further.

"No, it's not that. It's just . . . the memories of being tied up, of not being able to . . . "

"Shh, I'll make you forget." He pressed a soft kiss on her lips then pulled back and released her from his embrace. "We'll try something else."

Wondering what he had in mind, she watched him shed his pants, boxers and shoes, before sitting back. Her eyes moved past the hairless sculpted chest and went to his massive erection. Even in the dim light of the van, it was hard to overlook. It was thick and long. Her womb clenched at the thought of feeling him inside her.

"Straddle me," he demanded and leaned back.

Hesitantly, she followed his command and lifted one leg over his thighs, then braced herself on her knees. Oliver scooted forward to the edge of the seat, allowing his cock to point upwards like a tent pole.

"Now I want you to rub yourself against my cock." He looked into her eyes. "Don't take me inside you, just slide against me and find your rhythm."

"But you . . . "

"And don't worry about me." He grinned, making him look younger and so unlike a vampire. "I'm going to enjoy this just as much as I hope you will."

When she felt his hands on her hips, she allowed him to guide her into the first movement, lowering herself so her sex slid against his erect shaft. Her wetness coated his cock, making her glide smoothly along it.

Oliver's head fell back against the headrest. "Fuck!" he cursed, closing his eyes.

Encouraged by his reaction, she repeated the same movement. Up and down she moved, watching his face as he clenched his jaw and the cords in his neck bulged as if he were in pain. But she knew he wasn't in pain. He was trying to hold back. For her. So that she could find release. Would another man be this selfless, or would he simply have sex with her, not caring if she achieved an orgasm or not?

Ursula felt how her body took on its own unconscious rhythm, how she moved without thinking of it, as if something inside her had taken over the lead. With every stroke, his erection dragged against her sensitive clit. Tendrils of pleasure reached for her, vibrations hummed through her body, and flames started dancing on her skin, turning her hot. Her long hair, falling over her back, caressed her naked skin, the touch as delicate as if somebody were teasing her with a feather. And all the while, Oliver moaned out his pleasure, a sound that penetrated the walls of her heart.

"Oh, baby," he murmured, his hands stroking her breasts, his fingers playing with her hardened nipples, only adding to the lust that coursed through her body.

Needing more friction, Ursula reached for his hard-on and pressed it firmer against her flesh as she continued to slide against him. A loud moan escaped her lips when she felt a bolt of electricity shoot through her.

"Oh, yes . . . that's it . . . that's it," she coached herself.

Oliver's hand slid to the back of her neck and pulled her head to him. "God, you're beautiful."

Then he captured her mouth and seared her lips with a kiss. His tongue speared into her as he tilted his head and sought a deeper connection. Without hesitation she responded to him and allowed her mind to let go of everything. Nothing mattered right now except the man whose lips were fused to hers. His taste was drugging, his body tantalizing. And beneath her palm, his shaft was pulsing, indicating his need to take her.

On the next upward stroke, she sensed a heat wave slam into her out of nowhere. Then her entire body felt like floating. She let herself fall and felt the waves of her orgasm crash into her. Her heart stopped, and her breath deserted her.

As she rode out the waves that battered her body, Oliver released her lips and smiled at her, his hand combing through her hair. "See," he whispered. "I knew you could do it."

Ursula slung her arms around his neck and pulled him close. "Thank you."

His hand slid to her lower back. "I was happy to help."

She felt his cock twitch against her tender sex, reminding her that he was still hard.

"Would it be ok . . . " he started and drew his head back to look at her, before his eyes dropped down toward his erection. "I won't need long. I'm close to coming."

"You won't need long?" she asked.

He shook his head. "No, I promise. I know your body is exhausted right now. Thirty seconds tops," he said, his voice almost apologetic.

She had to smile and tipped his chin up with her hand. After all he'd done for her, he wanted to short-change himself? Not if she could help it! "That's a shame, because I'd love to feel you inside me longer than just thirty seconds. But if that's all you can do . . . "

He squared his shoulders, raising himself up from his slouching position. "No! That's not what I meant. I *could* do it in thirty seconds if you needed me to be quick, but if you don't . . . Baby, I can hold out for as long as you want me to." A devastatingly handsome grin spread over his face. "And maybe this time we can come together?"

"Don't you think that's a little ambitious?"

He drew her head closer to his, bringing his lips within kissing distance, self confidence now rolling off him in spades. "I love a challenge."

Then his lips were on hers, and his hands gripped her hips, urging her to lift up. The thick head of his cock probed at her sex, pushing inside her without resistance. When she sank onto him, impaling herself, he released her lips and groaned.

"That's even better than I imagined." His hand on her nape, he stroked his thumb over her cheek and pressed his forehead against hers. "This is more than I deserve."

"You saved me."

"Is that why you're sleeping with me?"

She slowly shook her head.

"Good, because I'm not into thank-you or pity sex. I'd rather like to think that you're sleeping with me because you're attracted to me."

She chuckled softly. "How would you know the difference?"

"By your reaction to this," he claimed, and lifted her hips higher, then slammed his cock upwards, driving hard into her to the hilt.

A loud moan left her lips, and her head fell back. Her knees felt like jelly and her heart raced. With one thrust, he could do this to her, turn her into a woman who was controlled by lust alone.

"See," he continued. "That's the reaction I was looking for."

She looked into his brilliantly blue eyes. "Then you'd better stop talking and start acting."

"As you wish."

His last word hadn't left his lips yet when she found herself flat on her back again, her legs in the air and Oliver above her, his cock poised at her sex.

Oliver looked into Ursula's big brown eyes and waited until she found her bearings. He had her where he wanted her: underneath him, so he could take her harder than he would be able to with her straddling him. The knowledge that she was just as keen on this as he, doubled his hunger for her. He would have contented himself with a quick thirty-second fuck if after her orgasm she had realized that it was all she had wanted, and that he had only been a means to an end. But luckily, she still wanted him, even after she'd climaxed.

His cock was still coated with her juices when he thrust back inside her, seating himself to the hilt. The tightness of her interior muscles nearly robbed him of his control, but he didn't allow himself to give into the urge to seek release. This was too sweet a victory to rush it. Her warmth and wetness enveloped him, welcoming him home like a sheath its blade.

Lowering himself over her body, he moved his hips back and forth, moving in and out of her in slow and measured strokes, ignoring the vampire inside him that demanded he go faster and harder. That part of him would win soon enough, but first he wanted his human side to enjoy the tender slide of flesh on flesh—something he hadn't experienced as a human: he'd always used condoms. But now, as a vampire, there was no need for those pesky things anymore. He could neither contract nor transmit diseases. As for an unwanted pregnancy: there was no chance of that either, since vampire males could impregnate only their blood-bonded mates.

Underneath him, Ursula's chest rose in concert with her breaths, and her skin shimmered with a thin sheen of perspiration. Her lips were parted, her lids half closed, and the sounds that came from her throat were deep moans and sighs that he gobbled up as if he were starving.

God, how he loved a responsive woman, and the Asian beauty beneath him was more than just responsive. Her movements mirrored the passion he'd seen in her eyes earlier and spoke of the fire that burned inside her. He could see the flames as they tried to reach the surface, and could sense the lust that she'd buried inside her for so long. The need that she'd had to suppress. No longer. With every thrust of his cock, he teased more of it out of her, demanded that she show him what lay behind those mysterious eyes and was hidden in her heart.

Without any conscious effort on his part, his body moved in sync with hers, adjusting his rhythm to her heartbeat and her breaths. He'd always wondered what it would be like to make love as a vampire. Now he knew: it was more intense. All sensations were amplified, each touch more meaningful, and each kiss more passionate. At the same time, his energy was boundless, even though he knew that his control wouldn't last forever.

The thing he'd never thought, however, was that the first time he made love as a vampire would be in the back of a van. But it didn't matter where they were, because all he could look at was Ursula, her flawless face, and her perfect body. Their surroundings melted into the background.

Being inside her and driving them both to ecstasy was all he was interested in. More and more, the vampire inside him pushed aside the selfless lover from earlier and took over the reins. With it, the hunger for blood moved to the forefront again, more urgent this time. His look veered to the vein at her neck. Her heartbeat pounded in his ears, the blood rushing through her veins sounding like a waterfall that cascaded down into a pool of sloshing water.

He ripped his gaze away from the tempting prize and took her lips instead, distracting himself by kissing her and by concentrating on the way she made his cock feel as her muscles gripped him with each inward stroke.

Pounding harder and deeper into her, he put all his thoughts into one goal: to find his release with her. It was the only thing that could ward off the need for blood for a little while longer.

Releasing her lips, he searched her eyes. "Baby, I'm coming. I can't . . . "

Before he could even finish his sentence, his balls tightened, signaling the approach of his climax. A second later, his seed shot through his cock, filling her as he continued thrusting into her.

He breathed hard when he finally collapsed onto her, bracing one leg on the floor in order not to crush her with his weight.

"Oh God," she sighed.

He lifted his head for a moment. "I'm sorry. You didn't come. I'll make it up to you later." After he'd fed. Right now, he couldn't risk it.

"It doesn't matter," she replied and combed her hand through his hair.

"It does." And he would find a way for them to climax together, even if it was the last thing he did. "Later." Right after he'd had his fill of blood. "Let's go home now."

Her eyes looked at him questioningly. "Home?"

"Yes, my home."

"What are you gonna do about the wallet?"

"Don't worry. I'll find the guy."

"Promise me you won't tell your colleagues about my blood. They can't find out," she begged.

How he could keep the information from his colleagues forever, he wasn't sure. Eventually, he would have to tell them what was going on—particularly if the man whom the wallet belonged to confirmed that Ursula's blood was a drug to vampires.

"Please."

Oliver nodded, unable to disappoint her. "I promise."

20

The nightclub was packed, and the music was blaring. Cain squeezed through the crowd, making a path for himself just as Zane and Amaury did, all the while scanning the throng of people for vampires.

"I don't see anything wrong," he yelled to get Zane's attention.

His boss turned. "The club has three floors and a few private rooms."

Cain nodded.

"Thomas and a few of our guards should be here already," Zane added. "But I don't see them. Amaury and I will go up a story. It looks quiet down here, but nevertheless, check all the rooms on this floor, then follow us if you don't find anything."

Cain grudgingly complied and watched them head for the stairs. It didn't appear that any fight was happening on this floor, and he would much rather join in whatever action was taking place farther up in the building.

"Fuck it," he cursed. With efficiency, he scanned the dance floor, noticing nothing out of place. Just a mass of people writhing against each other to a monotonous techno rhythm.

He pushed past the sweating bodies, ignoring the scent of heated blood that was more intense whenever a human's body was hot from exercise or dancing. An array of disparate perfumes mixed in the air-conditioned air of the club, but the air conditioning couldn't keep up with recycling the used air. The scent of alcohol mingled with it. The clubbers were drinking while dancing, spilling half their drinks on the floor.

Cain scanned the bar that lined the wall beyond the dance floor. Three bartenders were busy serving the never-ending thirst of their clients. Still, he saw nothing out of the ordinary. He was about to move on when his eyes were drawn to a man who pressed a young woman against him. Not a man—a vampire, as his aura suggested. Cain zoomed in, but there was nothing wild or uncontrolled about the other vampire's behavior.

Making his way through the crowd, Cain headed for the bar, wanting to take a closer look to make sure the woman wasn't in distress. He chose an angle of approach from which the other vampire couldn't see him, even though he was aware that the vampire would sense him.

When Cain was close enough to listen in on their conversation, he stopped and watched.

The woman was in her early twenties, pretty, and endowed with a set of boobs any Hollywood starlet would be envious of. Her hand was on the vampire's jeans-encased ass, and she was clearly pressing him against her—admittedly very enticing—body.

Cain heard the vampire groan. "Sugar, you keep on doing that, I'm gonna have to take you right here."

She giggled. "Well maybe then we should get out of here."

He sank his head to her neck. Cain went on alert. Would he bite her in full view of several hundreds of human witnesses? Cain's legs moved of their own volition, bringing him closer to the unknown vampire.

Suddenly, the vampire lifted his head from the girl's neck and turned to stare at Cain. Cain's eyes instantly homed in on the woman's skin, but it was unblemished. Then he met the other vampire's stare.

The stranger nodded briefly, letting Cain know that he'd seen him and knew that he was a vampire. Then he turned to the woman in his arms.

"I think it's past your bedtime," he said to her, making no effort to lower his voice.

Cain turned away. Clearly, the vampire was in possession of all his faculties, nothing crazy about him. That he wanted to take a human woman to bed was none of Cain's business, particularly since it appeared that the woman consented wholeheartedly.

"Have fun," Cain murmured, knowing that the other vampire would be able to hear him.

As the vampire left with his conquest for the night, Cain walked to the other side of the club which he hadn't covered yet. There, mirrored partitions separated the dance floor from an area with high tables and bar stools. It was only marginally quieter there, but just as crowded.

Again, Cain walked through the area, watching for any signs of vampires, but he didn't see the tell-tale aura that surrounded a vampire, something only other preternatural creatures could see. Having completed his sweep of the first floor, he headed for the stairs. When he set his foot on the first step, something in his peripheral vision caught his attention.

He whipped his head in its direction and noticed a door that was ajar. It could easily be overlooked, because it was made of the same material as the shiny black paneling that surrounded it. A dim light came from inside the room.

His heartbeat kicking up a notch, he walked toward the door, his eyes scanning the people around him, but nobody seemed to pay him any attention. With the tip of his finger, he opened the door another inch, then spied inside. From the little he could see from this angle, the room appeared to be a private party room, furnished with a large sectional.

Cain let his senses reach out, but couldn't sense the presence of a vampire. He inhaled. What he smelled made his gums itch violently: blood.

"Shit!" he cursed and pulled the door open wide enough so he could squeeze inside. He closed it behind him, holding his breath as he did so.

It took his eyes one second to assess the situation and his stomach an additional one to turn upside down.

***

Zane narrowed his eyes, focusing on a group of youngsters who screamed with the music and danced wildly, when he picked up a scent. Next to him, Amaury growled: he'd smelled the same thing.

Simultaneously, he and Amaury pushed through the crowd and cleared a path to where the smell of blood originated. Zane scanned the area. Beyond the bar, which was of similar size as the one on the first floor, smaller booths were tucked away in a corner, their entrances partially obstructed by mirrored screens. The booths were furnished with plush seating arrangements and low tables for drinks.

As he got closer, Zane sensed the aura of a vampire. He stormed into the booth, Amaury only steps behind him. A vampire was sucking on the neck of a young Asian woman, her struggles evidence that the bite was not a welcome one, and that the vampire wasn't employing his mind control skills to pacify her. His hand was clamped over her mouth so she couldn't scream, but her eyes did the screaming instead. He was making her suffer deliberately.

Zane jumped toward him, when the rogue vampire suddenly whirled around and glared at him, his fangs dripping with blood, his eyes red. The stranger pounced instantly and with such ferocity that Zane was thrown back against a wall, shattering the mirrored surface.

He caught himself quickly, but the vampire was wilder than he'd ever seen anyone. Like an animal he attacked again, growling; saliva and blood dripped from his mouth as his claws veered toward Zane's neck. Zane sidestepped him.

The girl's screams, which the rogue vampire had muffled before, now came from his victim's throat. From the corner of his eye, Zane verified that Amaury was taking care of the situation and concentrated on his attacker again.

Zane was no stranger to bloody fights, but this vampire was different—stronger and more dangerous—even though he was only of average size. Bloodlust, he figured. There was no other explanation for it.

Had this been any other fight, Zane would have simply reached for his stake and driven it into the jerk's heart, but he needed him alive. This was the first time they'd actually come face-to-face with one of the crazies that the mayor had asked them to watch out for. And if they wanted to know what was really going on and what was causing them to go berserk, he needed to catch one alive.

As he dodged another blow by his attacker, Zane swiveled and jumped behind him, then kicked him in the back of his knees. But instead of falling to his knees as Zane would have expected, the vampire jerked his elbows back and slammed them into Zane's ribcage, knocking the wind out of him.

"Fuck!" Zane ground out as he absorbed the violent jab.

"Chain!" Amaury yelled behind him.

Zane turned his head and saw how Amaury pulled on his gloves in vampire speed, then reached into this pocket. When he pulled the silver chain from it, Zane jumped aside, giving Amaury a straight line-of-sight to the attacker, who'd already turned and was ready to land more kicks and blows.

The hostile vampire's high leg kicks prevented Amaury from coming close enough to throw the chain around his neck. Flashing his fangs, the rogue snarled like a beast, then jumped toward Amaury. Zane, standing off to the side, saw his opportunity and kicked his leg up, hitting the vampire in the groin in mid-jump. He buckled.

Amaury didn't lose any time and wrapped the silver chain around his neck. The stench of singed hair and flesh immediately permeated the air.

"Fucking asshole!" Amaury cursed as he held the chain tight behind his neck and brought him down on the ground. The vampire was struggling, bringing his hands to the chain to remove it from his neck, but burned his fingers as he touched the only metal that was toxic to a vampire.

Zane kicked his boot against the rogue's hip, then helped Amaury tie him up with a second chain. Behind him, the girl was still crying. Zane stood and looked at her.

Her neck was bleeding profusely; her body was covered with bruises from the vampire's claws. He'd brutalized her.

"Shit!" Zane hissed.

A gaze to the entrance of the booth confirmed that none of the clubbers had noticed what was going on: the music was too loud for anybody to hear any of the fighting or the girl's screams, and the mirrored partition that partially covered the entrance to the booth hid the carnage behind.

Zane looked into the girl's eyes, focused on her mind and worked his magic, wiping every memory of this horrific event from her mind. But to stop the bleeding and heal her, he needed help. As a blood-bonded vampire he couldn't drink blood other than that of his hybrid mate, and if he were to lick the girl's wounds to close them, he would inadvertently consume some of her blood. It would make him violently ill. He needed a vampire who was either not blood-bonded or blood-bonded to another vampire—they were able to digest blood not coming from their mates.

Besides, the girl's injuries were severe. She needed vampire blood to heal, simply licking her wounds and allowing the vampire saliva to close them wouldn't be sufficient.

"We need Cain," he said to Amaury. "And where the fuck is Thomas?"

***

Cain refrained from holding his hand over his nose and mouth, but it was hard not to puke at the sight of gore that presented itself. The girl on the dirty floor of the room was dead. Her throat had been ripped out, and it was evident that a vampire had savagely fed from her, then finished her off with his claws. As if he'd been angry. No, not just angry: furious! He'd wanted to punish the girl for something.

Her almond-shaped eyes were open, still staring at him in horror. Proof enough that the vampire who'd done this hadn't bothered using mind control so she wouldn't realize what he was doing. The poor girl had known what was happening to her.

Cain turned away from the bloody scene and surveyed the room for any sign that could lead him to the vampire who'd done this. Instinctively he knew there would be none. He'd come too late.

He dropped his head when he noticed a small ray of light coming from under one of the mirrored panels. He walked toward it. There was no image in the mirror—even though he was used to it, it still startled him from time to time, making him wonder whether he truly existed, or whether he was only a shadow of his own imagination. Shaking off the wayward thought, he ran his hands along the mirror, searching for any indentations or hooks that might allow him to get behind it. There were no latches, but when he pressed against the panel, it moved away from the wall, revealing another room behind it, by the looks of it a storage room.

A figure jumped at him, the movement a blur, but Cain's reaction was instantaneous. He slammed his body against the attacker, whom he recognized as a vampire. The stench of blood still clung to him, and he was broader than Cain and a little heavier. Cain landed a right hook under his chin, whipping his attacker's head back, then followed it up with a balled fist against his windpipe, then a kick against his thigh.

But the guy didn't buckle as easily as other opponents had before him.

"Shit!"

The vampire shot him a nasty grin. "Better blood!"

Momentarily distracted by the odd comment, Cain couldn't avoid the hit to his neck that slammed him against the storage unit on one wall. Pain whipped through him, but it was only momentary. He pulled himself up immediately and was thus able to evade the next blow. Cain jumped to the side, kicking his attacker in the hip, catapulting him against the opposite wall.

"Fucking murderer!" he cursed, glaring at the jerk.

The vampire growled, narrowing his eyes as he prepared for a counterattack. "She didn't have the right blood! Bitch deserved it!"

The crazy vampire was clearly delirious, his mumblings not making any sense. Bloodlust was written all over him: his breathing was ragged, his eyes bloodshot, saliva dripping from his mouth as from a rabid dog. Unfortunately, another thing was true too: like other vampires in bloodlust, he seemed stronger and more ferocious.

As they fought, trading blows, kicks, and hits, Cain frantically looked for any weapons he could use to subdue his opponent without killing him. He had a stake in his jacket pocket, but he wasn't going to use it. Zane's order had been to take the crazy vampires they'd been hunting alive. If they could capture one alive, they would have a chance of figuring out what was going on.

With his next blow, the rogue vampire swiped Cain's neck with his claws. Blood ran from the stinging cuts.

Fury charged through him, and he pushed back, pulling up his knee and driving it into the guy's nuts. As his torso folded over, Cain kicked upwards once more, sending him against the cabinet behind him, making the supplies on it rattle and the items stacked in the shelves fall out.

Cain pinned him against the shelving unit, his arm across his opponent's neck. "Gotcha!"

The rogue's eyes danced first to the left then to the right, his arms reaching out. "No you don't!"

When his attacker's arm pulled forward, Cain saw him holding a piece of wood.

"Shit!"

Releasing the guy's neck, Cain reached into his pocket in the same instant as he made a half-turn getting out of the way of the swinging arm that held the makeshift stake. Palming his own stake now, he completed the turn and slammed it into the guy's chest.

Noise behind him made him turn on his heels, while his opponent disintegrated into dust. He raised his stake, ready to attack whoever had entered, when he sighed in relief.

"Thomas," he breathed. "About time!"

Next to Thomas, Eddie popped his head into the room. "Sorry, there was an accident involving a bus on Mission. We got stuck," Eddie explained.

"I had no choice," Cain said, looking back at the place where the vampire's dust now settled on the floor. "I guess there goes another chance at finding out what's going on." He'd failed, and he didn't like failure.

"Don't worry." Thomas motioned his head to the room where the dead girl lay massacred. "He deserved it. Besides, Zane and Amaury got a live one."

Cain let out a sigh of relief.

"Clean up time," Eddie suggested.

Cain squeezed his eyes shut for a moment. "She must have suffered terribly." When he looked up at his two colleagues, they answered his look with sad gazes of their own.

"He'll burn in hell for it," Thomas claimed.

Cain shook his head. "He's free now. I should have let him live to show him what hell really is." Because hell wasn't on some other plane. It was right in this world.

***

Cain left the cleanup to Thomas and the other vampires who'd arrived shortly after him, and transported the prisoner that Zane and Amaury had taken back to Scanguards' Headquarters in the Mission. While Zane and Amaury took the still-struggling vampire to one of the holding cells in the basement, Cain headed for the *V* lounge, a large room only accessible to vampires via their specially-coded ID cards.

He needed a distraction from what he'd seen tonight, and he knew the lounge would provide it.

As he entered, the calming atmosphere of the room instantly eased away the tension of the night. The lounge felt like an old gentlemen's club with comfortable seating arrangements, a fireplace and a bar with blood on tap.

This was where vampires rested between assignments, caught up with their colleagues, or enjoyed a quick snack. Visiting vampires who weren't part of Scanguards were also entertained here, but tonight Cain saw only colleagues. No visitors were present. He nodded to several of the vampires as he walked up to the bar and leaned against the counter. The woman behind it smiled at him.

He let his eyes travel over her black dress which hid none of her curves. His mouth watered at the sight. Even though he had no actual memory of it, he knew he preferred curvaceous women.

"What can I get you?" she asked politely.

How about you on a platter? he thought, but stopped himself. It would do no good screwing somebody in Scanguards' employ. After all, he wasn't interested in a relationship, and things could turn awkward if he had to see her again after a one-night-stand. She was a vampire and therefore wiping her memory after the act was not an option. That particular trick didn't work on vampires, only on humans.

He would have to go to a nightclub on his night off and pick up a human for some uncomplicated sex, just like the vampire he'd met earlier tonight had done. But the thought of visiting a nightclub didn't appeal to him right now, not after what he'd seen there tonight. Perhaps a visit to Vera's brothel would be in order. Her girls were pretty and asked no questions. And ever since he'd started working for Scanguards, he had enough money to spend on diversions like that.

Cain pointed to one of the taps. "AB positive, please."

His eyes continued to watch her as she poured the red liquid into a wine glass and put it in front of him, then tapped her register. Without having to be prompted, he swiped his ID to pay for his drink. The price of the blood was subsidized by Scanguards. In fact, Scanguards sold it to its employees at cost, a service they provided in order to convince more vampires to drink bottled blood rather than feed directly from humans.

Cain liked the convenience of bottled blood, but on occasion he went out to hunt. It wasn't something he flaunted, particularly in front of Oliver, who had enough problems with keeping himself in check. It wouldn't help him if he knew that Cain also enjoyed a little hunt now and then. He fully agreed with Quinn, though, that Oliver first had to learn to control himself before he could be let loose on the general public. And from what Cain could see, Oliver was as far away from that goal as he'd ever been.

Cain took his drink and slunk into an empty Wingback armchair in front of the fireplace.

The words of the vampire he'd killed echoed in his head. *She didn't have the right blood.*

What had he meant by that?

21

Ursula leaned back in the passenger seat as Oliver navigated the van through the nearly empty city streets. She felt tired and relaxed at the same time. As well as a tiny bit embarrassed about her behavior. She'd never been so . . . forward. And with a vampire of all creatures.

She could only hope that she hadn't made a mistake by trusting him.

"Do you regret it?" Oliver asked out of the blue, casting her a sideways glance. "Is that why you're frowning?"

"I'm frowning? I'm sorry. I was just wondering how you're going to find the vampire whose wallet I stole and what you'll say to him."

"Don't worry. That's what I'm trained for. He won't be hard to find. There's a driver's license in the wallet. That's where I'll start."

"And then?" She cast him a doubting look. "When you find him, what will you say?" Would the leech admit that he'd been to the blood brothel and fed off the girls? Or would he deny its existence?

"I'll make him talk. I promise you."

She nodded. "And if he doesn't know where they moved the operation to?"

"I have the feeling that he does. I would imagine that they told all regular clients where they were going. Why go looking for new clients when they can bring the old ones back? They must have a way of letting their existing cliental know where they can be found now."

"I hope you're right. We have to find where they've taken the other girls." She had to keep her promise toward them and help them get out of the hellhole they were in.

"You care about them," Oliver stated.

"We were like sisters. We weren't allowed much contact, but we found ways to communicate anyway. Going through the same pain binds you together." That's why she had to help them, because knowing they were still suffering hurt her.

"I'll do what I can. But you know that once we know where they're holed up, we have to involve Scanguards. It's not something I can do on my own."

Ursula knew what he was alluding to. "But you won't tell them about my special blood, will you?" She looked at him, but he continued to stare straight ahead.

"Why are you so afraid about them finding out? You told *me* about it."

"I don't know them. What if they're like the vampires who held me captive? What if they want the same?"

Oliver shook his head. "You don't know me either."

Her breath hitched. What was he trying to tell her? "You want my blood too?" Her voice broke. Had she made a huge mistake by trusting him?

She heard him breathe hard, then she noticed a shudder go through his body.

"It's not what you think. I want your blood, yes. Because of what we just did." He cast her a predatory look. "When a vampire makes love, he wants to take his woman every way he can. And that means sinking his fangs into her and drinking her blood."

Ursula shrunk back into her seat, inching closer to the door.

He seemed to notice and lifted his hand from the steering wheel. "You don't have to be afraid of me. I won't take your blood, because I can't."

With disbelief, she stared at him, not understanding what he was saying. "But you just said—"

"I know what I said," he interrupted. "But there's something you have to know. If your blood is like a drug, then it will be forever off limits to me. I was an addict a long time ago. When I was human. And I'm never going back to that. Never."

His blue eyes sought hers, looking at her with an intensity she'd never seen before.

"Because if I ever go back to drugs, no matter what kind of drug it is, I won't make it this time. It'll destroy me, but I won't throw away the second life I've been given."

His determined voice gave her pause. Was he really strong enough to resist the temptation?

"I'd rather forego the pleasure of feeding from you when making love to you than become an addict again." He paused for a moment.

"That is if you ever let me make love to you again."

One single word escaped her lips. "Oh." He wanted to make love to her again? She lowered her gaze.

"You don't have to answer me now. I only ask that you don't dismiss me outright because of what I just told you. But I thought you'd appreciate the truth."

She raised her eyes to look at him, wanting to tell him that she wanted nothing more than joining her body with his when she noticed a red glow in his eyes. It was something she was more than familiar with. Her gaze instantly dropped to his hands gripping the steering wheel. Claws started pushing through his fingertips.

She felt fear clamp down on her, tightening her throat and preventing her from speaking. She could only stare at him.

"I'm sorry, Ursula. I'm very hungry. But I won't attack you. I promise." He swallowed hard and when he opened his mouth again, she saw his fangs protruding.

A breath escaped her chest.

"We're almost home. I'll let you out at the curb. You'll have to go inside. Blake will be there. He'll protect you. Promise me you'll go right to him. Tell him however much or little you need to, but don't leave his side."

Oliver's voice sounded different now, strained as if he had trouble pronouncing the words.

She nodded automatically.

"I'll wait until you're inside. Please don't run away. If you do, my instinct will kick in and I'll chase you. And God help us then."

"I promise," she choked out. Anything so that he wouldn't bite her.

For the next few blocks, she watched his every move. Her own palms were sweaty, and her heart beat double as fast as usual. She knew he could hear it and smell her sweat if the clenching of his jaw and his white knuckles were any indication.

It seemed to take ages until Oliver pulled to a stop in front of his house.

"Go!"

Without looking back, she opened the car door and jumped out, slamming it behind her. Forcing herself to walk normally, she made it up the few steps to the entrance door, then rang the door bell several times in quick succession. As she waited impatiently, she looked over her shoulder. Oliver was still sitting in the van, the engine running.

Her heart nearly stopped when the entrance door to the house was ripped open from the inside.

"Ursula?"

"Let me in! Shut the door!" she demanded and pushed past Blake into the house.

Only when she heard the door being closed and bolted behind her did she breathe a sigh of relief.

"What happened?" Blake took her arm and turned her to face him.

"Oliver is hungry."

Fury spread in his face. "Fuck! Did he hurt you?" His eyes searched her neck. "Did he bite you?"

She quickly shook her head. "No."

But for some inexplicable reason she suddenly wondered what it would be like to feel his fangs in her neck while he was making love to her. A thought came and went: her captors had denied her and the other women sex, because they believed it would weaken the potency of their blood. She couldn't be sure of this being true, but she had told Oliver about it. Would he remember this detail? And if he did, would he try to bite her if he believed that the drug in her blood was less potent once she'd had sex? But most of all: would she let him?

How screwed up was she to even imagine this? Had she not suffered enough at the hands of her captors?

Tears brimmed in her eyes, and with her next breath, a sob tore from her chest.

22

After stilling his hunger for blood in an alley near Civic Center, Oliver got back into the van and headed for the address on the driver's license he'd found in the wallet. It was located in North Beach. As he drove, his thoughts went back to Ursula and her frightened look when she'd realized that he was in dire need of blood.

If he were honest with himself, he would admit that they had no future. Even if Ursula would allow him to bite her—which she clearly wouldn't—he could never risk it. Her blood was a drug, and he was a recovering addict. It wasn't any different from an alcoholic who would instantly fall back into his addictive behavior if he drank the tiniest drop of alcohol. Her blood would do the same to him. Not only would it destroy his own life by sending him into a tailspin, it would also end hers: knowing how addictive her blood would prove for him, he would eventually take too much and drain her. She would die in his arms.

That thought made him want to pull over at the side of the road and throw up. He forced the bile back down. No, he wouldn't be weak like that. He would resist—for her sake, and for his own. It left him with two choices: continue to feed off the less fortunate inhabitants of this city, or get used to bottled blood. Neither option sounded pleasing, when Ursula's blood provided the ultimate temptation.

After making love to her in the back of his van, he couldn't imagine anything better than to repeat it and this time sink his fangs into her lovely neck, making the connection even more intense than it had already been.

A fleeting thought tried to tempt him even further. Hadn't Ursula said that the reason why she wasn't allowed any sex was because her captors believed it would lessen the drugging effect of her blood? It seemed like a ludicrous suggestion, and he could only imagine that those vampires were sadists and took pleasure in seeing these women suffer, denying them any kind of pleasure for the hell of it. Following this idea that there could be a way of safely drinking Ursula's blood only made the temptation worse. This was only his addict-self talking, reaching for any straw, however thin, that presented itself. He couldn't allow himself to listen to it any longer—he had to shut it off or the "what-if" scenarios would drive him insane.

Oliver swallowed away the desire that coursed through him and concentrated on his next task.

Paul Corbin, the owner of the wallet Ursula had stolen, lived in a single family home in North Beach. The address pointed to him being wealthy, or at least well off, considering that single family homes in this sunny Italian neighborhood of San Francisco started at about two million dollars—for a fixer-upper.

Oliver parked the car in the driveway, blocking it, not just because there was never any available parking in the neighborhood, but also to prevent the man from escaping. Not that he had any suspicion that he would. After all, Oliver was only here to return the wallet and ask him what he knew about the blood brothel.

He got out of the car and locked it, then walked up to the entrance door of the impressive house. It appeared to have been fully renovated only a short while earlier. No expense had been spared, if he considered that the entrance steps were tiled with travertine and the entrance door was made of solid steel. He imagined the materials in the interior to be just as classy.

Oliver pressed the door bell and heard the pleasant chime from inside the house. A light came on over his head and he raised his eyes to it, noticing a camera that pointed at him. It appeared that Corbin preferred to know in advance who stood outside his door before he opened it.

Oliver let a casual smile play around his lips, wanting to appear non-threatening. He had no intention of scaring the other vampire off. He didn't have to wait long until he heard steps approaching the door. Then a lock was flipped and the door opened.

The tall man was a vampire, and according to the picture Oliver had seen on his driver's license, he was Paul Corbin himself. Somehow, he'd expected him to have a servant who would open the door for him. In a grand house like this, servants wouldn't have been out of place.

"Yes?" Corbin asked with a raised eyebrow.

"Mr. Corbin, it appears you lost your wallet," Oliver started, watching the man's reaction. "I'm happy to say that I've found it."

Surprised, he opened the door wider, allowing Oliver more of a glimpse inside. It was dark, but he could make out a hallway with doors to each side, then a large double door at the very end.

"You're here to return my wallet? I had already written it off as a complete loss," Corbin admitted.

Oliver smiled, pulling the wallet from his jacket pocket. He noticed an instant stiffening of the other vampire's shoulders, until he handed him the item.

"How can I thank you, Mr. . . uh . . . ?" Corbin asked politely and at the same time very stiffly.

Oliver shifted onto the other foot. "Oliver Parker," he lied. "Actually, I was wondering, whether I may ask you a couple of questions in relation to where I found the wallet."

The man's face remained impassive when he answered, "And where, Mr. Parker, did you find it?"

Oliver turned his head, looking around and noticed a man walking his dog. "I'd rather not talk about it out in the open." He motioned to the person with the pet. "Our kind has to be careful."

"Of course. How thoughtless of me. Please come in."

As he walked into the house, Oliver wondered how old the other vampire was. He appeared very old fashioned and stiff.

Corbin opened the double doors at the end of the corridor and motioned him to enter. While he closed the doors behind them, Oliver swiftly assessed his surroundings. They were in a generously appointed living room with a Baby Grand Piano, a large seating arrangement, and floor-to-ceiling windows with a view of Coit Tower, one of San Francisco's iconic landmarks.

"Not to rush you, but I have plans for tonight."

Oliver turned to face his host and cleared his throat. "I'll come straight to the point. I found your wallet in a building in Hunter's Point."

He paused, watching Corbin's reaction. There was a minute flicker of something, but already the other vampire had himself under control again.

"It's a place where some of our kind go to feed." Oliver deliberately didn't mention that the place was empty now, wanting to see how much the man knew.

"You've been there to feed?"

Oliver nodded. "It's quite special."

Corbin turned away, looking out the window. "So I guess you've discovered my dirty secret. It's not something I'm proud of."

Oliver waited patiently, not wanting to interrupt whatever the man wanted to confess.

"I went there once. An acquaintance told me about it. I thought it would provide some thrill, something to disrupt the monotony of my life." He laughed to himself, then motioned his hand to the room behind him, indicating that money alone didn't make him happy. "But, frankly, I didn't enjoy it. I didn't like the way it made me feel."

Oliver tried to hold back the emotions that were battling inside him: this man had drunk Ursula's blood. He'd had his fangs in her beautiful neck, her body underneath him. He clenched his jaw, trying not to let his fury show. "How did it make you feel?"

Corbin looked over his shoulder, meeting Oliver's gaze. "You tell me."

Remembering his days as an addict, he knew he could come up with a plausible answer. "Carefree, light."

Corbin nodded. "But I knew I couldn't go back. Already after the first time, I knew how addictive it was. I've never had blood like that. I had no idea it existed. But I couldn't allow it to change me. You understand, don't you?"

"So you only went once?"

"Yes. And I regret it. I guess it served me right that they stole my wallet there. It taught me a lesson." He shrugged. "Nevertheless, thanks for returning it."

He made a motion toward the door as if wanting to dismiss him, but Oliver wasn't done with his questions yet.

"I wonder whether you've been notified that the operations have moved to another location."

Corbin raised an eyebrow. "Moved? I hadn't heard."

"Yes, I'm afraid the building in Hunter's Point has been vacated."

"Maybe they closed the establishment. Good riddance."

"I doubt that very much. It was a lucrative business."

"Why do you care?"

Oliver gave Corbin a long look. He didn't appear to be an addict, making his claim that he'd been there only once plausible. But still, he was a former client of the blood brothel, and as such he might have a way of contacting the vampires who operated it.

"I need to get hold of the people who operate the place. But I'm afraid they haven't let me know where they moved the business to." Oliver dropped his lids, hoping he could fool the man. "You see, I do like the way I feel when I feed there."

"I'm afraid I can't help you. As I said, I was there only once."

"If they contacted you, let's say to let you know where they moved to, would you let me know?"

Corbin gave him a curious look. "If you've been to the place, and by the sounds of it more often than I have, why wouldn't they contact you directly? Surely they wouldn't want to lose a good client just because they moved?"

Oliver's mind worked quickly to come up with an excuse. "See, my contact information changed just recently and I'm afraid I'd forgotten to let them know. They have no way of contacting me. That's why I was so glad when I found your wallet and figured you might be able to help me."

Corbin nodded slowly. "Of course. But, as I said, I doubt they'll contact me."

Oliver pulled out a card from his pocket and handed it to him. It only had his first name and a phone number on it. Scanguards preferred it that way, not wanting to give away too much information.

Corbin took the card and looked at it. "Thank you. And, may I ask you for a favor in return?"

Oliver shot him a curious look. "Yes?"

"May I ask you to please not tell anybody about the fact that I went to a place where they keep women with drugged blood? I really don't want to be judged by my peers. I'm new in town, and you know how it is when gossip makes the rounds."

"Your secret is safe with me."

Oliver left the house, satisfied that he'd been able to confirm Ursula's claim. She had told him the truth, and that news made him feel a whole lot better. However, he wasn't any closer to finding out where Ursula's captors had taken the other girls.

23

Ursula eyed the two newcomers cautiously. They had arrived minutes earlier with big suitcases in tow and worried expressions on their faces. Blake had greeted them enthusiastically and introduced them as Rose and Quinn, his fourth great-grandparents.

Neither of the two looked any older than twenty-five. Rose was a classical beauty with long golden hair and a model figure to die for. Quinn wasn't any less handsome. His blond hair looked windswept, and his hazel eyes were alert and beautiful.

"You must be Ursula," he greeted her and offered his hand.

Not wanting to be impolite, considering she was staying in his house, she shook it. "Nice to meet you." Whether her statement would prove to be true wasn't decided yet.

When he released her hand, he addressed Blake, "Where is Oliver?"

"Out."

"Out where?"

Blake crossed his arms over his chest. "I don't know."

Before Quinn could say anything else, Rose put a hand on his arm, making him look at her. Instantly, the expression in his eyes softened, and he smiled at her.

"Don't, love. He'll be back." She motioned to Ursula. "I can't see him staying away for long."

Slowly, the tension in Quinn's shoulders seemed to ease. "You're right. I just feel that we should have never left. He's not ready yet to be left alone."

"Don't coddle him," Rose cautioned. "He's a grown man."

"I'm still responsible for him."

Ursula watched their exchange with interest. So this was Oliver's sire, the vampire who'd turned him. And by the looks of it, he was nothing like any of the vampires she'd encountered in the last three years. Rather, he looked like a concerned father. He reminded her of her own father, how he'd worried when she'd moved to New York to go to college. At the beginning, he'd called her daily to reassure himself that she was all right. Maybe that memory was the reason why she now wanted to soothe Quinn's concerns.

"Oliver went out to feed. He'll be back soon." She kept the fact that he was looking for the man whose wallet she'd stolen to herself. It wasn't something she could reveal without giving away things she wasn't willing to share. The situation was complicated enough.

Quinn let his eyes wander over her face. "So you know that he doesn't drink bottled blood. Does that scare you?"

She hesitated. When she'd seen Oliver only a short while ago with his extended fangs, his sharp claws, and his red eyes, she'd felt true fear course through her, but now, that memory seemed so distant that she couldn't recall the feeling. "I don't know," she answered honestly.

"Why don't we all sit down for a bit? I'm exhausted from the trip," Rose confessed and pointed toward the living room.

Having no reason to refuse her invitation, Ursula walked into the living room. She eyed the clock over the mantle. Oliver had been gone for a long time. Had he run into trouble with the vampire whose wallet she'd stolen? She knew she shouldn't worry about him. After all, he was a vampire and a trained bodyguard. And he was armed.

A prickling at her neck suddenly made her turn her head back to the door. Her heart nearly stopped: Oliver was back. He stood between door and frame and stared at Rose and Quinn, not even noticing her.

"What are you doing back so soon?" he asked, his voice clipped.

"Is that the way you welcome your family these days?" Rose replied, bracing her hands at her hips.

"Of course not," Oliver deflected quickly and walked toward her. "Welcome home, Rose, how was your honeymoon?" He pulled her into a quick embrace, when his eyes suddenly fell on Ursula.

When he freed himself from Rose, he nodded to his sire. "You must be tired from the trip. Why don't you two go upstairs and rest? I can carry up your suitcases."

Quinn frowned. "Oliver, I'm older than you. So don't think you can just brush me off. We're home early because of what's happening here."

Oliver tossed a glare at Blake. "I could've handled the situation without interference from anybody."

Blake squared his stance, glaring back. "Right!"

Quinn lifted his hand to stop their argument in its inception. "Blake didn't call us. Maya did. She was concerned about you two being alone with Ursula."

Oliver stared at his sire, clearly fuming. "I don't need a chaperone!"

"Neither do I!" Blake immediately took his half-brother's side.

Ursula almost had to chuckle. One minute the two were practically at each other's throats, the next they stood side by side against the head of their family.

Ursula caught how Rose rolled her eyes and shook her head. "Kids," she heard her murmur softly. Then Rose looked at her. "Ursula, why don't you and I go upstairs and leave these three alone to work out their differences? I for one can't stand any more display of testosterone right now."

Hesitantly, Ursula nodded.

"I'd better take all my clothes out of the guestroom so you'll be more comfortable," she added.

"But I was sleeping in Oliver's room," Ursula blurted, before she could stop herself.

Rose's head snapped toward Oliver, her eyes glaring at him. "Oliver! I can't believe you'd take advantage of a frightened young woman like that. That's despicable!"

Oliver thrust his hand through his hair. "I didn't do anything! I didn't sleep in my room!"

Rose huffed indignantly. "Of course you didn't *sleep*!"

Before Ursula could say anything else to defend Oliver, Rose pulled her out of the room.

Oliver watched as Rose and Ursula left the room. This was terrible timing: he didn't need Quinn and Rose sticking their noses into his affairs right now. He had too many things he had to keep quiet: the fact that he hadn't followed Zane's orders to put Ursula on the next plane to Washington DC, the fact that Ursula's blood was a drug, and that he'd been able to find an actual client of the blood brothel she'd been held at for three years. Until he knew how to proceed, he couldn't let anybody at Scanguards know about these things.

He hoped he could keep Quinn in the dark for long enough to figure out a strategy. If Maya was the one who'd told him about this situation, then Quinn didn't know very much yet. Maya didn't know what had transpired in Hunter's Point; neither did Blake. Therefore Quinn couldn't know that Zane had ordered him to send Ursula away. And he couldn't know yet that they had found nothing at the building in Hunter's Point and therefore dismissed Ursula's claims.

Shit, how had everything gotten so complicated?

"Everything is under control, Quinn, trust me." Oliver forced a confident look onto his face.

"Sure it is," Quinn said dryly. "Why don't you explain to me what's going on?"

"What did Maya tell you?"

"Enough for us to pack our bags and leave England to rush home. So, update me. What's happened since?"

Oliver swallowed. "We found the property in Hunter's Point where Ursula was held. But they had already cleaned everything out by the time we got there. I assume they figured she would come back with help, so they fled. We don't have any leads yet where they might have taken the operation."

He felt his body get hotter. How he hated having to lie to his sire. But the less he knew at this point the better. If he was aware of Zane's orders, there was a chance that Quinn would try to separate him from Ursula, and he couldn't risk that. She trusted him to protect her, and he could only do that when he was with her. Besides, he needed to speak to her in private to tell her that he'd been able to confirm her story.

"Hmm. What else?"

Oliver shrugged, trying to look casual. "Nothing else. We're working all our contacts to find out if anybody has heard of the place and knows where they might be now. They're holding a dozen other girls captive. They need our help."

"And the fact that you guys didn't find anything at the property in Hunter's Point didn't bother any of you?" Quinn wondered.

"Would have made me wonder if she's telling the truth," Blake threw in, looking at Oliver. "You know we all had doubts, even you."

"Go ahead and bother Zane by asking him if he still has doubts about her story. See how he likes it being questioned," Oliver bluffed. Would Blake fall for it? And more importantly, would Quinn stop asking questions?

"Fine, whatever. Just saying. I wish you guys would let me go with you to those raids. I never get to do anything fun," Blake complained. "No wonder I'm always out of the loop. Even Cain gets to patrol the city for those crazy vampires, and he's only been with Scanguards for a few months."

Quinn put his hand on Blake's arm. "What do you know about those crazies? It's classified information."

Blake grinned. "Cain told me 'cause I'm family. He said they were going crazy in the city, like some drugged out animals."

Oliver's ears perked up. Drugged out? He'd never heard them described that way—when the vampire staff at Scanguards talked about them, they used words like bloodlust, but what if those vampires were on drugs? Or rather drugged blood?

Was it possible that there was a connection between the blood brothel and those incidents they'd heard of where vampires had gone completely crazy as if they were suffering from bloodlust?

Tonight, Zane had gotten a call that several of those crazies had been spotted at a nightclub in town. Oliver had to find out what had transpired there. Maybe it would provide the lead he needed to find the new location of the blood brothel.

"Hey, Quinn," he interrupted. "Listen, it's great that you and Rose are back. We missed you. Didn't we, Blake?"

His half-brother nodded quickly.

"I'd better turn in. It's close to sunrise, and it's been a busy night." He hugged his sire.

"It's good to be home, son." Quinn smiled when he released him.

Oliver was about to turn, when Quinn put a hand on his shoulder. "About the girl." He motioned to the upper floor.

"What about her?"

"Don't do anything you might regret later. She's vulnerable."

Oliver was careful not to show that the remark irked him. He knew she was vulnerable; he didn't need Quinn to tell him that. "If you're insinuating that I might bite her, let me tell both of you once and for all: I won't."

And that was one promise he was determined to keep. No matter the cost.

***

Oliver waited for the noise in the house to settle down. Finally, it seemed Rose and Quinn had gone to bed and Blake had withdrawn to his room. Rose had set Ursula up in the guest room, clearly not wanting her to stay in his room again. But they would have to do a lot more to stop him from seeing her.

He waited an additional hour after all the noise had died down before he snuck out of his room and walked barefoot toward the guest room. The floorboards creaked under his feet, but nobody seemed to hear him.

When he reached the door to the guest room, he listened for any sound coming from inside, but heard none. He couldn't risk knocking, afraid that Rose or Quinn might hear him from the master bedroom across the corridor, so he simply eased the door open and squeezed inside, pulling it shut behind him.

The curtains were drawn, but some light filtered into the room, enough to clearly see that Ursula was sleeping, even if he weren't a vampire with night vision. He quietly approached the bed and sat on the edge, leaning over Ursula. With his mouth at her ear, he whispered to her, "Ursula, baby, it's me, Oliver."

A choked breath came from her. Afraid she might make too much noise, alerting everybody in the house, he slid his lips over hers and pressed a soft kiss onto them, ready to intensify it if necessary.

"Oliver?" she mumbled.

"Yes, baby."

"Mmm."

The humming sound she issued was reason enough for him to urge her lips apart with his tongue and delve into her inviting mouth. Within an instant, his hunger for her pushed to the surface. He had to force himself to pull back, reminding himself why he was here.

"I have news."

She opened her eyes and pulled herself up to a sitting position. She still wore one of his T-shirts, and that fact pleased him. Of course, if she were sleeping in his bed, she wouldn't be wearing anything. Instead, he would cover her with kisses and caresses.

"What happened?"

He listened for any sound from outside the door before he continued. "We have to be quiet. Quinn and Rose will be pissed if they find me in here."

"Are they very old fashioned?"

"No, just very protective of innocents."

"But I'm not—"

Even in the darkness, he noticed how she blushed. He couldn't resist pressing a kiss on her pink cheek. "I'm sorry about what happened earlier."

"You mean them showing up unannounced?"

He shook his head. "No, about what you saw in the van. When I was . . . hungry."

"Oh."

"I know I scared you. It won't happen again. I'll make sure I feed more often, so you won't have to see that again." When she didn't answer and dropped her lids instead, he wondered whether his words were making it worse. After all, he was still feeding off humans, even if he promised her not to bite *her*. "I am what I am, Ursula. I'm trying hard to change, but it's . . . difficult."

She laid her hand on his forearm. "I understand."

His heartbeat accelerated. "So we're okay? I mean, you and I, are we good?"

"We're good." She smiled up at him. "You said you had news."

"I found the vampire whose wallet you stole."

Oliver sensed the excitement that went through her.

"Please tell me what he said." Her eyes hung on his lips.

"He confirmed that he went there for the blood. He knows it has a drugging effect."

"Did he tell you where they went?"

"He says he doesn't know."

Disappointment spread over her face. He used his hand to tilt her face up. "Don't worry. It's early yet. If they moved the blood brothel somewhere else, then it might take them a few days to notify all their customers. We have to be patient."

She nodded, even though he could see that she wasn't fully convinced. "I hope you're right."

He stroked her cheek with his thumb. "In the meantime, I'll be checking out another lead."

"What other lead?"

"Leave it up to me. When I have something more concrete, I'll tell you about it. I just don't want you to get your hopes up in case it doesn't pan out. Please trust me, we'll find them."

"I hate waiting."

"It won't be long." Then he stood. "I'd better go."

She put a hand on his arm, holding him back. "Please stay for a little while, just until I've fallen asleep again."

"I shouldn't." But her eyes pleaded with him, and there was no way he could resist. "Just for a few minutes."

He pulled the blanket aside and slid underneath it, pulling Ursula against his fully clothed body. "Is that okay?"

"Yes," she whispered and snuggled up to him.

His arms went around her back, one sliding down to her backside. As he palmed it softly, she purred like a kitten and draped her leg over his thighs.

"Sleep now," he murmured and stroked his hand over her silken hair.

24

Cain sat in a small office behind a glass window that looked down into an interrogation room below. Next to him, Thomas gulped down the rest of his bottle of blood.

"About time that jerk is coming 'round. I need some shuteye."

Cain couldn't agree more. After they'd brought the rogue vampire to Scanguards' headquarters, the punk had passed out as if in a drunken stupor. At least that meant he'd stopped screaming for *real blood*, whatever he meant by that. For hours Thomas, Zane, and Cain himself had waited around in the V Lounge for the captive to gain consciousness. Amaury had long gone home after his mate had called him.

Even Cain had been able to hear Nina's seductive voice on the phone, describing to Amaury what she was wearing. He'd never seen his fellow vampire move faster. Not that they needed Amaury to question the rogue. Zane had volunteered for that particular job, and he was already tapping his foot impatiently, waiting for the rogue in the room below.

Cain snapped his head to the door of the interrogation room as it opened and two vampires dragged in the struggling captive. His hands were cuffed in front of him. In order not to cause him any unnecessary pain, the vampire's wrists had been bandaged so that the silver handcuffs wouldn't touch his exposed skin. Whether the bandages remained on his wrists during the interrogation depended on his cooperation. And by the look on Zane's face, Cain's superior clearly hoped that the prisoner didn't cooperate immediately so he could inflict some pain.

Thomas flipped a switch so the sounds from the interrogation room now came through the loudspeakers in the observation area.

"Leave him!" Zane ordered the two guards. They released the captive from their hold and left the room, shutting the door behind them.

Thomas pressed a button, locking the room remotely so it couldn't be opened from the inside. "You're locked in," he announced through the microphone by holding the speaker button down, then releasing it again.

Zane nodded in acknowledgement, then grabbed the prisoner by the neck and slammed him into the only chair in the room.

"Now we talk."

Cain watched intently, knowing that he could always learn something from Zane.

The captive looked up defiantly, his eyes wild. He bent forward on this chair, seemingly unable to keep still. His hands twitched, and the cords in his neck bulged.

"I want blood!" he demanded, his eyes narrowing.

"You had enough last night," Zane claimed. "You almost drained that girl. You're lucky she's alive."

"Or what?" he spat in response.

Zane jumped, grabbing his neck once more. The captive's hand came up. However, the silver handcuffs that made contact with Zane couldn't do him any harm: Zane wore a long-sleeved shirt and leather gloves.

"Or I would have ripped your heart out while you watched!"

Cain glanced at Thomas. "He's bluffing, right?"

"He's done it before. I don't see why he wouldn't do it again."

Cain tried not to show his shock at Thomas's words, and instead focused back on the events in the room below. It appeared that the prisoner was reasonably intimidated by Zane's claim and shrunk back into his seat.

"You won't feed until I have the information I'm looking for."

"You can't hold me here forever."

"Can't I?" Zane tossed his captive the semblance of a half-smile. "Piss me off and I'll throw you into an underground cell and forget you."

The wary look on the vampire's face was evidence that he started to believe that Zane was capable of doing just that.

"What's your name?" Zane asked.

There was a short hesitation, then the answer. "Michael Valentine."

"Not his real name," Thomas commented to Cain while he already typed it into the keyboard in front of him.

"Funny name! How about your real one?" Zane continued.

"That's my name. I was turned on Valentine's day in 1900. Somebody's idea of a sick joke. So I took the name."

"What was your name before that?"

"Garner," he pressed out.

Zane glanced up to the window, a silent question on his lips.

Thomas pressed the speaker. "Give me a minute." Releasing the speaker button, he continued typing on the keyboard. A moment later, he went back on the speaker again. "Checks out. Continue."

Cain looked at the computer screen where a message blinked. "No entry found," it said. He gave Thomas a questioning look.

Thomas shrugged. "Zane might not bluff, but I do. We just want him to think we can check on anything he tells us. It'll make him more likely to tell us the truth."

"But if Garner isn't his real name either, he would realize you have no way of checking on what he's saying."

Thomas smiled. "But Garner is his real name."

"How do you know?"

"Experience. I watched the movement of his eyes. It tells me a lot about whether a person is lying or not."

"I see. And what about the database then?"

"We don't have a complete database of all vampires past and present, nobody does. There must be hundreds of men named Michael Garner. It would be a waste of my precious time to go through all public databases and the internet to find the right one. However, I'm adding to my database every day. And that punk's name is in it now."

Cain looked back down to Zane and the vampire who called himself Michael Valentine. Zane stood only a few feet away from him now, his legs broad, his arms at his sides. He looked almost relaxed, but the captive would be a fool to assume such a thing. Zane was ready to pounce if Valentine made a single wrong move. Cain had seen Zane in action before. He knew what to expect.

"So, here's the deal, Michael Valentine: I ask a question, you answer it. Do you get that?"

Valentine nodded.

"What happened at the nightclub? Why did you feed in public?"

He lifted his head and grinned up at Zane. "That's two questions."

Before the last word had left his lips, the back of Zane's hand hit right across the idiot's cheek, whipping his head to the side so violently that Cain almost expected it to separate from his neck.

"Fuck!" the prisoner hissed as blood dripped from his nose. "You broke my nose!"

"Well then you'd better start talking before I'll break something more precious."

Finally, Valentine seemed to heed the warning and understand that Zane meant business. "Fine, I was ravenous. I needed a fix."

"A fix?" Zane repeated. "Elaborate!"

Valentine's eyes darted to the window as if he was worried about who was watching him.

Zane growled. "I'm waiting!"

"A fix, you know. Of blood. To get high. And the chick, she was Asian. I figured she might have what I needed. She looked like the others. But . . . "

"But what?"

"It was just ordinary blood. Nothing special. I couldn't get high. It wasn't the right stuff."

Zane looked up to the window, a strange look on his face, as if wanting to ask Thomas and Cain if they knew what Valentine was babbling about.

Cain pressed down the button for the speaker. "What makes you think the blood would get you high?"

Valentine jerked up at hearing the voice from the loudspeaker and looked up to the window. But Cain knew he couldn't see him, since the window was mirrored on the other side.

"Because I've had it many times. But they're not there anymore. And I needed a fix. I needed the rush. It's not my fault. Once you start, you can't stop."

Cain recognized an addict when he saw one. And this vampire was an addict. But what was he addicted to? Blood? Was he falling victim to bloodlust? Before he could ask anything else, Zane continued questioning him.

"Let me get this straight. You're claiming you're suffering from bloodlust and that's why you went berserk on that girl?"

Valentine shook his head. "No! I'm not in bloodlust! Are you crazy, man? I've just got a substance abuse problem. It's nothing major. I can handle it. I just need a fix and I'll be fine."

"A substance abuse problem? What the fuck are you talking about? Do you think I was born yesterday? Drugs have no effect on vampires. Every newborn knows that! So don't dish up crap like that or I'm gonna shove it back down your throat!"

Valentine jumped up from his chair. "But you have to believe me!"

Zane glared at him. "I don't *have* to do anything! You almost killed that girl! And whoever the other vampire was, he butchered another one downstairs. Or was that you too?"

Shocked, Valentine shrunk back. "No! I didn't kill her. Larry, he was even more in need of a fix than I. I swear! It was Larry, he killed that girl. He couldn't stop. And when he realized she didn't have the right blood, he went apeshit on her."

Zane snatched him by the collar of his shirt. "What *right blood*? A specific blood type?"

"No! Not a blood type. It's not that. It's just . . . "

"It's what?" Zane growled impatiently.

"I don't know what it is, but it's like a drug. It makes you high. It comes from those Chinese girls. They keep them in that place."

Cain let out a breath and exchanged a quick glance with Thomas. Was this conversation going in the direction he thought it was?

"What place?"

"Down there, an old building in Hunter's Point. They keep a bunch of them there. They rent them out. It's expensive, but that shit is good. But fuck, they're gone! They just left from one night to the next!"

A look of realization crossed Zane's face as he lifted his head to look up to the window.

"Are you saying that there's a place in Hunter's Point where vampires are keeping women for their blood?"

Valentine nodded. "It's not just ordinary blood. It's like a drug, like crack or heroine. And all the girls are Chinese. That's why we figured, Larry and I, that if we found some Asian chicks and fed from them, maybe we'd find one who has the same kind of blood. But it wasn't the same. It was just ordinary blood."

"Shit!" Zane cursed.

Cain looked at Thomas. "Ursula was telling the truth."

"Thomas, get the guards in here and have him taken back to his cell," Zane ordered.

Moments later, the guards picked up Valentine.

"What are you doing with me? You have to let me go!" Valentine whined as they dragged him from the room. "I told you everything you wanted to know!"

"What the fuck are we gonna do now?" Cain asked.

Thomas shoved a hand through his blond hair and leaned back in his chair. "Find those bastards."

"And Ursula?"

"There's nothing we can do now. Oliver wiped her memory, and she would have landed in Washington DC by now. Maybe it's for the better."

"But she would have been able to help us. She knows what they look like," Cain insisted. "We should—"

The ringing of the phone interrupted him. Thomas picked up the line. "Yeah?"

Cain heard a familiar voice, then Thomas's greeting. "Quinn, you're back? That's a nice surprise."

The door flew open and Zane tore into the room, cursing loudly. "Fuck, fuck, fuck!"

Cain refrained from saying anything, knowing that Zane was seething over his failure to recognize Ursula's claim as the truth.

"We have to come up with a strategy," Zane said, then turned to Thomas. "Get off the phone. This is more important."

Thomas pursed his lips. "It's Quinn, and I think you want to hear what he's got to say . . . Quinn, I'm putting you on speaker. Zane and Cain are here."

He pressed a button and put the receiver down. "Now tell them what you just told me."

"Hey guys. I'm a bit out of the loop—just got in a few hours ago—but the girl who says she was imprisoned by vampires, she's here."

Zane leaned over the desk. "Oliver didn't take her to the airport?"

"No, why would he?"

"Because I ordered him to!" Zane thundered.

There was a pause on the other line. "Guess he didn't like your order."

"Guess not," Cain murmured to himself, not a bit surprised at the turn of events. He'd seen the way Oliver had looked at the girl. She'd probably used her big brown eyes to wrap him around her little finger and make him do whatever she wanted to.

"Well, it doesn't matter now," Thomas said calmly. "She might still be useful, because we've just found out what the deal is with that brothel."

"Care to share?" Quinn asked.

Thomas shifted closer to the phone. "Apparently all the girls at the brothel have special blood. It acts as a drug to vampires. They go crazy for it, and when they're not getting any more, they're showing withdrawal symptoms. Like human drug addicts. It's not pretty."

Not pretty didn't even begin to describe it, Cain thought, remembering the scene in the nightclub.

"Are you sure about that?"

"Absolutely," Thomas confirmed.

"Then we have a problem," Quinn said gravely.

Zane put his hand on Thomas's shoulder, leaning over the speaker phone. "I know, Quinn. I was thinking the same thing."

Cain stared at Zane, then at Thomas who nodded.

"What?" Cain asked.

Zane sighed. "Oliver was a drug addict when he was human. He's susceptible to any kind of addiction. If he's with the girl and bites her, we have to assume the worst."

Thomas turned toward the phone. "Quinn, has he slept with her?"

"I'm not sure, but I'm suspecting it."

Zane cursed. "Fuck, then he's probably already bitten her!"

"No!" came Quinn's voice as if shot from a pistol. "He made a point to say he wasn't going to bite her."

"And you believe him?" Cain asked. "Quinn, I was there, I saw the girl, and I saw how he looked at her. He wanted her, not just her body, but also her blood."

A sigh came through the line. "Jesus, Rose and I should have never left."

"We'll take care of it," Zane assured him.

"What are you planning?"

"We have to separate them. It's for his own protection and for hers too. As soon as the sun sets, here's what I want you to do . . . "

25

Oliver felt warm breath blowing against his naked chest. The heartbeat of another person pounded against him, and the scent of a woman teased his nostrils.

He'd fallen asleep with Ursula in his arms, and sometime during the day rid himself of his shirt, because he'd gotten too hot. He should have left her bed then, but she had molded herself to him in such a trusting way that he hadn't been able to tear himself away.

The sun was setting already, and soon the house would be turning into a beehive. It was best that he went back to his room now before Rose and Quinn noticed him in Ursula's room.

As he gently removed Ursula's arm from his chest and rolled her onto her back, trying not to wake her, the door opened. Oliver's eyes shot to the figure standing in the doorframe: Quinn.

"That's just great!" Quinn said sarcastically. "You couldn't leave her alone, could you?"

Next to him, Ursula jerked awake, a scared gasp coming from her lips.

"Can't you knock?" Oliver growled at his sire.

"Damn it, Oliver, did you not listen to anything I said last night?"

"I haven't done anything!"

Quinn looked him up and down. "Oh, stop lying!"

Outraged at Quinn's wrong interpretation of the situation, Oliver grabbed one edge of the blanket, wanting to get out of bed, but Quinn lifted his hand in protest.

"Spare me the sight of your naked body!" Then he turned.

"But I'm not—" *Naked*, he'd wanted to say, but Quinn slammed the door.

From the corridor, he issued one last command. "Get dressed! Samson wants to see you. Now!"

Then his footsteps were swallowed by the rug in the hallway.

Oliver shoved a hand through his messy hair. "Ah, shit!" He looked at Ursula.

Her eyes were wide open in shock and embarrassment. "I'm sorry, I shouldn't have asked you to stay."

He smiled at her and stroked his knuckles over her cheek. "Don't be silly. He'll calm down. He's just not used to me having a girl over."

Oliver dished up the explanation even though he knew it wasn't true. Quinn was worried about what he would do to Ursula if his hunger for blood became too much. He'd made his concerns clear earlier. But that still didn't excuse him bursting into the room without knocking. Something else must have gotten Quinn all riled up.

"You don't have many girls stay over?"

He bent to her and pressed a kiss on her cheek. "No. You're the first." Then he straightened. "And as much as I would love to stay with you right now, I'd better see what my boss wants."

A frightened look crossed her features. "You're leaving me alone with them?"

"You have nothing to fear. They won't harm you." In fact, she would be much safer with Quinn, Rose, and Blake than with him. At least, none of those three was tempted by her blood. But he kept his thoughts to himself.

With another reassuring look at her, he swung himself out of bed, snatched his shirt from the floor and left her room. He went to his room, and ten minutes later he was ready to face his boss. It wasn't unusual that Samson wanted to see him. Samson often called him to his private residence to check in with him and see how he was doing. After working as his personal assistant for over three years, Oliver still had an especially close relationship with his boss, even though he was now assigned to other duties.

Unfortunately, this meeting with Samson was damn inconvenient. Oliver had wanted to stop by headquarters to see if he could find out more about what had gone down with those crazy vampires at the nightclub.

Quinn was in the foyer when Oliver descended the stairs. His sire gave him an odd look. Still annoyed about his rude intrusion—which was so unlike Quinn's impeccable manners—he lifted his chin and glared at him.

"Next time get your facts straight: I wasn't naked!"

Then he sailed past him and slammed the door, realizing too late that he had parked the car in the garage. "Damn it!"

But he was too proud to turn around and go back inside. Samson's Victorian house was only a stone's throw away in neighboring Nob Hill. He would just have to walk there.

Delilah, Samson's wife opened the door for him when he arrived. She looked as lovely as ever and had completely regained her figure after the birth of her daughter Isabelle only six months earlier.

"Hi Oliver, how are you?"

He smiled at her and entered the house, pulling the door shut behind him. "Nice to see you, Delilah. How's Isabelle? Is she sleeping?"

Delilah sighed, motioning him to follow her into the living room. "I wish! But I'm afraid she's keeping her father's hours!"

"Samson wanted to see me."

Delilah crouched down to the floor where a large blanket had been spread out. "He's still on the phone. Why don't you keep me company in the meantime?"

She tossed a little ball in Isabelle's direction, and the girl reached for it, but a Labrador puppy suddenly jumped onto it and snatched it.

"Coco!" she chided the dog. "You don't give her a chance."

But the toddler didn't seem to mind having been bested by her pet. Isabelle laughed, and it sounded more like a gurgle, but her eyes beamed when she smiled up at Oliver, flashing tiny fangs at him.

"God, she gets bigger every week." He bent down and stretched his arms out to her. "Do you want to come to Uncle Oliver?"

"Maybe later," Samson's voice interrupted him from behind.

Oliver turned instantly and rose. "Samson."

"Join me in my office."

Oliver walked along the wood-paneled corridor that led to the back of the house, where Samson's study was located. As he entered it behind his boss, he was instantly reminded of when he'd worked here as a human. He'd spent many hours in this house, taking care of Samson's needs and protecting him while he slept during the day.

"Take a seat."

Oliver sat down in the chair opposite the massive desk that housed two computer monitors and various other electronic devices. Samson took his seat behind the desk and steepled his fingers.

"I called you because we've got problems," Samson started in a calm voice, his expression serious.

Oliver lifted an eyebrow and moved forward on his chair, a sinking feeling rising from his gut. Conversations that started like that never ended well. "Yes?"

Samson rested his arms on the desk, folding his hands as he leaned forward. "I'm disappointed in you, Oliver."

Oliver's heart missed a beat. Shit! What was Samson referring to?

"You didn't follow the orders you were given. The girl was supposed to be on a plane to Washington."

Oliver jumped up, his heart racing. How did he already know this? Fuck! Who had ratted him out? "Blake! He couldn't keep his mouth shut!"

"Sit down!" Samson ordered.

Reluctantly, he slunk back into his seat.

"Blake has nothing to do with this. And it doesn't matter how we found out. The point is: you didn't follow Zane's orders, and by doing so, you've put yourself in danger."

"I'm not in danger!"

"You might not think so because you don't know the whole story, so let me tell you what's going on: at a raid of a nightclub last night, we apprehended one of the rogue vampires we've been hunting for weeks. A second one was destroyed by Cain, but not before that rogue butchered a young Asian woman, leaving her dead. Both of those vampires were showing withdrawal symptoms."

The wheels in Oliver's brain were clicking into place. He knew where this was leading.

"They wanted to get high on blood. On special blood that they were addicted to. They'd been feeding at a blood brothel in Hunter's Point, the very place that Ursula led you to, and that you found empty. When they couldn't get any more blood from the girls who were being held at the brothel, because they didn't know where it had been relocated, they started attacking Asian girls."

Oliver squeezed his eyes shut. He realized what the rogues had been trying to do: find Asian women who had the same kind of blood as Ursula.

"But when it turned out that the women they encountered in the nightclub didn't have blood that got them high, they went berserk! I don't want the same to happen to you."

Oliver met Samson's intense gaze. "Why would that happen to me?"

"Oliver, Ursula has special blood. It will get you high, and you'll become addicted to it. We all know how vulnerable you are. And I know you better than most. You can't be allowed to be near her. One bite, and your fate might already be sealed."

"No! You're wrong. I won't bite her."

"Please, Oliver," Samson implored him, his voice more soothing now. "I've been told how you look at her. It's not a secret that you want to sleep with her, if you haven't already done so. You know what that means. You'll want to bite her as part of making love to her. And then, you won't be able to stop. We can't risk that, because we don't want to lose you."

Oliver shook his head, furious. "I'm not like that! I didn't bite her the first time. I promised myself not to, because I couldn't go down that road again! I knew I had to be strong. And I was. I am!"

Samson narrowed his eyes, his expression changing. "You knew? You knew all along what her blood does and you didn't tell anybody?"

Oliver suppressed a curse. Crap! He'd inadvertently blurted out too much.

"Why didn't you come to me? You should have told me!" Samson thundered.

"I promised her not to tell anybody."

"She entrusted you with her secret?"

Oliver nodded. "She's scared of all of you. She told only me so I would help her, but she's afraid that if you all knew, you'd just imprison her for her blood, just like the other vampires did." He ran his hand through his hair.

"But you know we would never do that!"

"*I* know that! But she doesn't! Do you know what she's been through? What those animals did to her for three years?" He clenched his fists. "I'm going to kill them for it!"

"You're not going to do anything right now! From now on you'll follow orders."

"If I'd followed Zane's stupid order, Ursula would be back in Washington and we wouldn't be any further. Instead—"

Samson held up his hand, stopping him. "Granted, in hindsight Zane's order was wrong, but given the information he had then, it was the only logical solution." He leaned over the desk. "I'm not upset that Ursula is still here. In fact, I think she might turn out to be useful in trying to find the nest of those vampires. But what does piss me off is that you didn't have enough trust in me to come and tell me what's going on. And that you continued to expose yourself to the temptation of her blood. It's irresponsible. You of all people should know that an alcoholic can't be in charge of a liquor store."

Oliver felt his blood boil. "It's not like that! I can handle it."

"For how long? Until you overestimate how long you can go without blood? Until your hunger for it gets too strong? Until you can't think straight anymore and can only think of sinking your fangs into her neck?"

Oliver felt his gums itch at the very thought of drinking from Ursula, while she was panting beneath him. "She needs me."

"She's a danger to you. Have you slept with her?"

Oliver avoided Samson's gaze. "That's none of your business!"

"So you have," Samson concluded. "And you'll do it again, and what if your control snaps next time? What if you feed from her? You have no idea what her blood will do to you. Zane and the others saw it at the club. Those vampires were crazy. Violent. Uncontrollable. We can't allow that to happen to you. I'm sorry."

An icy shiver crept up his spine. Narrowing his eyes, Oliver glared at his boss. "What are you saying?"

"You know what I'm saying. You can't be allowed near her. She's off limits for you."

"You can't do that!"

Samson gave him a serious look. "Please try to see my side. I didn't rescue you from a life as a drug addict and criminal to let you slide down into the same kind of cesspit I found you in. You have a promising life ahead of you. Wasn't that what you always wanted? Be one of us? Become a great bodyguard? Have exciting assignments?" Samson shook his head. "You would be throwing all this away if you bit her and became an addict again. As a vampire, your desires and needs are much stronger. You won't be able to shake the addiction this time. You won't be strong enough. That's why I can't allow you to see her again."

Oliver thrust his chin up, ready for a counterattack. "What if somebody had told you the same thing about Delilah?"

Samson pounded his fist on the desk. "That's uncalled for and you know it! You can hardly compare Delilah with a girl you met two nights ago!"

Oliver jumped up. He knew he was treading on thin ice, but he had nothing to lose. "If I recall correctly, you didn't know Delilah much longer than I've known Ursula before you went all possessive on her!"

Slowly, like a stalking tiger, Samson rose from behind his desk. "I advise you to be very careful about what you say. Another word of insubordination, and I will strip you of your position within Scanguards, and you'll be back to chauffeuring people around."

Fuming, Oliver went nose to nose with Samson. "Go ahead! But you can't keep me from Ursula!"

"I already have. By the time you get home, she'll be gone."

Oliver jolted backwards. Samson had tricked him. He'd asked him to his home so the others could grab Ursula behind his back. "Fuck you!"

"You'll thank me for it later."

Oliver glared at him, then turned on his heels and ran out of the house, ignoring Delilah and the baby playing in the front room.

He had to make it back to stop them from taking Ursula.

26

Ursula heard the doorbell as she finished dressing after a quick shower. She hadn't wanted to linger in the bathtub, feeling uneasy because she was alone in the house with Quinn, Rose, and Blake. While she wasn't worried about Blake or Rose, Quinn barging into the room had rattled her. He'd looked angry, and for whatever reason, she didn't think it was because he'd found them in bed together. From everything she knew about vampires, she didn't think that they had such high moral standards and cared who slept with whom.

Besides, Oliver and she hadn't even had sex this time. He'd simply held her in his sleep. Just thinking about it made her feel all warm and safe. Safe in the arms of a vampire. Only three days ago she would have laughed hysterically at this notion.

A sound in the corridor outside her room made her snap her heard toward it and relinquish her thoughts. A knock at the door came a second later.

"Ursula? Are you dressed?" Quinn asked.

"Yes."

The door swung open and Quinn entered. Behind him, Zane stepped into the room. The sight of the bald vampire twisted her stomach into knots. What did Zane want here?

"Zane has come to bring you to a safe place."

Ursula almost choked on her saliva. Instinctively, she backed away, hitting her legs against the bed frame. "W-what?" she stuttered. She was safe here, with Oliver.

Quinn looked as if he was sorry for her, when he continued, "We have to move you someplace else. You can't stay here."

She shook her head. "Why? I don't understand. Is it because you found Oliver in my bed? I'm sorry, but it's not what you think. We didn't—"

"It doesn't matter what I think. And it's not about that." He tossed a look at Zane.

"What is it? Please!"

Zane took a step toward her. "You should have told us about your special blood from the beginning. It would have saved us a lot of time."

Her heart stopped beating as shock coursed through her. It hit her all at once: not only did Zane know that Oliver hadn't brought her to the airport and put her on a plane to Washington, he also knew about her blood. He knew her secret!

Disappointment and fear collided inside her, welling up, driving tears into her eyes. She tried to hold them back.

"No!" she choked out.

How could Oliver have done this to her? How could he have broken his promise to keep her secret safe? To keep *her* safe? She had trusted him. She had believed that he was different, that he was good and true. That he cared about her. How stupid of her to think that.

No vampire could be trusted, no matter how sweet he appeared, how caring he seemed.

Oliver had betrayed her.

"I hate Oliver! And I hate you all!" she cried out.

Zane shrugged. "Yeah, well, I don't give a damn. You lied to us! Is that a way to treat people who are helping you? You were wasting our time! If you had told us right away what we were dealing with, we wouldn't have lost time."

Lost time? She knew what that meant. "So you want my blood for yourselves, is that it?"

Zane gave her a disgusted look. "Dream on, kiddo! I don't want your blood: I'm blood-bonded. I only drink my mate's blood. I wouldn't touch yours if my life depended on it. Don't you get it?"

She stared at him, not understanding. A blood-bonded vampire only drank his mate's blood? He didn't attack others for it? "Then you'll just hire me out like the other vampires did. Same difference!"

Zane exchanged a look with Quinn. "I hadn't thought her dim-witted, but hey, even I can be wrong sometimes."

"I'm not dim-witted!" she screamed, fisting her hands at her hips.

"Then get this into your thick skull: nobody at Scanguards wants to drink blood that acts like a drug! We don't want any addicts in our midst. We have a job to do and we can't do it if we're all drugged out and high on something. We need to have clear heads."

She listened to his words, but had a hard time believing him. Why would Scanguards pass up something as valuable as her blood when they could make lots of money with it? No, they were probably just pacifying her now until they had figured out what to do with her. She couldn't trust them. She'd made that mistake once, trusting Oliver, and he had betrayed her.

Her heart clenched at the thought of him. Why had he done it?

She dropped her head. "What are you going to do with me?"

"You'll be brought to a safe house."

"For how long?"

"For however long it takes to find the other girls and destroy the other vampires," Zane replied.

A sob tore from her chest. And once they had the other girls, they could start the operation themselves. Was that what they were planning? Or were they truly going to rescue her and the other women? If only she could trust them, but that particular sentiment eluded her. She'd given all her trust to Oliver, and he'd misused it by telling his colleagues about her secret.

Zane took a step closer. "And you might come in handy to flush out your captors."

Quinn raised an eyebrow. "You want to use her as bait?"

"We might have to. We'll discuss it later." He motioned to Ursula. "Now, let's go."

She walked to the door, passing Zane and Quinn, keeping her head high, not wanting to show the pain inside her.

"Is there anything you want me to tell Oliver from you?" Quinn asked.

The softness in his voice almost made her want to burst into tears, but she clenched her jaw instead and stared straight ahead into the hallway. "You can tell him to go to hell."

She didn't attempt to escape when Zane led her to his Hummer and opened the passenger door for her. She knew it would be wasted energy. He was infinitely faster than her, and by the looks of it mean enough to inflict pain should she not comply with his wishes. She wasn't in the mood for physical pain right now—the emotional pain she felt was hard enough to cope with.

And there she'd thought she was falling in love with Oliver. Oh

God, how stupid! And all the while he'd been deceiving her as to his intentions. At the first opportunity, he'd ratted her out to his colleagues. How could she have been so wrong about him?

"I need some more information from you. How many guards were on the premises?" Zane asked as he set the car in motion.

"There were always four of them guarding the top floor where we all lived and where they fed from us. But there were more of them."

"How many more?" Zane insisted.

"At least seven or eight others. They rotated in and out."

"And how many girls besides you?"

She hesitated. "Why do you want to know that?"

He tossed her a sideways glance. "Because I need to know what we're dealing with."

Unease crept up her spine. How would he use this information? To plan what to do with the girls? Where to set up shop once Scanguards had *freed* them?

"I asked you a question."

"I don't know how many."

He clenched his teeth. "Talk, or I'll make you talk."

She had no doubt that he would, and she also knew that she had no strength left to fight him. "I can't be sure, a dozen, but there's one girl I hadn't seen in a while. I can't be sure that she's still alive. And two new ones arrived recently. But I think it's twelve."

"All Chinese?"

Ursula nodded.

"Good."

Then Zane fell silent. Clearly he wasn't the type to make small talk. And luckily she wasn't in the mood for it either.

During the rest of the short drive, she stared out the window. When Zane pulled the Hummer to a stop only a few minutes after they'd left Quinn's house, she took in her surroundings. They were parked in front of a large corner building. It had four floors from what she could tell, and it looked like it was built around the turn of the century, or maybe a few years after it.

Zane motioned her to exit the car. Ursula closed the car door behind her, then looked at the large entrance door. Next to it, a brass sign was affixed to the wall. When she reached the door with Zane by her side, she read it. *Executive Services*, it said. Zane rang the door bell while she wondered what kind of business was located behind those elegant doors.

The intercom crackled. "Yes?"

"Zane for Vera."

The buzzer sounded, and Zane pressed against the door, holding it open for her. Hesitantly, Ursula stepped inside. An elegant and opulent foyer leading up to a majestic staircase greeted her. To her left there was a lounge of sorts from which soft music and voices drifted to her. Along the right side, she noticed several doors.

Ursula followed Zane as he walked closer to the large staircase that dominated the far end of the foyer, her eyes still scanning her surroundings. As she walked past the lounge, she slowed her steps and focused her eyes. Women in revealing dresses sidled up to men who sat on comfortable chairs and sofas. She homed in on one couple. As the man drank from his glass, the beautiful black woman next to him draped her leg over his thighs, rubbing his crotch.

Ursula's gaze whipped to the people who sat on another sofa not far from them. A similar picture presented itself. The woman was opening the man's shirt, slipping her hand inside, while he, in full view of everybody, pushed the spaghetti strap of her dress off one shoulder and palmed her suddenly exposed breast.

Ursula turned to Zane and glared at him. "Ohhh! You brought me to a brothel! How could you?"

Not even from Zane would she have expected such cruelty, but apparently her skill at assessing people sucked. Zane *was* that cruel to bring her to the same kind of place she'd only just escaped from. That here, the merchandise was sex rather than blood didn't matter. It was still the same thing.

Zane shrugged as if he didn't even understand her objection. "It's safe. And it's run by an ally. But what's most important, nobody will suspect you here."

At the sound of footsteps coming from the stairs, Ursula turned her head. A gorgeous Chinese woman in an elegant business suit glided down the staircase, her walk as graceful as that of a princess. Her black hair was piled high on her head, and her face was enhanced with subtle make-up, emphasizing her expressive eyes. She looked no older than thirty.

"Zane," she greeted the vampire in a husky voice.

Zane simply nodded, then pointed to Ursula. "Vera, thank you for agreeing to this. This is Ursula."

Vera let her eyes run over Ursula, giving her a thorough inspection. "So you're the special one. I'm Vera. I run this place."

She stretched out her hand, and Ursula felt compelled to shake it. Despite the polite gesture she couldn't suppress her next comment. "So you're my new jailor."

"Ouch!" she replied dramatically, pressing a hand to her chest, before glancing at Zane. "What have you done to her that she has such a bad opinion of us?"

Zane grunted. "Nothing."

"I see, so you were your usual pleasant self."

When Zane glared back at her, Ursula almost wanted to smile. It appeared that Vera wasn't afraid of him. She had to be a vampire herself. No human would dare piss off Zane, nor would many vampires.

"As Samson requested: keep her here, don't let her out of your sight, and don't give her any access to a phone or any other means of communication. She's not to have any contact with anybody from Scanguards, particularly not with Oliver."

Vera raised her lids. "Oh? What's the poor guy done now?"

Ursula huffed at that. Poor guy? "Jerk!" she let out under her breath. First he'd seduced her and then he'd betrayed her.

"Ah, I see. Well, leave it to me. I'll take good care of her."

Without another word, Zane turned on his heels and left. When the entrance door fell shut, Vera put her hand on Ursula's arm and motioned her up the stairs.

"I'm having a room made up for you on the top floor. It's very secure and comfortable."

Ursula tossed her a sideways glance. "You mean I won't be able to escape."

Vera gave her a chiding look. "Now, now. Why so hostile? I was planning to treat you like a guest. If you'd rather be treated like a prisoner, however, that can be arranged."

Ursula pressed her lips together.

"Listen, my dear, I've been told what you've been through, and it's something I wouldn't wish on anybody. But it happened, and you have to let it go. I look at you and I see myself when I was your age."

They reached the second floor and continued on to the next flight of stairs.

"Only I was pregnant then," Vera confessed.

Surprised, Ursula looked at her. "But you're a vampire, aren't you? If you know all this about me and are associated with Scanguards, you must be one of them."

She smiled. "Yes, of course. But I was human once. And young like you."

"You're still young. Look at you."

"My shell is young, but inside, I've aged. I've grieved for the child I was never able to raise. And the years I wasted trying to get revenge for the wrong that was done to me. Don't make the same mistake I did. It's time to live."

Ursula dropped her lids. "I wish it were that easy. But I'm not alone in this. There are others like me, and as long as they're suffering, I'm suffering." She hadn't forgotten the women who'd become her sisters over those years, the women who'd endured the same hardships as she had.

"Let Scanguards take care of them." Vera opened a door to a room and motioned Ursula to enter.

A young woman was putting finishing touches on the bed, then moved into the adjacent bathroom.

"Do you trust Scanguards?" Ursula asked.

"With my life. They're honest and dependable. You won't find anybody with higher ethics than the men who work for Scanguards."

Ursula huffed indignantly just as the young woman exited the bathroom. "Well, if that's the case, then I guess Oliver is the one bad apple that spoils the batch!"

"Oliver?" Vera asked, clearly surprised, and even the other woman stopped in her movements and stared at her. "Oliver is the sweetest man anybody could wish for. Full of integrity, honor, and—"

"Integrity? Hah! He betrayed me the first chance he got!"

Vera lifted her eyebrows, then turned to the girl who'd made up the room. "Is everything done?"

"Yes, Vera. The linen is fresh, and there are warm towels in the bathroom. Everything's clean."

Vera nodded. "Thank you, Karen, it's very kind of you to help out. I know that's not your job."

"I don't mind." Karen left the room and pulled the door shut behind her.

The moment they were alone again, Vera's face turned serious. "I'm sorry that you feel like that about Oliver. Maybe you've seen a side of him that I didn't know. Anyway . . . " She pointed to the nightstand. "This is a house phone, it only connects within the building. If you need anything—toiletries, food, or anything at all—just dial zero, and one of the staff will bring you what you need. There's a selection of clothes in the closet. I'm afraid some of it won't be to your liking, but there are some tame nightgowns and T-shirts among the items that will suit you."

Vera turned to the door.

"I'm sorry. I'm not angry at you," Ursula apologized, feeling bad because the woman had been open and friendly and all Ursula had done so far was complain. "I'm just . . . "

"No need to explain. It's none of my business, I'm sure."

When the door fell shut behind her, Ursula threw herself onto the soft queen-sized bed and allowed her tears to flow freely. All she could think of was Oliver and the fact that he'd betrayed her.

27

Oliver ran faster than he ever had. Vampire speed could reach up to forty miles an hour for short bursts, and he was glad for it now. He didn't care who may have seen him, questioning their sanity. All he was concerned with was to get home before his colleagues could whisk Ursula away.

His heart beat like a jackhammer, and his breaths rushed in and out of his lungs as he finally turned onto his street and ran up to the entrance door of his home. He jammed the key into the lock and opened it, then bolted into the foyer.

"Ursula? Ursula!" he cried out.

No reply. The beast inside him howled in frustration.

"Ursula, where are you?" he repeated and ran to the stairs when he caught a movement to his right. He whipped his head toward it.

Quinn stood in the door to the living room, his hands buried in his pockets. "She's gone."

Furious, Oliver stormed toward Quinn and pushed him against the doorframe. "Where is she?"

His sire shook him off with ease. "They took her to a safe place."

"Where?"

"I can't tell you."

Oliver narrowed his eyes. "You can't or you won't?"

"Both."

"Then you're against me."

Quinn shook his head and gave him a stern look. "I'm protecting you. The state you're in there's no telling what you'll do. Do you really think I would allow this kind of temptation to remain right under your nose and watch how you destroy yourself? I didn't sire you to see you throw away your life!"

"You have no idea what's going on inside me!"

He noticed that Rose and Blake had come out from the living room.

"None of you! You have no trust in me! I can make my own

decisions. But you don't believe that I can resist temptation. You think me weak! I'm not a child, goddamn it! I know what's right and wrong! But you all believe that you have to think for me! Give me some fucking credit! All I wanted was your support and your love! And instead you suffocate me! You treat me like a juvenile delinquent who's about to commit a crime! Damn it! I was never going to hurt Ursula! I care about her!" He took a breath of air, filling his lungs, before he continued, "She trusted me! And now?"

He knew what Ursula thought of him now. He didn't have to be a brain surgeon to figure that out. She hated him—he was certain of it—because she thought that he'd betrayed her trust and broken his word. He'd promised her to keep her secret safe.

Oliver pointed his finger at Quinn. "If anything happens to her, I'm making you responsible."

Then he turned and ran to the door that led to the garage. He descended the stairs, jumped into the minivan, then raced out of the garage and into the night. He had to find Ursula.

He reached Scanguards' headquarters in the Mission a short while later and drove into the underground parking garage, letting himself in with his access card. After parking in his assigned space, he took the elevator to the executive floor. When the elevator doors opened, he noticed the frantic activity that made the normally-quiet floor buzz like a beehive.

Oliver approached the large meeting room, where many of his vampire colleagues were hovering. He tapped one of them on the shoulder.

"What's going on, Jay?"

"Zane's called a meeting. Looks like we have some info on those crazies we've been patrolling the city for. Rumor has it, Zane captured one last night. I guess we'll be handed new assignments."

Oliver nodded. He was already aware that they'd captured one of the leeches, as Ursula called the vampires who'd frequented the blood brothel. "It's not a rumor. Where's Zane now?"

Jay shrugged. "Beats me." He glanced at his watch. "Meeting is supposed to start in fifteen minutes." He grinned at the crowd that had already formed. "Everybody's licking their chops already, eager to get some action."

"I can see that." At least it meant that Scanguards was now engaging with full force, trying to find out where the blood brothel had relocated. It made him feel marginally better. But it wasn't his priority at this moment. Finding Ursula's whereabouts was. "Have you seen Thomas?"

Jay jerked his thumb over his shoulder. "Probably in his office."

"Thanks!"

Oliver marched down the hall and stopped in front of Thomas's office, knocking briefly.

"Come," he heard Thomas's voice from inside.

He pressed the door handle down and pushed the door open, entering quickly. Thomas looked up from the computer.

"Uh, figured you'd show up eventually."

"Where is she?"

Thomas tsked. "What, no niceties? You've gotten downright rude since you've been turned."

Narrowing his eyes, he glared at Thomas. "Well, we can't all be as nice as Eddie, can we?"

Thomas's expression turned to displeasure. "If you think by pissing me off you'll get me to tell you where Ursula is, you're a worse strategist than I thought."

Oliver placed his hands on the desk and leaned over it. "Where are you hiding her? Here in the building? In one of the cells?" The thought sent a shiver down his spine. Knowing that Ursula was locked up somewhere made him angry. He felt his gums itch as a result, his fangs eager to descend.

"How stupid do you think we are? Do you think we'd hide her in plain sight where you can just waltz in with your access card and get to her?"

"Is that why Zane isn't back yet? Because he's out hiding her somewhere?"

Thomas didn't flinch. He was too experienced to give away anything, but Oliver knew nevertheless. Zane was the one who'd taken Ursula.

"What does it matter? All that's important is that you're safe."

Oliver let out a bitter laugh. "Safe? From what? Her blood? Don't you get it? I won't bite her. I promised her that. Do you think I'd go ahead and do what these assholes did to her? Use her for her blood?"

Which didn't mean that he didn't want her body—underneath him, panting in ecstasy.

"You say that now, but wait until the temptation becomes too strong." Thomas rose. "If you don't mind, I have a meeting to attend. And you'd do well to join us. After all, it was your case to start with. If only you had told us the truth about Ursula when you found out, it would still be your case. Tell me, Oliver, where do your loyalties lie? With us or with her?"

Then Thomas pressed a few buttons on his keyboard, presumably locking his computer screen, and walked out of his office, not waiting for an answer.

Contemplating Thomas's words, Oliver dropped his head and studied his shoes. Scanguards was his life and his family. But over the last few hours he'd fought practically with every member of his extended family and basically told them that he hated them. All because of a woman. He'd never thought that it would come to that. He'd never believed that a woman could come between him and Scanguards.

Knowing he had to do something, he left Thomas's office and stalked down the hallway. He stopped in his tracks when he saw the door to the emergency exit open. A second later, Blake emerged from it and snuck onto the executive floor.

Looking around himself, Oliver verified that nobody had seen his half-brother yet and quickly walked over to him. Blake jolted when he saw Oliver approach, but caught himself quickly.

"Are you crazy?" Oliver asked under his breath as he dragged him into a nook which housed a refrigerator and a few shelves. "You're not allowed up here."

"When you stormed out I felt bad. I just want to help," Blake justified his actions.

Oliver shoved a hand through his hair. "You can't. This case is strictly vampires only."

"Damn it, I can help. I know enough about it to be of use. There must be something I can do."

Oliver felt his frown deepen. "You can find Ursula; that's what you can do." Even though he knew that Blake had even less of a chance of finding her than Oliver did himself.

"Man, I had no idea they would just take her away. Doesn't seem fair. You were the one who protected her in the first place."

Oliver nodded, somewhat surprised that his half-brother was taking his side. "I did. She trusts me. Can you imagine what she must be thinking now?"

"But Zane's never gonna tell us where he took her. You know him."

"Hmm."

"Who else knows?"

Oliver motioned his head toward the corridor behind him. "Thomas. But he isn't talking either. I already tried. Unfortunately he isn't gonna tell *you* either."

Suddenly Blake grinned. "But he might tell Eddie."

"Eddie?" Oliver echoed, when he felt a light bulb go on above his head. "My god, you're right. Why didn't I think of that? Thomas would tell Eddie anything. Everybody knows he's got the hots for him."

A movement to his left made Oliver snap his head to the side.

He stared right into Eddie's wide open eyes.

"Oh shit!" Oliver cursed.

Blake let out a heavy breath.

It had been an open secret for a while now that Thomas harbored more than just friendship for the young vampire who lived with him. Everybody could see it, no matter how hard Thomas tried to suppress his feelings for the straight young man. The only one who didn't know was Eddie himself—well, until now.

Eddie stared at him, frozen in place and shocked to his core. "Thomas . . . he . . . " As if trying to shake off the words, Eddie shook his head. He looked distraught.

"Listen, Eddie, forget what you heard."

The cords in Eddie's neck bulged. "How the fuck can I just forget that?"

"Believe me, Thomas is an honorable man. He'll never act on his feelings since he knows they're not reciprocated."

Shit! Not only was he not going to get Eddie to get any information out of Thomas, now he found himself defending Thomas even though he was pissed at him for denying him access to Ursula. But what he was telling Eddie was the truth: Thomas would never make a pass at Eddie. He'd kept his feelings under wraps ever since Eddie had been turned, and there was no reason to think he'd ever try to make the young vampire uncomfortable by exposing him to his feelings.

"God, I wish I'd never found out."

"I'm sorry." Oliver put a hand on his shoulder, wanting to calm him down, but Eddie pushed him off.

"Don't touch me!"

Eddie turned on his heels and left.

Oliver exchanged a look with Blake who seemed just as sorry about this incident as Oliver.

"Fuck!" Oliver cursed again. He'd made a mess of things. A royal mess. How was he ever going to clean this up again?

28

After convincing Blake that it was unwise to stay on the executive floor, and making sure he left the way he'd arrived, Oliver headed for the meeting room, where the meeting was already under way. The least he could do right now was see if he could help apprehend the vampires who ran the blood brothel. After all, he had some information that he hadn't shared with his colleagues yet. It didn't mean, however, that he would stop looking for Ursula.

Oliver stopped at the open door to the meeting room and peered inside. Over a dozen vampires were assembled, and since there was no empty seat, he remained standing at the door.

Zane had arrived in the meantime, and he and Thomas jointly led the meeting, filling in the assembled vampires on what had happened at the nightclub and whatever information Ursula must have given them about the blood brothel. Surprised murmurs went through the crowd.

"We must assume that one sip of the blood these women carry can turn you into an addict," Zane continued.

"I beg to differ," Oliver interrupted, drawing the crowd's attention to him.

"So you decided to join us after all," Thomas said.

Oliver ignored the stab and stared back at Zane. "I met a previous client of the blood brothel earlier tonight."

"Why are we being informed of this only now?" Zane griped, clenching his teeth.

"If you hadn't been so busy getting me out of the way so you could snatch Ursula behind my back, maybe I would have told you earlier!"

Zane made a hand movement, indicating him to shut up. "That's nobody's business. So, get to the point, unless this is another attempt to convince us to let you see her."

Oliver narrowed his eyes, but decided not to fight him on this. There was time for that later. "The vampire was a leech. That's what the girls at the blood brothel called the clients. Very fitting, I guess. He claimed to have only visited the brothel once, and I could see no signs of addiction."

Zane huffed as if he didn't believe him. "What else?"

"He was cooperative and agreed to contact us if he's notified of the new location of the brothel."

"How did you verify that he's a former client? How did you find him when according to you he exhibited no signs of addiction or behavior that made him stand out?"

"I found his wallet."

Zane raised an eyebrow. "Where?"

"In the building in Hunter's Point."

"The building was empty."

"Not quite," Oliver shot back, "it had a wallet in it. Ursula had stolen it from a client and then hidden it beneath the floorboards in her cell. I took her back there to search for it."

"When you were supposed to drive her to the airport," Zane added.

Oliver folded his arms over his chest and squared his stance. "Which we all know now was the wrong decision. If I had done that, I wouldn't have found the wallet or the leech."

But Zane didn't take the bait and remained cool on the outside. "And when were you going to present us with this evidence?"

"I'm presenting it now, aren't I?"

"After this meeting, I want to see you in my office, alone." Then Zane looked back at the assembled vampires. "Now to your assignments. We have no lead yet as to where they might have relocated, but we assume they're still in the Bay Area, because this is where their clients are." He pointed to one of the vampires in the crowd. "Jay, you'll be checking out the background of this Michael Valentine we apprehended. He's still in our custody. Search his apartment, his mail, his computer; go through his phone, his address books, anything you can find. See if he's received anything in the last two days that would indicate where the brothel has moved to."

Jay nodded. "Consider it done."

"Benjamin, have Jay give you a list of all of Valentine's friends and acquaintances. Then you, Andrew, and Greg will check up on all the names on that list and see if any of them are also clients of the blood brothel. If they are, put some pressure on them and make them talk. See if they've received any text messages or emails with the new address of the blood brothel. We need to find the place. There are still a dozen women imprisoned there. We have to get them out. Quickly."

Then he let his eyes roam. "The rest of you, you're on regular patrol duty for those . . . *leeches*. Go to the clubs and watch out particularly for vampires feeding off Asian women, or even speaking with them. From what we know, they seem to be the only carriers of this blood. If you must, drop a few hints and pretend you know where a vampire can get high. Make sure you have backup. Are we clear?"

Several answered with a resounding "yes"; others simply nodded.

Oliver glanced to his side, having noticed that Eddie had approached. He now looked into the room, his eyes darting toward Thomas, who stood in one corner of the room, talking to Zane as the other vampires got up from their chairs.

As if Thomas could feel Eddie's eyes on him, he turned his head and looked straight at him. There was an awkward pause before Eddie turned on his heels and left.

After the meeting, Thomas walked up to Oliver, tossing a long look down the hallway where Eddie had disappeared to.

"I need the name and address of that vampire you found."

Oliver nodded. "Got something to write?"

Thomas handed him his notepad and pen, and Oliver started to scribble down the information.

"Something wrong with Eddie?" Thomas asked casually.

Oliver was glad that he was still busy writing the address down, so he didn't have to look at Thomas when he answered him. "Didn't notice anything." Still feeling bad about what he'd blurted out for Eddie to overhear, he handed Thomas the pad and pen and changed the subject. "Don't let Corbin know you're checking his background. He's cooperative, so don't mess up the progress I've made already."

"I'm not an amateur."

A moment later Oliver stood in Zane's office, tapping his foot while he waited for the bald vampire to make an appearance. He knew he was in for a dressing down, but he didn't care what Zane had to say to him.

He didn't have to wait long. Zane barged into the office, slamming the door behind him, reminding Oliver of the mood he was in. Pissed off didn't even begin to describe it.

Zane pinned him with a glare. "Insubordination. Withholding of evidence. Refusal to follow orders . . . "

"You're repeating yourself. Insubordination and refusal to follow orders I believe are the same thing." Oliver knew he was treading on thin ice, but he couldn't help himself. Zane needed to be cut down from his high horse.

"Oh, you think you're so smart! What happened to you, Oliver? What happened to the nice young guy who couldn't do any wrong? Who looked up to us?"

Oliver fisted his hands at his hips. "That guy became one of you and realized you're all made out of flesh and bone, just like the rest of us. You're not any better than me! You're just a bigger asshole! So, go ahead, be yourself! Behave like an asshole like you always do, and let's get this over with. You wanna dress me down? Take a swing! See if I care."

The standoff took several seconds, then Zane sighed. "You haven't changed at all. You're still a hothead, just like when you were human. Only then, you still had some respect for us. Or maybe you were afraid of us."

"I was never afraid of you," Oliver hissed.

"Well then it's time to make sure you're afraid of us now. So let me tell you this: you can kiss your job and your association with Scanguards goodbye if you don't fall in line now. Orders issued by a Scanguards superior are to be followed. That goes for everybody, including you!"

Oliver crossed his arms over his chest. "That's funny coming from you. Considering that not too long ago you defied direct orders from Gabriel and Samson to be with Portia."

Zane's chest rose. "Keep Portia out of this."

Satisfied that he'd hit a nerve, Oliver continued, "It's the same thing, so don't make it sound like I'm the first one in this company who's ever defied an order when he knew it was wrong. You of all people should understand. But no, you've suddenly turned into the establishment. When did you stop using your gut to figure out what's right or wrong?"

"Don't tell me who you think I am!" Zane thundered. "I know what you're trying to do and it's not working. I won't tell you where she is.

No discussion. You're in no condition to be around her. Her blood will destroy you. And we all—all of us at Scanguards—care too much about you to let that happen."

"You have a funny way of showing that!" Oliver grumbled and turned on his heels.

Before Zane could stop him, he was out the door, slamming it even louder than Zane had only moments earlier.

29

A persistent ringing sound penetrated his sleep. Blindly, Oliver reached for his alarm clock and slapped his hand over it, hitting the snooze button. But the ringing didn't stop. He forced open one eyelid and glanced at the clock. It was just past three in the afternoon. Who had set his alarm clock to three p.m. and why the hell didn't it stop?

He shot up to sit and glanced around the dark room, with every second more awake, until he finally realized that the ringing wasn't coming from the alarm clock but from the heap where he'd tossed his clothes when he'd come home shortly before sunrise.

He lunged for it, and pulled his cell phone out of his jeans pocket. "Yes?" he answered it without even checking caller ID.

"Hey Oliver," a female voice cooed.

"Huh? Who's this?"

A chuckle on the other end of the line. "Karen, of course. Don't tell me you were sleeping."

"Hey, Karen," he answered quickly. She was one of Vera's girls—probably the chattiest of them—and she had no idea that he was a vampire. Nobody who knew what he was dared calling him during daytime hours. "I had a late night. What's up?"

Did she want him to come over to Vera's tonight? While he was a regular at Vera's establishment, all the girls there knew that he never came for sex. He simply loved hanging out with Vera and flirting with the women in her employ. Even though he'd gotten plenty of offers from several of the women—freebies so to speak—he'd never taken any of them up on it. He wouldn't start now.

"We haven't seen you all week. Are you cheating on us?"

"Would I do that to you?" He forced a chuckle, even though he wanted to get back to sleep so he would be refreshed by sunset to continue searching for Ursula. The night before, he'd stopped by Amaury's place, finding only Nina at home. He'd eliminated their home as Ursula's hiding place after his visit and driven to Zane's house. The dog had been the only one at home. Nobody had answered the doorbell, and after climbing a fire escape and peeking into the windows on the upper floor, he'd determined that there was no trace of Ursula. Besides, Zane would never leave her alone in his house, knowing that she would probably try to escape.

" . . . so I figured I'd call you." Karen's voice drifted to him.

Shit, he'd missed half the conversation!

"Mmm," he answered, wondering what she'd been telling him.

"So what's the deal? Why doesn't she like you?"

Confused, Oliver scratched his head. "Who?"

"That girl of course. Have you even been listening?"

"Of course I have. What girl?" If this was one of her long-winded stories that could go on forever, then he had to make up an excuse to get out of this pointless conversation. "Listen, I've gotta go."

"Come on, just tell me. Did she come on to you and get pissed off because you're not into Chinese girls?"

Oliver was instantly alert. "Chinese? What's she look like?"

"Well, Chinese of course. Long black hair. Pretty."

Could he be so lucky? Was Karen talking about Ursula? "What did she say to you?"

"Well, she didn't say it to *me*, but I overheard her. She said you betrayed her the first chance you got. Sounded pretty pissed off to me."

He wasn't surprised at that, but he cursed nevertheless. "Ah, shit! You wouldn't know where she is now, would you?"

"She's staying up in room 407."

Shock made him catapult from his bed. "In the brothel?"

An annoyed huff came from Karen. "We don't call it that!"

Oliver backpedaled. "I meant, at Vera's . . . uh . . . establishment?" But he didn't listen to Karen's next comment, because all he could think of was that he knew where Ursula was. Of all places, Zane had hidden her in a brothel. Did that big oaf have no concern for Ursula's feelings? To hide her in a brothel, when she'd been imprisoned in one for three years!

"Thanks Karen, you're a sweetheart. Please, may I ask you for a favor?"

" 'Course you may, hon."

"Don't tell anybody you told me about her. I've gotta keep a low profile on this. Promise?"

"What do I get for it?" she negotiated.

Oliver thought about it for a moment, wondering what would pacify her. "Flowers? Tickets to a show?"

"The best seats?"

"Only the best for you."

When he disconnected the call, he was ready for action. He went into the bathroom and jumped in the shower. It was no surprise to him that his cock was already fully erect the moment he soaped up. No wonder—he was imagining Ursula's hands touching him. Of course, before that could happen, he had to first explain to her that he hadn't betrayed her secret. Considering her current opinion of him, he doubted she'd let him hold her hand, let alone make love to her.

For the remaining hours until sunset, he paced in his room, practicing in his mind what he would say to her, how he would start his explanation to make sure she believed him.

The time seemed to stretch forever, but finally, the sun set over the Pacific Ocean. On his way out, Oliver stopped in the library and unlocked the supply cabinet where Quinn kept spare electronic gadgets. He grabbed a cell phone and headed out the door. He left the car behind, wanting to be as inconspicuous as possible. Just in case anybody from Scanguards showed up at Vera's, he didn't want them noticing his car parked in the area. Besides, Vera's was in Nob Hill, which lay adjacent to Russian Hill and was therefore only a short walk away.

Since it was still early evening, it would be quiet at Vera's. Most clients would show up later as the evening progressed. Therefore, he had to be extra quiet. Knowing he couldn't simply march into the place, he walked around to the small alley that framed one side of the building, where a fire escape was located. Room 407 overlooked this alley, but there was no fire escape leading down from it. Instead it had a tiny balcony.

Oliver quickly assessed the situation. The closest fire escape led to the room next to it, but since it was an anteroom to Vera's office, he could not enter that room to get into Ursula's room from the inside. He had to get to Ursula's balcony.

The fire escape only reached to the second floor where a quick release lever allowed anybody escaping from the building to bring the remainder of the ladder down to the ground. But from his position in the alley he couldn't reach up high enough to grab onto any part of the fire escape. Testing how high he could jump, Oliver took a few steps back, then ran and leapt upwards, stretching his arms, but his fingers didn't quite reach the metal fire escape. He tried again for good measure, but his second try didn't prove any more fruitful than his first. He was out of shape. Maybe if he ran from farther back and got up to a higher speed, he could reach the ladder.

His eyes roamed the alley. A large dumpster stood less than twelve feet from the fire escape. He walked to it and inspected it. There were no rollers underneath it, and while he could have moved the heavy thing with his vampire strength to shift it closer to the fire escape, the noise of the metal scratching against the concrete underneath would wake the entire neighborhood.

Oliver climbed the dumpster, pushing the lid closed with his foot, then stepped onto it. He was almost eyelevel with the ladder now. He assessed the distance quickly and decided it was worth a try. Taking one step back, he lunged forward, jumping toward the fire escape, his arms reaching upward and forward. His fingers connected with the metal platform, instantly tightening around a rod as his body continued to swing.

"Gotcha!" he murmured under his breath and swung his legs up. Helped by his strong stomach muscles, he was able to lift himself onto the platform and stand up.

He looked up and took the two flights of the metal ladder up to the fourth floor, then stopped there. He pressed himself against the wall, making sure that he couldn't be seen from the window of Vera's anteroom. As he looked across to the small balcony in front of room 407, he realized that he had underestimated its distance to the platform he now stood on. There was no way he could jump from his current position and land on the balcony.

Looking for another solution, he glanced up. If he could get to the roof, he could jump straight down to the balcony. He focused his eyes and noticed several short metal rods sticking out from the wall, where at some point another ladder leading to the roof must have been affixed. For some reason it had been removed, but some of the metal rods that were anchored in the brick facade—and were no longer than three inches—had been left.

Oliver ducked to pass by the window and get to the other side of it, then lifted himself up onto the railing that surrounded the fire escape. From there, he stepped onto the first rod, gripping a higher one with his hand. Like a cat burglar, he worked his way up, careful not to lose his grip and fall and draw attention to himself.

Within seconds, he reached the roof and pulled himself onto it. Trying not to make too much noise, he treaded lightly and walked over to where the window to Ursula's room was. He looked down. He was right above the slim balcony.

Oliver jumped, bending his knees all the way into a crouch to absorb the shock and sound as he landed squarely in the middle of the balcony. He quickly tossed a look toward the fire escape, but nobody had seen or heard him. The curtains were drawn in Ursula's room, and the windows were closed. However, Oliver knew from experience, that the building was old and that many of the windows didn't lock, since the old sash windows had warped over the years.

Praying that this was the case with this window, he gripped the frame and pushed upwards. It moved. As fast as he could, he lifted it and squeezed inside, knowing that Ursula would have already heard the noise. He couldn't allow her to scream.

Frantically he parted the curtains. The light in the room was muted. Only a small bedside lamp was lit, the TV was running. Ursula had jumped up from the bed, the remote control lifted over her head as if she wanted to strike him with it.

"Ursula, it's me. Oliver," he announced himself.

She gasped and opened her mouth wider as if she wanted to scream. Out of instinct, he leapt and grabbed her, bringing them both down onto the bed, while he simultaneously pressed his hand over her mouth.

She struggled against him, beating her small fists against his chest.

"Shh! Ursula, stop, I'm not here to hurt you."

She glared at him, fury blazing in her eyes. A second later, her teeth dug into his palm. She was biting him!

"Ouch! What are you doing that for?" He didn't release her mouth though. "Are you promising not to scream if I take my hand off your mouth?"

She narrowed her eyes at him, then her leg suddenly wedged itself between his thighs and kicked up. But he was faster, shifting his weight and imprisoning her legs so she couldn't try again to kick him in the balls.

"What was that for?" He let go of her mouth.

"You jerk! You betrayed me! You told them about my blood!" she spat.

"It wasn't me! I never told them a syllable of what you confided in me."

"Bullshit!" She hit him with a defiant glare. "Now get off me or I'll scream for Vera."

"You try to scream, I'll kiss you! And trust me, I'm faster than you." He was, and he wasn't bluffing.

Ursula stilled under him. Slowly he shifted his weight onto his knees and elbows, making sure he wasn't crushing her. But he had no intention of releasing her until he could be certain that she wouldn't scream or escape him.

Ursula seemed to realize that he meant what he said and pressed her lips into a thin line. It appeared that he would be subjected to the silent treatment.

"Listen, baby, I was called to Samson's—"

"I'm not your baby!" she griped.

"You were when you slept in my arms."

She turned her face away to avoid him. But with his fingers on her chin he made her look at him. "I can see that you're angry with me."

"No shit, Sherlock!"

He had to smile despite himself. "You're a wild cat, Ursula. Maybe we'll take advantage of that later when we make love. I wouldn't mind those sharp claws of yours digging into me when I'm inside you."

She sucked in an outraged breath. "If you think I'm going to sleep with you after all you've done, you're wrong!"

"Am I?" he murmured and lowered his head, allowing his lips to hover over hers. "I bet if I kissed you now, you would kiss me back." Then he pulled his head back again. "But I won't kiss you, because you need to know what really happened."

He sat back on his haunches, allowing her more freedom of movement. Instantly, she shuffled backwards, pulling herself up into a sitting position.

"I was called to Samson's house—it was a ruse to get me out of the house and away from you. Do you remember when Zane and the others were called away the night we checked out the building in Hunter's Point?"

She nodded reluctantly, her eyes watching his every move.

"They were called to a nightclub. Apparently some vampires were causing trouble. Turns out that they were two of your clients. Leeches."

Her eyes widened with interest.

"They were both feeding off Chinese girls. My colleagues had to do a lot of damage control, wipe memories, clean up. One of the leeches killed a girl. Cain staked him."

A gasp escaped from Ursula's throat. "Oh God no!"

Oliver gave her a sad look. "I'm afraid my colleagues couldn't save her. She was already dead when they got there. But they saved the other girl. And they captured that crazy vampire. They took him back to HQ and questioned him. He told them everything: that he wanted special blood, blood that drugged, that the blood brothel in Hunter's Point he'd been going to was gone. He was an addict, Ursula. He was suffering from withdrawal—that's why he was so crazy. When Zane and the others realized what was going on, they knew instantly that you had to have special blood too."

He looked into her eyes and saw realization there. She knew he was telling the truth. "That's why Zane came for me."

Oliver nodded. "After seeing what the blood does to vampires, they wanted to make sure I wasn't anywhere near you. That's why they took you. They were afraid that I would bite you and end up like those crazy drugged-out vampires."

"So they really don't want my blood. Your colleagues, they're not keeping me because of that," she said as if talking to herself.

"No. They wanted to protect me. Even though they were royally pissed when they found out that I already knew about your blood and didn't tell them. Anyway, now that they think they've kept me from you, they're busy combing the city for any evidence of where the blood brothel moved to. They want to destroy those vampires. I promise you."

"And the girls and I? What will they do with us?" There was a trace of fear in her voice.

Oliver had worked for Scanguards long enough to know what they were planning, even though nobody had talked about the ultimate plan. "Once we've found them, we'll make sure they go back to their families, and if need be, we'll set up new identifies for them so nobody will ever find out about them and what makes them special."

"They will do that? For us? For humans?"

Oliver stroked his knuckles over her cheek. "Yes. They're here to protect you. Just like I am."

She inched closer. "How did you even find me?"

"One of the girls here overhead when you said something about me, and she called me."

Her eyes widened and she jerked back from him. "You're a client here?"

Oliver leaned closer. "No, I'm not. I just come here for . . . uh company."

"Company?!" She looked at him, clearly not believing him.

"I'm friends with Vera, and her girls like me. But I've never come here for sex." He grinned. "At least not until tonight."

30

Oliver wanted to sleep with her. Ursula felt a wave of heat shoot from her belly all the way into her head and spread in her cheeks. If she looked anything like she felt right now, she'd say she was blushing like a ripe tomato. Her anger at Oliver had vanished when he'd recounted what had happened at the nightclub and afterwards. Oliver hadn't betrayed her secret. He'd kept his word. Even though by doing so he'd drawn the wrath of his colleagues upon him.

When Oliver leaned in even closer, she dropped her lids. "I'm sorry I cursed you behind your back."

His lips approached her mouth, his breath ghosting over her skin. "I can live with that if you're willing to make it up to me."

She opened her eyes fully, meeting his sensual gaze. The blue of his eyes was almost blinding. "How?"

"A kiss would be a good start."

"What else?" she asked, meeting him halfway.

"You, naked." He glanced behind her, a wicked smile forming on his face. "Preferably tied to this wrought iron headboard."

Her breath caught in her chest. Instinctively, she pulled back a fraction. "Why?"

"To teach you to trust me. To teach you that even if you're tied up and vulnerable, I would never do anything to hurt you. That even when you're at my mercy, you still have your free will, you're still the one in charge of your body and your mind."

She stared at him, scared, because she'd spent three years of her life with her hands tied to her bed, being robbed of her free will. She shivered. "It won't work. I can't let you tie me up. They did that to me. They—"

He put his finger over her lips. "I know what they did to you. That's why you and I will do this together now. To wipe away the bad memories. When we're done here, you'll associate being tied up with pleasure, not with fear, frustration, and pain. Because I'll make sure that all you'll feel is pleasure. Nothing else."

She didn't doubt that he wanted to shower her with pleasure, but she couldn't imagine ever being able to forget those days when she'd been chained to her bed. "What makes you think it will work? Psych 101?"

He smiled. "I never went to college. But I've always been able to read women. And when we made love in my van, you couldn't let go of the chains they bound you with. They're still there." He softly knocked at her temple. "Still in there. And as long as you can't shake them, you'll never be able to share your body freely. Call me selfish, but when I make love to you, I want to feel all of you. I don't want you to hold back because you're afraid. I want you to be free."

Free, the word sounded so good. But could she ever truly feel free? Even now she was still incarcerated, even though it was for her own protection. "And that's why you want to tie me up?"

Oliver's eyes darkened. "That and . . . because the idea of you at my mercy makes me so hard that I'm ready to burst."

He took her hand and led it to the front of his jeans. When he pressed it onto the bulge that had formed there, she felt heat underneath her palm where his erection pulsed.

"And if I asked you to untie me, would you do it immediately?" she asked, her voice trembling, because she was considering something she should never contemplate. But whenever Oliver looked at her with desire and lust in his eyes, a different side of her took over and made decisions for her.

He shook his head, bringing her heart to a complete stop. "No. You'll be able to untie yourself. I'll only use silk scarves to tie your hands to the headboard. But the knots will be so loose that you'll be able to slip from them whenever you feel the need."

Relief made her release the breath she'd held. She looked at him and remembered the things he'd done for her to achieve an orgasm in the back of his van, how selfless he'd been, how giving. So if this game of bondage was something he wanted, she could try it. He hadn't hurt her so far. There was no reason he would do so now. Slowly she nodded, praying that she wasn't making the biggest mistake of her life. "Yes."

Oliver pulled her into his arms and hugged her close. "Oh baby, thank you. You won't regret it!"

Then his mouth was on hers, searing her lips with a passionate kiss.

He was different from the time in his van: more passionate, wilder, and more untamed. Had she made the right decision? But she had no occasion to contemplate it any further, because Oliver's kiss robbed her of the ability to think. Instead, all sensory receptors in her body seemed to switch on as if he'd flicked a switch.

His hot breath seared her, his tongue delved deep into her, leaving no corner unexplored, and his hands roamed her body, commanded by a man who knew he would encounter no resistance. With confidence and determination, he pulled her T-shirt over her head, exposing her naked skin beneath. Skin that tingled pleasantly. When the zipper of his jacket rubbed against her breast, she cried out, making him release her instantly.

"Your jacket," she said. "Take it off. Take all of it off."

Oliver jumped from the bed and rid himself of his clothes. She'd never seen anybody undress himself with such speed and grace. When he stood in front of her with only his boxer briefs, she licked her lips, and her eyes moved to the impressive outline of his cock. The bulbous head of his erection peeked out from the waistband of his underwear, too large to be contained by the fabric that stretched too tightly to truly conceal anything.

"I love the way you look at me," he claimed.

"How do I look at you?"

He growled softly. "Hungry."

Before she could reply to him, he stripped her of her jeans, leaving her with only her bikini panties. But instead of joining her on the bed again, he turned to the chest of drawers behind him and opened the top drawer. He rummaged around in it.

"What are you doing?"

He turned, and she saw him holding up a virtually see-through negligee. He tossed it at her. "Put this on. I think you'll look good in red."

She took the gauzy fabric that hid nothing and slipped it over her head. It was surprisingly soft. But as soon as she wore it, she also realized that the area where it should cover her breasts was devoid of fabric. She felt scandalous in the outfit and was about to take it off again when she noticed Oliver staring at her, unbridled desire burning in his eyes.

"You're beautiful," he whispered, and the admiring sheen in his eyes made her heart beat faster. At the same time her nipples tightened into hard little buds, and she felt moisture collect at her core.

Slowly, she lowered herself back onto the mattress, aware that she was presenting herself as if on a silver platter, her breasts sticking out through the holes in the negligee. Suddenly she felt powerful. She felt like she was the one in charge, the one who pulled the strings. Ursula licked her lips.

"Fuck, baby!" Oliver cursed and jerked open the second drawer, pulling out a couple of silk scarves, before he walked to the bed and joined her.

He straddled her midsection, then leaned over her, the erection behind his boxer briefs brushing against her stomach. "Stretch your arms over your head."

"In a moment." She would comply with his wish, but there was something she wanted first.

Without embarrassment she tugged on the waistband of his boxer briefs, pulling them down as far as his position allowed. Then she closed her palm around his hard cock and squeezed the firm flesh.

Oliver moaned loudly, his eyes closing, his head falling back. His breathing accelerated as she stroked him, running her hand up and down his length.

"You've gotta stop," he begged, "or I'll spill all over you." His eyes opened and met hers.

"And would that be so terrible?"

He gripped her hand and gently pried it off him. "Yes. Because I want to come inside you when you're climaxing."

Then he took both her hands and pinned them over her head. With swift and surprisingly practiced moves, he tied both her hands to the bed frame. She pulled on them slightly and noticed that they were loose, just like he'd promised. If she curled her hands, she could slip from the bonds.

"Promise me something."

She looked up into his blue eyes. "Yes?"

"Pretend you can't escape those bonds. I'd like to believe that you're at my mercy, even though I know that I'm at yours."

She nodded, surprised at his words. Did he really think he was at her mercy? Or was this all part of the sexual game they were playing? Either way, she liked the feeling of power that suddenly coursed through her. For so long, she'd had none. Now, she felt strong and invincible.

"In that case, come a little closer." She dropped her gaze to his cock, noticing how he did the same.

A sharp intake of air signaled that he'd caught on to her thinking. "You're not . . . "

Deliberately slowly, she ran her tongue over her lower lip, then lifted her eyelids to meet his surprised look. "You did it to me."

"This isn't exactly how bondage works," he said as he scooted farther up her body, lifting himself onto his knees in the process. "I'm supposed to be the one telling you what I want you to do."

"Well, then maybe you should command me."

Oliver gripped the headboard behind her and leaned forward, bringing the tip of his erection to her mouth. "Suck me!"

"Thought you'd never ask." On her last word she licked over the mushroomed head, tasting the salty drop of moisture that had collected there. Then she slid her lips around the tip and opened wider.

Oliver eased forward, pushing his cock into her mouth, moaning out his pleasure all the while. He was only halfway inside her, when he pulled back and repeated the movement. His skin was velvety soft, but beneath it, he was hard as steel. When she looked up at his face, she saw how he watched her with fascination. His eyes were filled with lust, his lips parted. She could see the tips of his fangs. They had lengthened. At the thought of what he could do to her, a flame shot through her core. But instead of sending her into a panic, she felt her womb pulsate with need.

Instinctively, she sucked harder, pulling more of his shaft into her mouth. Oliver's head fell back, and he groaned loudly. "Oh, God, Ursula!" His hand slid underneath her nape, holding her there as his tempo increased. But he didn't push any deeper into her, aware that his cock was too big for her mouth, and that she would choke if he did.

Then suddenly, with a suppressed curse, he pulled out of her and moved backwards.

"Fuck, baby, you're too good."

She smiled and licked her lips. They felt tender now. As if he knew what she needed, he bent down to her and kissed her softly to soothe them.

Moving his mouth to her ear, he whispered to her, "You have a very wicked streak, trying to get me to lose control like that. And wicked women have to be punished."

Her breath caught and instinctively, she pulled at her bonds. But his hand came up, stopping her from slipping from the bindings. A shiver ran down her body, and her heart began beating frantically.

"Easy."

His lips connected with the heated skin on her neck as he planted soft kisses on it. Slowly, she relaxed and released the tension in her shoulders and arms.

"Better," he murmured and moved down her body.

His lips found her nipple and captured it. He sucked it into his mouth, giving it a strong pull. Ursula cried out at the unexpected sensation, her pelvis tilting toward him in the same instant.

"Like that?"

"More," she demanded instead of an answer.

When he repeated his action, pleasure speared through her, sending a shockwave into her clit. Her body arched toward him.

Oliver licked his tongue over her hardened nipple. "How about this then?" She felt something hard against her breast: teeth touching her skin, brushing over her nipple.

She reared up, but the scarves around her wrists tightened with her action.

Oliver pressed her back into the mattress and licked over her tender nipple once more. Then he shifted and his leg pushed her thighs farther apart. His hand slid down her body. When he reached her panties, he slipped his fingers under the fabric and ran them through her coarse hair. But he didn't linger there. Instead, he moved deeper and touched her female folds, which were drenched with her juices.

"Oh, baby," he praised, "you're all wet for me."

He dropped his head to her other breast and kissed it, while he thrust one finger into her tight sheath. She let out a moan. "Oliver!"

It seemed to spur him on, because he licked her breast with even more fervor. He nibbled, sucked and kissed her flesh until it felt tender and raw. All the while, his finger drove in and out of her sex.

"See, you can't escape me," he murmured. "You're at my mercy."

Then he suddenly pulled his finger from her clenching sex and ripped her panties from her body. Cool air blew against her heated flesh. Before she could even take another breath, the blunt head of his cock probed at the entrance to her body and plunged forward.

31

He hadn't bothered taking off his boxer briefs completely. They still rested just below his butt. That's how hot Ursula had gotten him. So turned on that he couldn't prevent his fangs from descending. She'd sucked him like a champion in oral gymnastics, and the outfit that exposed her boobs made her look sexier than anything he'd ever seen. Maybe he should have opted for her being naked, but no, he'd thought he could handle a little dress-up with her. Apparently he couldn't.

If he hadn't sunk his cock into her when he had, he would have bitten her. His plan of making her come first had gone right out the window. Now all he could do to stop himself from sinking his fangs into her, was to drive his cock into her over and over again.

"I'm sorry, Ursula, but I'm gonna have to fuck you really hard." Because he needed to pacify the beast inside him. And it would only be appeased if he exerted his power over her in another way, since he couldn't bite her.

Ursula's lips parted on a breath, her eyes darkening with lust. "How hard?"

"Hard." He pulled back and rammed his cock into her, pushing her a few inches closer to the headboard.

She gasped, but didn't try to get away from him. Instead, she slung her legs around him, crossing her ankles behind his butt, and pulled him closer.

"You can do better than that."

Heat flared inside him when he heard her taunt. "Oh, yeah? Not enough for you?" He pulled himself out of her and flipped her on her stomach. As a result, the silk scarves that tied her to the bed frame crossed and tightened around her wrists. He realized instantly, that this meant she wouldn't be able to untie herself in this position, and even though this had been unintentional, the beast in him liked that thought.

Swiftly, he pulled her onto her knees, her beautiful heart-shaped ass pointing up. Her moist petals glistened invitingly. Without hesitation, he drove into her from behind, holding her hips steady so she would absorb the impact fully and not crash against the headboard.

Ursula moaned into the pillow.

"Fuck! You're even tighter that way."

"And you're bigger," she claimed, panting as she tried to support herself on her elbows.

Her interior muscles gripped him tightly, squeezed him as hard as if she were holding him in her fist. Her warm heat lubricated him and made every thrust a smooth slide into silk, into heaven. His body worked without any conscious thought, his breaths coming in rapid succession, his heart beating like a jackhammer. His cock moved back and forth in a rapid rhythm, his hands holding so tightly onto her hips that he knew he would leave marks. But he couldn't stop himself.

Ursula was laid out in front of him, vulnerable and enticing. She gave him the same feeling he experienced when hunting for blood. The same sensation overcame him now: he felt powerful and invincible as he fucked her, knowing that she was at his mercy. That he alone determined her fate. Yet at the same time, he knew what he wanted for her was nothing evil: he wanted her pleasure, to lead her into ecstasy. He had power over her body now, the power to make her feel desired. The beast inside him started to withdraw.

Finally, he was able to slow his thrusts and slide in and out of her with gentler motions. He looked down to where his cock disappeared in her body, the sight of her pink flesh exciting him. To know that she had enough trust in him to let him put her into this vulnerable position filled his heart with pride. His hands loosened their grip on her hips, and he stroked her beautiful ass.

He slid his hands under the red negligee and moved them along her back, caressing her. Then he touched her chest, filling both his hands with her breasts. They weren't big, not as voluptuous as those of other women he'd known, but he didn't mind. They were enough for his hands, and they were firm and young, and her nipples responsive.

The small buds were still hard. Rolling them between thumb and forefinger, he tugged at them, making her cry out again.

"You're the sexiest woman I've ever made love to."

At his words, she met his thrust with an equal but opposite reaction, doubling the impact. It sent a bolt of lightning into his balls, adding fuel to the fire that was raging inside him. He wouldn't be able to last much longer if she kept this up. But he couldn't slow himself down either, and on the next thrust, he felt his balls tightening. The rush of semen shooting through his cock was the last thing he felt before he exploded inside her, his body going into spasms as he experienced the most amazing orgasm he'd ever had.

As he collapsed on top of her, he realized with horror that Ursula hadn't come with him. He hadn't delivered the pleasure he'd promised. Dismayed, he pulled out of her and rolled her onto her back.

"I'm sorry," he said, looking into her eyes.

"Why?"

"Because you didn't come."

"I told you, it's difficult for me."

He couldn't accept that as a fact. And he wouldn't rest, until he had rectified this situation. He rid himself of the boxer briefs that hindered his movements, then he pushed her thighs apart once more and settled between them, bringing his still-hard cock to her sex.

"But you're done," Ursula protested.

"But you're not." He drove back into her. "And as I see it—" He glanced at the silk scarves around her wrists. "—you're still tied up, which means, you're still at my mercy."

She smiled. "So what are you planning now?"

He delivered a gentle thrust with his cock. There was one way to heighten her arousal and make it easier for her to climax. "I want you to feel my bite."

Oliver watched as her face turned from excitement to apprehension. Her lips started to trembled.

"Oliver, please . . . "

"Hear me out, Ursula." He gently brushed his finger over her lips. "It won't be a real bite. My fangs will never touch your flesh."

Her forehead worked itself into a frown. "How?"

He'd never tried what he was about to suggest, but he hoped it would work. "I'll use mind control to make you feel the bite without actually biting you. You'll feel all the same sensations, the arousal, the excitement."

She looked at him, her eyes widening in surprise. "You can do that?"

"You know about mind control."

Ursula nodded. "They used it on me to stop me from . . . "

"From touching yourself. And I can use it now to help you climax." If he could manage. His attempts at mind control had been hit-and-miss up till now. But he wasn't going to burden Ursula with that.

"But why would you do that? You won't feel the bite yourself, will you?"

Oliver let his fingers trail down to her neck, caressing the tender skin where her pulse beat against his touch. "No, I won't feel it, but I'll be seeing it in your eyes, I'll hear it in your moans, and I'll feel it in the way your body moves. And then, when you come, I'll feel it, because your muscles will spasm around my cock, squeezing me so tightly that I'll come a second time."

He noticed her chest rise and fall and her eyelids flutter.

"All I want is your pleasure." He reminded her of his cock, which was still inside her, by plunging deeper into her. "Do you trust me?"

Her voice was breathless, when she answered after what seemed like an eternity. "Do it."

His heart expanded when he heard her answer. The trust she offered him was the greatest gift he could have ever expected from her. Overwhelmed, he closed his eyes for a moment. When he opened them again, he gazed into her dark orbs.

"I think I could fall in love with you." Unless it had happened already. He didn't know. What he felt for Ursula was new and so utterly exciting that he felt like he was on a high. As if he'd drunk her drugged blood. But did that mean he was falling in love with her? Or did he simply feel that way because sex with her was spectacular?

"Oliver . . . " A moist sheen spread in her eyes.

He bent down to her, brushing his lips over hers for a feather light kiss. "I wish I could sink my fangs into you and taste you, feel that connection with you that only the bite can provide. But the risk is too great. For both of us." He kissed his way to her neck, sensing her tremble under his lips. "So you'll have to experience this for both of us."

He lifted his head and looked deep into her eyes. Then he channeled his thoughts, feeling the warmth that collected in his center.

He sent his first thought to her mind. While she wouldn't hear his actual words, her body would feel the sensations he was conveying. *Ursula, you feel my lips on your neck.*

A corresponding hitch in her breath told him that he'd reached her. He noticed how she shivered.

It's warm and pleasant. My tongue is licking over your skin. You feel the sharp edge of my teeth scraping against your flesh. It excites you.

Ursula's body arched toward him, and he recommenced the slow thrusts of his cock inside her warm sex. Her hips moved in sync with him.

"Yes," she whispered.

You feel my mouth opening wider and my fangs piercing your skin. It's like a pin prick. It doesn't hurt. They sink deeper, lodging in your flesh, just like my cock is buried inside you.

She moaned and her lids lowered halfway.

Your body yearns for this. You feel the pull on your vein, and it feels like I'm licking your clit. Like I'm sucking your sweet pussy. You want me to take more.

"Oh God!" she cried out, her eyes searching his. All fear in them had vanished, and all he could see now was desire.

With every pull on your vein, you sense my touch more intensely. You feel me licking you. You feel every inch of my cock as I'm driving into you. Your heart beats in sync with mine.

He could hear how her heartbeat adjusted to his, how she allowed him to control her reactions, to guide her in the sensual exploration of her body.

Your breasts are aching. Your nipples are hardening, burning. They can feel the tingling that spreads all over your body, the slow waves that wash over you. Heat engulfs you. The fire inside you is burning ever higher. You need me. You feel my cock filling you, my tongue licking your swollen clit.

Faster and harder. You feel the pressure build.

Oliver watched in rapt fascination how her body reacted to his suggestions. He'd never seen anything like this: every thought he planted in her mind took root and transformed Ursula into a woman burning with passion and desire. Her eyes shone with lust, her entire body was glistening with moisture, and her lips released sounds of pleasure he'd never heard from her. Her moans and sighs, her soft cries, they all aroused him, hardening his cock again. Even though he'd come only a few short minutes ago, he was ready again. All because Ursula excited him.

You feel my fangs pulling harder. Wanting more. And you want more too. You want to give me everything you have. You open up. You lay yourself bare. And then you feel everything at once. My fangs in your neck, my hands on your breasts, my tongue on your clit, and my cock in your pussy. Then the waves hit you like a tsunami. They wash over you.

Ursula's interior muscles clenched around him, squeezing him just as tightly as he'd predicted when she climaxed, an expression of wonder in her eyes.

Oliver let go of his own control and joined her in her moment of bliss, shooting more semen into her welcoming body until they finally both stilled. He hugged her to him, pressing gentle kisses on her face and neck.

"Oh, my god," she murmured, still breathless. "I never thought . . . "

He lifted his head and smiled. "I've never experienced anything better." It was the truth.

32

Ursula enjoyed the way Oliver's arms held her to his body as he lay behind her in the bathtub. The warm water sloshed around them, and she felt more relaxed than she had in a very long time. After they'd made love, he'd apologized for being so rough with her and had insisted that they take a bath together so he could soothe her sore body. It was true, he'd been a little rougher than the first time, when they'd had sex in the van, but he hadn't hurt her.

"How did you become a vampire?"

She turned her head to look at him, and Oliver brushed a wet strand of hair from her cheek. His gestures were so tender and gentle that it was hard for her to reconcile them with the fact that he was a vampire.

"I had an accident. I was driving down a winding road with Quinn. We'd just left a party. I saw the car that came toward me too late and swerved. We hit a crane. I was thrown through the windshield."

"You weren't wearing a seatbelt?"

He shook his head. "I'd forgotten to put it on. I don't know why—I always wore one. Maybe it was meant to be." He forced a grim smile. "I was impaled on the shovel of an excavator."

Ursula pulled in a deep breath. "Oh my god!" She could only imagine how painful it must have been.

"I don't remember the impact or what followed. I was dying. If Quinn hadn't been there, I wouldn't be here today. He turned me right there and then."

"He saved you." She stroked her hand over his cheek. "Why were you with him in the first place?"

"I worked for Scanguards. I think I might have told you about that before. I was the personal assistant of the owner, Samson. He took me under his wing, and he trusted me." A pained expression came over his face.

"What's wrong?"

Oliver closed his eyes for a moment. "When I realized that they were going to hide you from me, I was so angry I said terrible things to Samson."

She tipped his chin up. "You have to apologize to him."

"I know. But I can't let him know that I found you. If I do, they'll most likely move you somewhere else. I hate lying to my colleagues, but they don't give me much of a choice."

She faced away from him again and leaned against his chest. "They don't believe that you can control your urges, is that it?"

Oliver combed his hands through her hair. "To them, I'm young and inexperienced. They think they know better." He sighed. "Come, I'll wash your hair."

He pushed her lower in the tub so her hair sank into the water then pulled her up again. As he shampooed it, he continued, "Most of my colleagues have been around for a very long time. They've lived so many lifetimes that I think sometimes they forget what it's like to be young."

As Oliver massaged her head gently, she sighed contently. "You might be young, but you're very good."

He chuckled. "Good at making love?"

Ursula laughed. "Good at washing my hair."

He huffed in mock-protest. "Wait until I get you underneath me again."

"What if I want to be on top next time?"

"Oh, I'm totally open to that."

"Are you?" she teased, enjoying the lighthearted banter between them.

"Mhm." His hands continued to massage her scalp, and he fell silent for a few seconds. Then he cleared his throat. "Uh, Ursula. There's something I wanted to ask you."

Surprised at his hesitant tone, she tensed slightly. "Yes?"

"Remember when you told me that your captors wouldn't allow you any sexual gratification?"

She nodded.

"You said that the reason was that they thought your blood wouldn't be potent anymore."

Ursula's breath hitched. She knew where this conversation was going. And she didn't know whether she dreaded it or welcomed it.

"That's what they claimed."

"I was wondering . . . if that meant, the drugging affect of your blood would be gone forever, or just for a period of time, like maybe a few hours or days. Have you ever given it any thought?"

"I never thought of it. Not while I was imprisoned." Though she'd been thinking of it since—ever since he'd told her in the van that he wanted to bite her while making love to her.

Oliver's hands removed some of the foam from her hair, dropping it into the bathwater. Then his hands came up again, caressing her neck.

"Did you like my bite?"

A shiver ran down her spine, making her entire body tingle. "It was different from all the other bites. It was . . . gentle." And she had loved it. But she was scared to admit it openly. Because it would invite too many problems.

Oliver pulled her back, dipping the back of her head into the water to rinse her hair. When she sat up again, he drew her back against his chest, circling his arms around her torso, his cheek next to hers.

Excitement and fear collided inside her when he dipped his head to kiss her neck. She held her breath, half dreading, half hoping that he would sink his fangs into her, but he removed his lips from her skin again.

"You were beautiful when I watched you react to my virtual bite. But I was envious too. Because you experienced it first hand and I didn't." His voice was husky, and one of his hands now slid down to her belly and lower still until he reached her sex. He cupped it, then extended his middle finger and drove into her.

She let out a stifled moan. "Oliver, I . . . it's too risky. We don't know what'll happen." She couldn't let him bite her, not just for her own sake, but also for his. She didn't want him to become a drug addict. She cared too much about him to let this happen. "Please, you don't know how you'll react to it."

She sensed him freeze, then withdraw his hand from her sex. "Baby, did you think I was going to bite you now? I'm not."

She turned her head, surprised. "You're not? But why . . . I thought you were asking me."

Oliver shook his head and smiled. "I wanted to know if you would allow me to take a sample of your blood and have it tested."

"Tested?"

"Yes, you know that Maya is a doctor. We could give her samples of your blood from before we have sex and then again from after. And then she can see if there's a difference. Maybe then we can figure out if what they said is true, and if it is, for how long your blood is safe after sex."

The hopeful glint in his eyes was undeniable.

"Do you really think that Maya can do that?"

"She's a good doctor. And she's done a lot of research on what affects vampires and what doesn't. I trust her."

Slowly, she let the implications of his request sink in. "And if it's safe, what will you do then?"

His blue eyes looked mesmerizing when he gazed at her with scarcely-restrained desire. She barely felt how he sat up and turned her body so that she straddled him. Underneath her, she felt the hard ridge of his erection probe at her core. Slowly, he pulled her down onto him, impaling her on his shaft.

"That'll depend on you. It's your decision." He kissed her gently. "You already know what I want; now the question is: what do you want?"

A few days ago, her answer would have been clear cut and instantaneous, but tonight things were more complicated. She was falling in love with Oliver, and she wanted to give him everything he wanted. But did that include her blood? Was she willing to give him what her captors had stolen from her for three years? And if she did—if there was indeed a way for him to drink her blood without being affected by the drug within—would he be able to hold on to his control without falling into bloodlust and sucking her dry? She'd seen him when he'd craved blood before. What would happen when he couldn't control that craving any longer?

"I don't know what I want," she murmured, tears forming in her eyes.

Oliver brushed his thumb over her cheek. "You have all the time in the world to make a decision. I'll be waiting for as long as it takes."

Then his lips were on hers, kissing her first softly, then more passionately, while his cock moved inside her in the same rhythm.

33

"Here," Oliver said after he and Ursula had gotten dressed. He pulled a cell phone from his jacket pocket and handed it to her.

"What's that for?"

"It's a spare I have. It's untraceable. I've programmed in my number so you can reach me, and I can contact you." He motioned to the phone on the nightstand. "I'm guessing that phone is only a house phone. I've put the ringer on vibrate. Make sure nobody finds it. Hide it from Vera and the others, but keep it close enough so you know when I'm trying to contact you."

"Thank you." She lifted herself on her toes and kissed him.

"One thing: I know you want to talk to your parents, but it'll have to wait." He pointed to the phone in her hands. "The phone is locked. The only number you can call is mine. I'm sorry, but I had to do it. I know you'll be tempted, and sometimes it's just better to remove temptation before it has a chance to take root."

She nodded. "I understand. Really, I do." Her eyes confirmed her words.

He drew her into an embrace, holding her to his chest for several minutes without speaking. Then he kissed her forehead. "I'll be back tomorrow night."

After leaving Ursula, Oliver checked in with Cain and went patrolling with him. Cain was one of the few colleagues whom he hadn't pissed off yet, and Oliver took great pains not to say anything that would lead to an argument.

"Glad you joined me; it's not as boring that way," Cain said as they walked toward the entrance of another nightclub, where a couple of dozen clubbers lined up to be let inside.

"Guess it was different the other night. How bad was it?" Oliver tossed him a sideways glance then let his eyes wander over the young people outside the club to scan for anything unusual.

"It wasn't pretty, let me tell you that." He lowered his voice, so the humans around them couldn't hear him. "She looked like he'd butchered her."

Oliver spoke just as quietly. "Worse than one of our kind in bloodlust?"

Cain shoved his hands in his pockets. "And so useless. What a waste of a life. It's terrible what drugs can do. It's evil, pure evil."

Oliver thought back to the time when he'd taken drugs as a human. "Yes, senseless." And if Samson hadn't pulled him out of it, he would have perished. Thinking about it now brought back the guilt he felt about how he'd parted with Samson. He stopped just before they reached the entrance to the nightclub.

"Listen, Cain, do you mind if I leave you for a while? I need to talk to Samson."

Cain rocked back on his heels. "Something important?"

"Something very important."

"No worries. I've still got a few more clubs to check out. Call me if you want to rejoin me later. That is, if you're done before sunrise."

Oliver checked his watch. He'd spent half the night with Ursula, and this was already the third club he and Cain were checking out. "It's late. I'll call you if I'm done in time."

It took Oliver twenty minutes to get to Samson's house. When he stood in front of the entrance door, he hesitated for a moment. He took a deep breath, filling his lungs with cool night air, before he rang the door bell.

"Here goes," he mumbled to himself.

The door was opened by Samson himself. His boss stared at him, his face serious. For a long moment they simply looked at each other, neither saying a word. Then Samson broke the silence. "Come in then."

Samson stood to the side to let him enter, then shut the door behind him.

Oliver stood in the hallway, shifting his weight from one foot to the other, not knowing how to start. He hadn't exactly thought this through. He wasn't like any of his colleagues who had a way with words. He was much simpler than that. Less sophisticated.

He sucked in a breath, then raised his eyes and looked at his boss. "I'm sorry, Samson. For what I said."

Samson sighed and shoved a hand through his hair. Seconds ticked by. "It's not easy seeing you grow up and become a man with his own opinions. I guess I still see you as the kid I picked up from the street one night, to make myself feel better."

Oliver stared at him with curiosity. "What do you mean?"

A sad smile played around Samson's lips. "I was at a low point in my life, thinking of all the bad things I'd done in my past. I wanted to do good, and suddenly just running Scanguards wasn't enough anymore. I wanted to save somebody. To turn their life around. So I chose you. For my own selfish purposes. I wanted to prove to myself that I could be selfless, that I could do something for a human being without expecting anything in return."

"You chose me?"

"I did it to make myself feel better. To be proud of something."

Oliver dropped his head. "And now you're disappointed in me. I can understand that."

Samson put his hand on Oliver's shoulder, making him look up. "No. I'm not disappointed in you. It's not that. I wasn't selfless. It was selfish to think that I could make decisions for you. And when I realized that you'd started making your own decisions, I got defensive. I couldn't let go, when I knew I had to. Oliver, Quinn might be your sire, but you're like a son to me."

Oliver felt a stinging in his eyes and realized that they were welling up with tears. He pushed them back. "I've always looked up to you."

Samson pulled him into a hug. "I know that."

Oliver felt the tension in his body ease. "Are we okay?"

Samson released him and ruffled Oliver's hair. "We're okay. Now tell me why you're smelling like a spa."

Shock coursed through him, making him freeze in place for a moment. What else was Samson smelling besides the bubble bath he'd shared with Ursula? Could he still smell Ursula's scent on him?

"There's nothing wrong with a man taking a bath," Oliver said in a light tone then winked. "Just don't tell Rose that I'm borrowing her expensive gels and lotions."

Samson leaned a little closer, sniffing again. "She must have changed brands. It doesn't smell like her."

Oliver forced a chuckle, hoping his boss wouldn't realize he was lying. But there was no way he could let him know that he'd seen

Ursula. "Women. As soon as you think you've got them figured out, they change things around."

Samson laughed. "Wiser words have never been spoken."

This small crisis was averted. Relief flooded him just as his cell phone buzzed. Oliver pulled it from his pocket and checked caller ID, but it only said *Private Caller*. At least that meant it wasn't Ursula, otherwise the number of the cell phone he'd given her would show up. Talking to her when Samson would be able to listen in on the call wouldn't be smart.

"Let me see who wants something from me," he said to Samson, then pressed the talk button and answered the phone. "Yes?"

"Oliver Parker?" the male voiced asked.

He recognized it immediately. "Mr. Corbin!" Oliver motioned to Samson, indicating that he wanted him to listen in. "What a nice surprise."

"Yes, yes. Are you still interested in that address we talked about?"

"Absolutely."

"Do you have something to write?"

He noticed Samson snatch a notepad off the sideboard and pull out a pen from the drawer.

"Shoot," Oliver instructed the vampire on the other end of the line.

Corbin dictated an address in the East Bay, and Oliver watched as Samson wrote it down.

"Thank you so much."

"No problem. Just one thing: if you're going there, you should probably go soon. The email blast I received said that it was only a temporary address. Looks like they might be moving again."

"Thanks for the tip."

"Sure."

Then the line went dead. Oliver stared at Samson then pointed to the phone. "That was the vampire whose wallet Ursula stole."

"I figured." He pointed to the address on the notepad. "Let's alert HQ and get this show on the road."

34

On the way to Scanguards' headquarters, Samson already alerted the staff by phone and started giving instructions to call everybody off patrol duty and have them come in before sunrise. Nobody would be going home to sleep today, because the day would be spent working out a plan of how to extract the dozen incarcerated girls and destroy the vampires who ran the operation.

Oliver thrived on this part of his job. Like a well-oiled machine, all wheels in Scanguards' big machine clicked into place. Everybody knew what they had to do.

The entire building was buzzing with activity when they arrived. As he and Samson walked through the corridors, busy staff members greeted them as they passed.

"Let's see what information the others have for us already," Samson said as he walked into the situation room, a large, windowless office with several monitors mounted on the walls. A number of computers stood on desks on one side. A large table dominated the middle of the room.

Thomas sat at one of the computers, his fingers flying over the keyboard so fast that the movement would have been a blur to the human eye. Cain was hovering behind him, staring at the monitor above Thomas's head. It showed a split screen with various angles of a street corner.

Quinn leaned against the table in the middle, listening to Amaury and Zane who stood talking with Gabriel.

"You're back," Samson greeted his second-in-command.

When Gabriel turned to return the greeting, light shone on the scar on the right side of his face, showing it more prominently than normally. His long dark brown hair was bound together in a pony tail.

"Hey Samson, Oliver. Got back a few hours ago. Just in time as it turns out. Wouldn't want to miss the action." He grinned.

"Good to see you. Where's everybody else?" Samson asked.

Zane walked to the table. "Jay is still sieving through the stuff he brought back from Valentine's apartment. The place was a pigsty. Not everybody is back from their patrol yet, but they've been notified. Eddie is in the computer lab downstairs, cracking the password on a second cell phone we found in Valentine's place." Then he jerked his thumb in Thomas's direction. "Thomas is trying to get us camera feeds for the outside of the building."

Oliver stepped closer. "How?"

Thomas briefly looked over his shoulder. "The address you gave us is an old warehouse in one of the less savory neighborhoods of Oakland. There might be some surveillance cameras in the area, maybe a gas station, or some other business. I'm scanning the area for it."

"What else do we have?" Oliver looked back at Zane.

Zane curled his lip up. "You running the show now?"

Oliver squared his stance, but refrained from fisting his hands at his hips, not wanting to look like a puffed up peacock. Instead he simply glared at his colleague. "Remember, I was the reason we got this break."

The standoff took several tense seconds during which nobody spoke and only Thomas's tapping on the keyboard was audible. From the corner of his eye, Oliver noticed that even Quinn tensed. Was his sire rooting for him?

Then Zane relaxed his shoulders and looked at Samson and Gabriel. "Guess the kid will have to run point eventually. Might as well do it with a case he cares about."

Surprised that Zane had conceded, Oliver was speechless for a moment. Then he kicked into action.

"Cain, tell Eddie to lay off the cell phone for now and get us blueprints of the building."

Cain nodded and picked up the receiver, dialing a two digit number.

For the next few hours, they set up surveillance of the warehouse and brainstormed ideas on how to attack without endangering the women and what to do with any clients found on the premises. They were in agreement about what the fate of the vampires who ran the brothel would be: they would be destroyed on sight. The punishment for the clients was a little less clear cut.

"We have no idea how many clients they even have," Amaury said. "We can't just go around and dust them all."

"Hmm." Samson rubbed the back of his neck.

Oliver paced. "They must have a client list. Otherwise they couldn't have contacted Corbin to let him know about the new address. We'll have to find the list. It's the only way to find all affected vampires in the city."

Gabriel sighed. "And then what? Bring them in and lock them up until they've gone through withdrawal and are clean?"

"It might be the only way," Oliver mused. "Samson, how about we talk to Drake about it? He might be able to help us there. After all, addiction is in part mental. As a psychiatrist, he might have some ideas."

Samson gave him an encouraging look. "That's a good idea. I'll talk to him."

That problem dealt with for now, Oliver brought the focus back on the main task: how to get the women out safely.

"Thomas. Pipe the feed into the large screen so we can see what we're dealing with."

Thomas did as he was asked, and a moment later, a grainy black and white image appeared on the main TV screen in the room.

"What are we looking at?" Oliver asked.

Thomas stood and used a laser pointer to project a red dot onto the video image. He moved it over the screen as he spoke.

"That's the warehouse. There's an entrance door to the right here, but from the blueprint we know that there are two other doors in the back. There's been no activity, which would be consistent with the information we have: since it's still daylight, nobody is going in or coming out. And even if it were night already, this video wouldn't help us. Unfortunately as we all know you can't tell on a video feed whether you're dealing with a vampire or not. Their auras can't be captured on camera. So we'll need to send somebody there to confirm first."

Oliver shook his head. "And waste more time? No. Corbin said that this might only be a temporary address. We can't risk them slipping through our fingers."

"I agree," Samson said. "Nevertheless, let's send over a couple of our best human guards while it's daytime and have them do some reconnaissance for us. That won't cost us any time."

Oliver nodded. "Fine."

"And I think to be cautious we should get confirmation of the address from another source." Samson turned to Thomas. "How's Eddie coming along with breaking that password on Valentine's second phone?"

"He said he's got it under control."

"Okay, then let's go over weaponry," Oliver suggested. There were many ways to kill a vampire, and while he would love to see those bastards suffer the most horrible deaths possible, he was smart enough to know that Scanguards had to employ the most efficient methods to ensure the safety of the women.

Small caliber handguns with silver bullets were still the most effective way to kill a large number of vampires without having to get too close. Several of their group were sharpshooters, Thomas being one of them. While everybody discussed the merits of one weapon versus another, Quinn leaned in, speaking quietly.

"I'm very proud of you. And I'm sorry we doubted you. I always knew that when push came to shove, you would pull through."

"It's not over yet."

"I know. But it's a good start." He tossed a look at the screen and the blueprints that were spread over the table. "When all this is over, we'll talk about Ursula."

Absentmindedly Oliver nodded. Shit, he hadn't told Ursula yet about the latest developments. And he had to tell her that he wouldn't be able to stop by tonight since they would be going on the attack tonight. He didn't want her to wait for him in vain and possibly worry.

It was almost sunset by the time Oliver was able to slip out of the situation room and find a quiet office where he could make a phone call without being overheard.

He dialed the pre-programmed number while keeping an eye on the door.

"Oliver?" Ursula's voice came through the line.

"Yes, baby, it's me."

She sighed.

"I have exciting news. We know where the blood brothel has relocated to. It's over in Oakland now. We're going to attack tonight and get the women out."

"Oh my god! I can't believe it!" Excitement colored her choked up voice.

"It'll all be all right soon."

"What will you do? It's going to be dangerous, isn't it?"

He chuckled. "Are you worried about me?"

"What if I am?"

Pride made his chest swell. Ursula cared about him. "I promise you I know what I'm doing. And my colleagues do to. We're discussing strategy right now. Don't worry, we're going in with guns blazing."

Her breath hitched. "But the girls. You can't hurt them."

"We won't. We have some excellent sharpshooters on our team. None of the girls will be harmed. I promise you."

"It's so good to know it'll soon be over. How did you even manage to find the place?"

"I got a call from Corbin, the vampire you stole the wallet from."

"He found out where they moved to?"

"Yes, he got an email notifying him of the new address. Damn lucky too! Since he'd only been to the place once, he didn't think they'd even notify him."

"What?"

"I said damn lucky—"

"Oliver, Corbin didn't just come once. I saw him many times. He was a regular."

Surprise flooded him. "But he said . . . are you sure?"

"Believe me . . . Oh damn, I think Vera is at the door. I've gotta go."

"Wait—" But the line went dead. "Fuck!"

Why would Corbin lie about the fact that he'd been a frequent client at the brothel? Why pretend that he'd only been there once and didn't like the special blood? Was it possible that Ursula confused him with another client? No, he couldn't allow himself to doubt her words. Whenever he'd done so, it had turned out that he was wrong and she was right.

He had to follow his gut.

Oliver stormed into the situation room just as Eddie entered too.

"Corbin is lying."

All heads turned to him.

"I just got off the phone with Ursula. She confirmed that Corbin was a regular—"

Zane interrupted him. "You spoke to Ursula? I specifically ordered—"

"That's not important now!" Oliver cried out. "I found her. What she told me makes me believe that Corbin is lying. He was a regular at the blood brothel while he told me he'd been there only once and didn't like it. He's been deceiving us! The warehouse in Oakland has to be a trap."

"There are many reasons why he wouldn't want to admit that he was a regular client," Samson cautioned.

"I agree," Gabriel said. "That doesn't mean the blood brothel isn't where Corbin says it is right now. Besides—" He motioned to the monitor where the live video of the warehouse was still showing. "Our human guards have confirmed that they found evidence of activity there. There must be at least a dozen guys holed up inside."

"But no evidence of the women," Oliver noted. "That makes it a trap."

"We should still go in," Zane said. "We'll just take more men with us."

"No! Corbin first."

Amaury shrugged. "It doesn't hurt to send a few people to his house and check on him while the rest of us make our way to Oakland. It'll take us a while to get there anyway." Then he looked at Eddie. "Anything from that second phone Valentine had?"

"I cracked the password," Eddie replied. "But he didn't get any texts or emails about the blood brothel."

Oliver pointed to Eddie. "See, even more reason not to go to Oakland. Why would one client get an email with the new address, but not the other? And Valentine was definitely a regular, considering how addicted he is." He stared at his colleagues, whose expressions had darkened.

Samson and Gabriel exchanged a look. Then Samson stood up. "Change of plans."

35

Paul Corbin put the finishing touches on his impeccable outfit. He loved dressing well, and for tonight's occasion he'd outdone himself.

As soon as the sun set, he sped away in his black Mercedes. Everything was arranged. It took him less than ten minutes to reach the address on Nob Hill. He parked on the opposite side of the street and killed the engine.

When he got out of his car and shut the door behind him, he smoothed the creases from his black suit, while his legs ate up the distance to the entrance of the large building. Next to the brass sign was an intercom system. He pressed the bell and didn't have to wait long until a crackling and the voice of a woman came through it.

"Yes?"

He bent toward the speaker. "Paul Corbin. I'm a new client."

There was a slight hesitation, then the buzzer sounded. He pressed against the door and entered. The foyer was lush. He quickly assessed his surroundings: a lounge to the left, two doors to his right, then a large staircase at the end of the hall. One of the doors to his right opened and an Asian woman dressed in a smart business suit exited and walked toward him.

She stretched her hand out in greeting. "Mr. Corbin?"

Corbin shook her hand, not at all surprised that the woman was a vampire. "Good evening."

"I'm Vera," she introduced herself. "May I ask who referred you?"

Prepared for the question, he answered evenly, "Oliver was so kind."

She smiled instantly and relaxed seemingly. "You know Oliver?"

He nodded politely. "Charming young man."

"He is, isn't he?" Then she looked him up and down, sizing him up.

Corbin kept his cool. He knew he would pass muster.

"What may I offer you for your pleasure? We cater to all tastes."

He smiled nonchalantly. "I'm a man of many tastes. Surprise me."

He tossed a glance to the lounge where several women entertained the men present. "All I require is some privacy, away from all the . . . uh, entertainment, shall we say?"

"A private room, of course. This way," Vera directed him.

He followed her along the hallway until she knocked at another door then entered. Inside the comfortable living area sat half a dozen women, all beautiful in their own right, and all tastefully dressed, some showing more flesh than others.

Vera motioned to the girls and gave him a sideway's glance. "The choice is yours."

He let his eyes wander over the women, then pointed at one of them. "This one."

Vera waved the woman to come to them. She was voluptuous, her curves full and enticing. Her gaze swept over him, lingering briefly on his crotch. He allowed a half-smile to cross his lips before he took the beauty's hand and brought it to his mouth.

She appeared surprised at the old-fashioned gesture and giggled.

"This is Ophelia. She will lead you upstairs to a private room. Ophelia, please wait at the bottom of the staircase for Mr. Corbin."

The woman nodded and left the room. Vera followed her, motioning him to do the same, then stopped in the corridor where she turned to him once Ophelia was out of earshot. "Will this be cash or credit card?"

He looked at her and pulled out his wallet, opening it. He'd had the presence of mind to stuff his wallet with large bills before leaving his house and pulled them out now. "Cash."

Vera stretched out her open palm, and one after the other he placed hundred dollar bills on it until she was satisfied and closed her hand around the money.

"Enjoy your evening. And should you require anything, there's a house phone in the room. Dial zero, and let us know how we can make your stay more enjoyable."

"I'm already certain that this will turn into a very satisfying evening." He would make sure of that.

When he reached the stairs, Ophelia was waiting for him. He snaked his arm around her luscious curves and allowed her to lead him upstairs. On the third floor, she made a turn and led him down a corridor with several rooms. She stopped in front of one of them and opened the door.

Giving him a seductive look, she entered and motioned him to follow her. "This is it."

Corbin gave the room a cursory look. It was tastefully furnished with a large bed, bedside tables and a dresser. There was a chair, presumably so clients could put their clothes there while they indulged in the offerings the women provided.

"Perfect," he answered.

She brushed against him, her hand reaching for his tie. "What would you like?" She licked her lips.

"What do you do?"

"Everything," she replied and pressed her hips against his groin.

"Good," he murmured. "Then how about this?"

He brought his hands up to her head, cupping it. Expectantly she gazed at him. Then, with one swift, but powerful move, he turned her head, snapping her neck.

She collapsed instantly, and he caught her, depositing her on the bed. It was a shame that he was in a hurry, otherwise he would have fucked her first, but business was more important.

Readjusting his tie, he turned back to the door. "Now the evening can start."

***

Ursula flicked through the channels on the TV but found nothing interesting to watch. She was too hyped up to concentrate on anything. Tonight, Scanguards would free her sisters, the women who'd been locked up like her. Their ordeal would be over soon, and everybody would be back with their families. She prayed that Oliver and his colleagues would be able to defeat the other vampires and not get hurt.

Sighing, she closed her eyes and recalled the memories of the previous night, but a sound at the door interrupted her. Was her dinner ready so soon? Ursula heard a noise as if somebody forced the key into the lock, but had trouble turning it. Then the door was jerked open.

What she saw then was a blurry movement, then a man appearing inside her room, shutting the door behind him.

Stunned, she scrambled to jump up from the bed, trying to put some distance between her and the intruder, but he was faster and snatched her arm, squeezing it painfully.

"Not so fast, my little blood whore," he said with an evil smile on his face.

Oh God, she knew who he was! She recognized him. He was the leech whose wallet she'd stolen: Paul Corbin.

Air rushed from her lungs. "What do you want?"

He issued a non-committal smile. "Well, isn't that obvious? I didn't buy you whores to have you escape me. I've come to bring you back to the flock."

"Bring me back?" She didn't understand what he was talking about. Why would he want to bring her back? He was a client of the brothel, not a guard.

Corbin chuckled. "I own you and all the others. You work for me! You make money for me, and I won't have some young vampire upstart steal you from me so he can get the goods for free. Whoever wants your blood, will have to pay me for it!"

Her eyes widened with understanding. "You're their leader! You own the brothel."

"Smart girl. Maybe even smarter than some of my guards. They never caught on to the fact that I was checking up on them by pretending to be a client. They never suspected a thing."

Ursula felt shivers race through her. So it was true then that the owner had a spy who would report whether the guards were doing their jobs, only that the spy was the owner himself. Clever. And now he was here to take her back. Frantically, she searched her brain for what to do. She had to stall him. If she was lucky, her dinner would arrive soon, and with any luck, Vera would be the one to bring it and be able to help her.

"How did you find me?"

Corbin laughed softly. "Your boyfriend brought me the wallet you stole from me. I knew that somebody in the brothel had stolen it and had the place searched, but nobody could find it. When Oliver brought it to me, I knew it had to have come from you. You were the only one who got out. I knew then that I would find you."

She swallowed.

"And then your little friend claimed he's a client. How stupid do you people think I am? I know every client by name. There was no Oliver Parker among them, if that's even his real name." He glared at her. "So I followed him, and guess where he leads me to?" He looked around the room. "This beautiful establishment. So, what did you give him to help you? Just your pussy? Or did he drink your blood too? Did you promise him a lifelong supply if he helped you?"

Corbin jerked at her arm, pulling her closer to him. His eyes were red now, and she saw how his facial muscles hardened, and his fingers started turning into claws.

"No!"

"No matter. Because he's not getting anything at all from you. Because you're coming back with me."

"You have nowhere to run! He's freeing the other women tonight!" she cried out.

Corbin let out an evil laugh. "Oh, you mean at the warehouse in Oakland that I gave him the address to?"

Oh shit! Oliver had told her over the phone that Corbin had been the one to provide him with the address. He would be running into a trap. They would kill him and his colleagues. "Oh God no!" She had to help him, get a message to him. But her cell phone was tucked underneath her pillow and out of her reach, not that Corbin would give her any opportunity to even press the call button.

"Yes, when your friend and his colleagues arrive at the warehouse in Oakland, they will be annihilated. There'll be a dozen heavily armed vampires waiting for them. They'll be walking into a bloodbath. And in the meantime, the girls are being packed up and loaded up. We're leaving town tonight, and you're coming with us."

She shook her head, but he grinned.

"Let's go!"

He tried to pull her up, but she kicked her leg against him. He cursed, but his grip loosened by a minute fraction and she twisted, stretching her arm out to reach under the pillow. Her fingers gripped the cell phone. But he jerked her back, and the phone slipped from her fingers, sliding to the edge of the bed, before she could press the call button.

Corbin's eyes fell on it. "Disobeying again? I've heard that about you! You were a trouble maker from the start! Never knew what was good for her! Now take this and see how you like it!"

He slapped the back of his hand across her cheek, whipping her head to the side. Pain radiated through her, making her feel so dizzy she thought she'd lose consciousness.

She groaned.

"I'll teach you to disobey me!"

He raised his hand once more.

"Do it and I'll make you suffer!" a male voice warned from the window.

Was she hallucinating already, or had he really come to save her?

36

Oliver watched in horror as Corbin pulled Ursula in front of his body like a shield. Oliver had reached for his gun the moment he'd entered the room from the balcony, but he hesitated now. He wasn't a crack shot, and if Corbin moved in vampire speed, dragging Ursula with him, the bullet could hit her instead. He couldn't take that risk.

"Look who's joined us!" Corbin said to Ursula. "Your boyfriend. Shame he's too late."

Corbin reached into his pocket producing a handgun which he now held to Ursula's temple.

Shock coursed through Oliver, but he forced himself to remain calm and sound unconcerned, when he answered, "That's not how I see it. I came just in time. Granted, I found your house empty when I got there. Are you moving?" Oliver asked casually. "What a shame. That was a nice house."

Corbin forced a smile. "In my profession moving comes with the territory."

"Where to this time?"

"That's my business, if you don't mind. Now drop your gun."

"You won't shoot her. She's too valuable to you."

An evil grin spread over Corbin's face. "The bullet won't kill her, but it'll hurt nevertheless." He lowered his gun to her shoulder.

Realizing that Corbin wasn't bluffing, Oliver dropped his weapon to the floor.

Then he watched in panic as Corbin took a couple of steps backwards toward the door, keeping Ursula pressed closely to his front.

"One last question before I leave: how did you know it was me?" Corbin asked.

"You shouldn't have said you only went to the blood brothel once. When I realized you were lying about that, I figured you could be lying about other things too. Like the new address of the blood brothel. Particularly since nobody else got an email with the address. Funny that you would be the only client who did."

Corbin lifted an eyebrow then shrugged. "Ah, well, next time I'll know."

"There won't be a next time," Oliver prophesized.

But Corbin reached behind him and opened the door. Ursula stared at Oliver, her eyes wide with fear, her hands trying to pry off Corbin's arm, to no avail.

Oliver perceived a movement behind Corbin in the hallway when the door swung open wider. "Corbin, you made one other fatal mistake."

For a second, Corbin stopped in his movements. "Nice try."

"You assumed I came alone."

A shot rang out. Corbin's right arm, holding the gun, dropped as he cried out in pain, blood seeping from his shoulder. Ursula wrenched free of him, falling forward in the struggle. Corbin's face distorted into a grimace, but it appeared that the bullet had exited his shoulder and was therefore doing no further damage.

Aided by his left hand, Corbin raised his gun arm again, aiming at Ursula as she tried to crawl to safety.

"You'll never get her or the other girls."

Oliver lunged and barreled into Corbin, knocking him to the ground. As Corbin hit the floor with his injured shoulder, he lost the gun. It skidded underneath the bed, out of reach of either one of them. Oliver was on him in an instant. They struggled, exchanging blows and punches too fast for the human eye to follow.

Oliver repeatedly pounded into Corbin's wound, but the bastard was strong, and his left hook whipped Oliver's head to the side. Using the momentum he had, Corbin rolled, and Oliver suddenly found himself underneath him, being pounded by the evil vampire's fists.

Oliver kicked his leg up and managed to drive his knee into Corbin's thigh, making him pull back for a moment. It was enough to get out from underneath him and roll to the side.

Corbin's next blow missed, and Oliver knew his enemy's strength was waning. Corbin knew it too. Oliver pinned him down with one arm against Corbin's throat. Then he reached into his pocket and pulled out a stake. Corbin's hand moved, jerking something from his pocket. From the corner of his eye, Oliver saw what it was: not a weapon, but a cell phone. Corbin's arm pulled back like a pitcher, even though his range was limited.

"You'll never find them!" he vowed and tried to smash the phone against the wall.

But Oliver slammed the stake into his heart and whipped around in vampire speed, catching the phone in mid-flight before it could hit the wall and smash to pieces. Beneath him Corbin disintegrated into dust.

Breathing heavily, Oliver clutched the iPhone tightly and stared back to where Corbin's dust settled. "Maybe I should have mentioned that I was the catcher for my baseball team, asshole."

Cain burst into the room, still holding his gun. "Guess I'm a worse shot than I thought."

"Should have waited for me," Thomas admonished on rushing into the room behind him.

"What took you guys so long?" Oliver growled at his colleagues, but didn't wait for an answer and instead rushed to Ursula. "Ursula, baby. Are you okay? Are you hurt?"

She reached for him, and he pulled her into an embrace. "I'm okay," she whispered. Then her hands fisted in his shirt. "There'll be a dozen vampires waiting for you at the warehouse in Oakland."

"We've got it under control."

She took a few deep breaths. "The girls. He said he's taking them away. They were being loaded up somewhere. But he didn't say where."

Oliver raised his hand that held Corbin's cell phone, then turned to face his colleagues.

"Thomas, can you crack the password on Corbin's phone and see if you can find a trail? He wanted to destroy it, which makes me think there's information on it as to the girls' whereabouts." Oliver ran his hand over Ursula's hair.

Thomas took the phone. "No problem. Give me a few minutes." He sat down on the bed and pulled out a small electronic device from his leather jacket, then plugged the attached cable into Corbin's iPhone.

Ursula wrapped her arms around Oliver's neck. "You saved me."

Oliver smiled and motioned to Cain. "Technically, Cain helped me, but if you want to kiss me instead, I'm game."

He had barely finished his last word, when Ursula pressed her lips on his and seared them with a kiss. Had Cain not been standing there, watching them, Oliver would have allowed himself to indulge in more than just a kiss. But the situation wasn't over yet, and there were still innocents that needed saving.

As he looked to the hallway, he noticed several of Vera's girls approach. "Shit, they must have heard the gunshot. Cain, I think you'll have some cleaning up to do."

Cain nodded when all of a sudden Vera burst into the room. Her gaze darted from Oliver and Ursula to Cain and Thomas then back to Oliver. "I found Ophelia dead in one of the rooms," she murmured, shutting the door behind her. "A broken neck."

Oliver closed his eyes. "Oh, shit. Corbin must have killed her."

"Corbin? The new client you referred?" Vera asked.

"So that's how he got in."

Cain lifted his hand. "I'll fill you in shortly, Vera. But first you and I will need to clean up." He motioned to the door behind which Vera's girls were still hovering. Oliver could hear their concerned voices through the door.

Cain ushered Vera out of the room, following her.

Oliver looked at Thomas who stared at his gadget, deep in concentration. Knowing he shouldn't disturb him, he pulled Ursula aside.

"How did you know that Corbin would come for me?" she asked quietly.

"When I found Corbin had moved everything out of his house, I was close to going insane. I knew then that he'd set up the trap to get two birds with one stone: get me and Scanguards off his back, while snatching you to take you and the girls away."

"I never suspected him being the boss," Ursula admitted. "He was just like any other leech. He didn't stand out."

"I guess that was the point. He wanted to blend in so that he could keep an eye on things. I'm just wondering how he could hide the fact that he was an addict. I saw no signs in him." Oliver couldn't believe that he'd been so blind.

"Maybe he wasn't an addict."

"But how?"

"What if he never drank much of our blood?"

"Go on," Oliver said with interest.

She lowered her voice even more, obviously not wanting to be overheard by Thomas, even though Oliver knew that his colleague could hear her if he was inclined to listen. "Remember when you used mind control to make me think you bit me?"

He nodded. How could he forget? "But mind control doesn't work on vampires. The guards would have noticed."

"He could simply have dug his fangs in on that side of the neck that was turned away from the guard, but never sucked on the vein. The guard would have smelled the blood because he punctured our skin, but we would have never known that he didn't drink from us because he used mind control to make us think we sensed him sucking on our vein."

"My god, you might be right. How else could he have maintained control?" He smiled at her. "You're very smart."

She returned his smile then turned serious again. "Will we find them?"

Instead of an answer, he turned to look at Thomas, who looked up from the phone at the same moment, a triumphant grin on his face.

"Got it!"

37

The truck stop along the freeway was busy. More than two dozen large trucks, most of them eighteen-wheelers, were parked in neat rows, many of them presumably resting there for the night. Some of the drivers were most likely already sleeping in their cabs, others still sat in the diner eating a late dinner.

Oliver pulled the minivan into the parking lot and turned off the engine. Next to him, Thomas peered out toward the trucks. Gabriel, along with Amaury, who'd come back from Oakland a short while earlier, having left a contingent of their staff watching the warehouse, sat on the back bench.

Ursula sat between the two large vampires, still not entirely comfortable with them, but she knew she would eventually get used to them. Oliver's presence made her feel safe. He turned his head, as did Thomas.

"I'm afraid we have no information on what the truck looks like, but the email we found on Corbin's phone said that somebody would deliver Ursula to this spot. Guess Corbin was still trying to protect his identity, because his note refers to a new guard bringing her in," Oliver said.

"In that case," Gabriel answered. "Why not give them what they expect? It'll draw them out."

Oliver nodded. "That's what I was thinking." He looked at her. "You'll be perfectly safe. My colleagues will be ready to jump as soon as the guards reveal themselves. They'll never even get close to you."

Ursula nodded, having come to the same conclusion. "I agree."

"Good. I'll take Ursula out and walk toward the diner, crossing in front of the trucks and—"

"No!" she interrupted him.

A confused look crossed Oliver's face. "I thought you agreed."

"I want Gabriel to take me."

When Oliver tried to protest, she held up her hand. "Hear me out.

Corbin followed you, which means most likely he saw where Scanguards operates from. What if he's seen your colleagues too? And what if he snapped pictures to give them to his staff so they can be on the lookout?" She pointed to Gabriel. "You told me that Gabriel came back from New York only a few hours ago, when Corbin was most likely already planning to snatch me from Vera's place. He wouldn't have seen Gabriel."

Then she gave Gabriel a sideways glance and smiled at him. "No offense, but you look like you could be working for Corbin." Her eyes wandered to the large scar on his face.

After a moment, Gabriel looked at Oliver. "She's right. On both counts: Corbin wouldn't have seen me, and I guess I do look a bit like a thug."

Grudgingly Oliver conceded and stared at Gabriel. "Fine. But if anything happens to her, I'm coming after you."

Gabriel rolled his eyes and reached for the door. He slid it open.

"Wait," Oliver said and reached in his pocket, pulling out a stake. He handed it to her. "Just in case." With one last smile at him, Ursula followed Gabriel out of the car. She stuffed the stake into her jacket pocket.

"I think you should grab my arm and pull me along," she murmured under her breath. "Corbin's guards weren't exactly friendly."

Gabriel took her arm and gave her a gentle shove forward. They rounded a few cars and came into view of the trucks. Slowly and deliberately, Gabriel led her between the two rows of parked trucks. From the corner of her eyes, she scanned the trucks for any movement as they continued walking. The headlights of one truck blinked on, then were extinguished again.

"This must be it," Gabriel said under his breath and pulled her toward it as she pretended to move reluctantly. Despite the knowledge that she was safe and that the other men from Scanguards weren't far, her heartbeat accelerated, and her palms became damp. With every step they took toward the truck that had flashed its lights, her pulse raced faster.

Suddenly the cab of the truck opened, and a man stepped down from it. When he hit the ground and walked forward, Ursula recognized him as one of the guards. Instantly, she froze. The guard, whose name she remembered as Marcus, flashed a nasty grin, having recognized her too. Then his eyes wandered to her companion, looking Gabriel up and down.

The click of a gun cut through the silence. Before she could react, a familiar voice addressed them from behind. "Ursula, my favorite of all."

"Dirk," she choked out before turning.

He stood several feet away from them, and was just emerging from between two parked trucks.

Dirk waved his gun in Gabriel's direction. Ursula noticed that a silencer was attached to its nozzle. "And who's this?"

"Must be the new guard the boss was mentioning," the other guard replied.

"No, he's not," Dirk claimed.

Ursula's heart stopped. Behind Dirk another man emerged from the shadows. Dirk motioned his head toward the man. "That's the new guard. When the boss didn't show up to hand Ursula over to him he followed his orders and alerted me."

Marcus pulled his gun, pointing it at Gabriel who hadn't moved. Now Gabriel spoke for the first time. "What makes you think that that guy is the new guard? Way I see it, I brought the girl, he didn't."

Marcus, clearly confused, moved his gun, pointing it at the stranger who'd sidled up to Dirk.

Dirk tilted his head to the vampire next to him. "Give my colleague the code word."

"Emperors' blood," the stranger said.

"Fuck!" Marcus hissed and aimed his gun back at Gabriel, ready to shoot.

Faster than her eyes could follow, Gabriel lunged at Marcus, kicking the gun from his hand as a scuffle ensued. Fists went flying in such rapid pace that it almost made her dizzy. Their movements were a blur to her eyes.

To her left she saw two men barreling toward them: Oliver and Amaury. Thomas was nowhere to be seen. Seeing them too, Dirk dove for her, his intent clear: he wanted to use her as a human shield. He slammed his body against hers, temporarily robbing her of her breath.

Shots rang out, and with horror she saw that the new guard was firing in Oliver's and Amaury's direction. Her heart stopped.

"No!" she screamed, praying that none of the bullets would hit Oliver.

Dirk whipped her around, dragging her toward the truck, preventing her from seeing what was happening to her rescuers. She struggled against him, kicking her foot into his shin, but it appeared that it made no difference to her attacker.

"Ursula, no!!!" she heard Oliver yell behind her just as another shot was fired.

"Fuck!" Dirk hissed under his breath, but continued dragging her toward the door of the truck. "We're leaving, bitch!"

She turned her head as much as she could and saw Gabriel still fight with Marcus. The new guard was engaging Amaury in a fist fight, and Oliver was nowhere to be seen.

"No!" she wailed, anger and pain surging within her. Where was Oliver? She couldn't allow her mind to continue her next thought. Instead, she acted on pure instinct.

When Dirk slammed her against the door of the truck and released her for a second to reach for the handle, she slipped her hand into her jacket pocket. She turned, glaring at him. "Of all the guards I hate you most!"

When he grinned, mocking her, she spit in this face.

Her action distracted him for a tiny moment, but it was all she needed: she rammed the stake into his chest. With satisfaction, she watched as he turned into dust before her eyes.

Behind him, Oliver emerged out of nowhere, gun drawn. He froze in his movement, jerking the gun to the side, away from her. He'd been about to shoot Dirk in the back.

He rushed to her, pulling her into his arms. By the time he released her, everything was quiet again. Her eyes searched the area where the fight had taken place. None of their enemies were left.

Gabriel and Amaury stood there, breathing a little heavier than before, but there was no scratch on them.

"And Thomas?" she asked, holding her breath.

"I'm here," came Thomas's voice from between two trucks. He emerged a second later. "Humans. They were approaching. I had to make sure they turned back, or they might have gotten killed."

She nodded, relieved, then she felt Oliver shelve her chin and turn her face to make her look at him. "I'm so proud of you, Ursula."

She tossed a glance at the spot where Dirk's ashes had settled on the ground. "He was the one who taunted me every night."

"Nobody will ever hurt you again," Oliver promised and hugged her tightly. "Now let's get the girls."

Together with Oliver's colleagues, they walked to the back of the truck. Amaury gripped the lever, opening the lock. Then he and Gabriel swung the double doors open.

It was dark inside, but Ursula heard silent gasps coming from the farthest end.

"Come out, you're free," Gabriel called into the truck, but nobody moved.

"They're scared," Ursula explained. Then she stepped up on a metal step to lift herself higher and addressed them in Chinese. "It's me: Wei Ling. You're safe, sisters. Come out, we're going home."

"Wei Ling," she heard them reply. "Wei Ling came back for us."

One-by-one, the women walked to the opening, looking first at her, then eyed the men behind her. "They're our friends," she assured them in Chinese.

The vampires helped the girls from the truck. When they'd all exited their temporary prison, they huddled around her. Ursula's eyes searched for one girl in particular. "Lanfen," she whispered. "Where are you?"

A hand touched her shoulder, and she turned.

"I'm here," Lanfen answered.

Relief washed over her. "I thought you were gone."

"I was sick," Lanfen continued. "But I made it."

They hugged, holding each other close. Tears shot to Ursula's eyes.

"We're going home," she whispered again and allowed herself to cry in the bosom of her sisters.

38

After more minivans from Scanguards showed up, they transported all of the rescued women to a safe house in San Francisco. Several of Scanguards' staff went to work, contacting the women's families and arranging for their return home.

The rest of Scanguards had one more task ahead of them.

Oliver sat waiting in the situation room, tapping his foot impatiently. Even though he knew that Ursula was tired and needed to sleep, she had insisted on watching how the rest of her tormentors would finally meet their end.

"When do you want to call your parents?" he asked, knowing that there was no more reason to keep her from them. Just like all the other girls, she would want to return home.

And she would leave him and go back to where she belonged.

Ursula motioned to the monitor that still showed a live feed of the warehouse in Oakland. "After they're dead."

He nodded, his chest tightening. "You can fly to New York with the other women if you want. Samson has authorized the jet for it. Or you can fly out later . . . if you want to stay a few days longer."

He looked away, not wanting to show how eager he was for her answer.

"I really want to see my parents. I miss them," she said.

Oliver choked back the disappointment, knowing that within a few hours she would be gone. "Of course, I understand."

"About the other women . . . "

"What about them?"

"Will they remember what happened to them?"

Oliver looked up, shaking his head. "We can't allow them to keep those memories. They might promise today never to breathe a single word about vampires, but under pressure, they'll tell their families, their friends. They'll want to explain things to them. But our secrets must be kept."

"I understand. What about me? The memories you and I made?" Her big eyes looked at him, affection and trust shining back at him.

He swallowed hard. His next words were the most difficult ones he'd ever had to utter. "When you leave here, I'll have to make sure you won't remember anything."

"What if you got on that plane with me? Just for a week or two."

His heart suddenly beat a hundred miles a minute. "You want me to come with you?"

She stretched her hand out to clasp his. "I know that logistically it'll be tricky to hide from my parents that you're a vampire, but I'm sure we can figure something out."

He sat up and leaned closer to her. "You want me to meet your parents?"

"I can't guarantee that they'll take to you immediately. They're a little old fashioned, and me bringing home a Caucasian boyfriend might be tough to swallow at first, but I figured since they'll be so happy to know that I'm alive, they'll probably—"

"Boyfriend?" he cut her off. "You want to introduce me as your boyfriend?"

"And as the man who saved me, of course, that too."

He pulled her hand to his lips and kissed her fingertips. "Tell me something before I agree to this: are you planning on dumping this boyfriend after those two weeks, or can he hope to stick around for a while longer?"

Ursula's lids lowered halfway. "I was hoping to come back to San Francisco for something longer term. Maybe finish my studies here . . . "

"How long?"

"Can we maybe discuss this in a year or two and see how we're doing by then?"

Oliver pulled her onto his lap and brought his mouth to hers. "That's definitely doable."

"Does that mean I get to keep my memories?"

"I can do better than that: I'll help you make new ones." He kissed her softly, then felt her pull away.

"There's something else."

He brushed a strand of hair behind her ear. "Yes?"

"I want your friend Maya to do that blood test on me."

Her words rang in his ears, making him virtually dizzy with excitement. "Are you sure?"

Instead of an answer, she kissed him.

The clearing of a throat interrupted them. Oliver drew his head back to see who was disturbing his pleasant interlude with Ursula.

Thomas rolled his eyes as he entered, followed by half of Scanguards, Oliver's sire included. "Don't mind us, we're just here to watch the operation go down." He pointed to the big monitor on the wall.

Ursula scrambled off Oliver's lap, her cheeks bright red. Quickly, Oliver scooted his chair closer to the table so his lower half was hidden beneath it. If his colleagues saw his hard-on, they would tease him for the rest of his life.

"Let's get the show on the road then," Oliver said instead and watched as everybody filed into the room and took their seats.

"Sunrise is in two minutes. The charges were set earlier in the night, and we made sure that the security cameras in the area were obstructed at the time. Nobody will assume foul play. They'll blame it on PG&E as usual," Thomas summarized as he typed something on the keyboard he was sitting at.

"All our staff have cleared out of the area?" Samson asked.

"Everybody's far enough away."

Samson added, "Any innocent bystanders?"

Thomas shook his head. "We made sure nobody is in the vicinity. We received the "all clear" a few minutes ago."

Ursula's eyes were glued to the monitor, when the live feed went black. "What's happening?"

The monitor flickered, then a video feed from a different angle showed up on the screen. "We've switched from the camera at the gas station across the warehouse to our own camera which we've installed on a telephone pole. It has its own power source. All power on this block will go out once we give the go-ahead. That way we can assure that there will be no footage on the security cameras."

They had thought of everything. Nothing would be traced back to them or expose any vampires to humans. Their secret would be safe.

"I think Ursula should give the command," Oliver suggested. He looked at his colleagues, and one-by-one they all nodded.

Thomas waved Ursula to change seats with him. "Take the mouse and point it to this icon here."

Oliver watched as the first rays of the sun started illuminating the street in front of the building. More seconds passed. "Sunrise," he announced.

Ursula glanced back at him, then all that could be heard in the room was the click of the mouse.

"The electricity to the block is being shut off now," Thomas explained, and simultaneously all streetlamps and other building lights around the warehouse went out.

Oliver watched the screen, when suddenly an explosion rocked the warehouse. Even though he'd been expecting it, it still jolted him.

The fire spread, engulfing the building quickly and fully as expected: according to the blueprints, the building wasn't equipped with sprinklers.

The few vampires who tried to escape by braving daylight didn't get far. To assure none escaped, human sharpshooters, trusted Scanguards employees, had been positioned at strategic points, their weapons loaded with silver bullets. But no shots were fired in the end. Instead, the sun took care of the escaping vampires, adding their ashes to the dirt on the pavement.

The blood brothel and its jailors were finally history.

The police would investigate, no doubt, as would other government agencies, but Scanguards had enough connections who would make sure that nothing would come of these investigations.

"Now our real work starts," Samson said, his voice serious. Everybody nodded.

When Ursula gave Oliver a questioning look, he explained, "We found Corbin's client list. Each and every one of those clients is a potential risk to the human population of San Francisco. We'll have to monitor them and lock those up who are most at risk until they've gone through all stages of withdrawal."

It would be an enormous task, but the mayor had offered Scanguards all resources at his disposal. Within a few weeks, the situation would stabilize, and San Francisco would be as safe as before.

39

Two weeks later

Oliver carried the two suitcases into the house and dropped them in the foyer. Behind him, Ursula set a small bag onto the floor. After almost two weeks in Washington DC, visiting Ursula's parents, he was ready for some major relaxation. He'd never been so tense in his entire life.

While Ursula had stayed with her parents, Oliver had resided in the house of a vampire Gabriel knew and only joined them in the evenings. After discussing it at length, Ursula had agreed to his suggestion to wipe her parents' memories of the past three years and plant new ones in their minds. All their pain would be forgotten as if it had never happened. They now believed that Ursula had transferred to UC Berkeley to study for her master's degree, and that she visited her parents at least twice a year. In addition, Oliver made sure that he was part of their new memories too, so that they would easily accept him as their daughter's boyfriend. Mind control had become easier for him after he'd used it to make Ursula feel his bite. Almost as if he'd simply needed the right motivation for it.

But simply wiping her parents' memories had not been enough: Oliver had had to enlist the help of Scanguards staff in Washington and New York to do the same with friends and family of Ursula's parents, staff at the embassy where her father worked, as well as the police detectives and reporters involved in the case. Thomas had hacked into the police computers and deleted all files of Ursula's disappearance and also erased the records at the newspapers who ran the story. It was a colossal task, but one that was necessary so Ursula could be with him. Had Oliver and his colleagues not erased every memory of her disappearance, her parents would have never let her leave again.

Apart from a few stolen kisses during their stay in Washington DC, Oliver hadn't touched Ursula until they'd boarded Scanguards' private jet to return to San Francisco. He'd practically mauled her during the flight home, but since they'd had to share the plane with a few staff members of Scanguards, there had been no occasion to have sex with her, and his cock was still as hard as ever.

"Where is everybody?" Ursula asked.

"Rose? Quinn?" he called out, secretly hoping that they were out for the evening, saving him from having to tell them about their trip when he'd rather lug Ursula over his shoulder to drag her into bed. "Blake?"

"Upstairs," Quinn's voice finally sounded from the upper floor.

Frustration howled through him. He had no idea how much longer he could pretend to be civilized before he would fall over Ursula and bury himself deep inside her.

"Come on up, we want to show you something," Rose called down.

Oliver grimaced and took Ursula's hand. "Let's go then."

When they reached the third floor, Rose and Quinn were standing in front of his bedroom.

"Welcome home!" they both said.

Hugs were exchanged before Quinn opened the door to Oliver's bedroom and motioned him and Ursula to enter.

Quinn rocked back on his heels. "We thought with Ursula here, you both needed a little more space, so we knocked out the wall to Blake's room and moved him onto the second floor instead. That way, you'll have a little sitting area for yourselves."

Oliver let his eyes roam, taking in his newly decorated room. Not only was it almost twice as large as before, it had also been updated. An extra closet had been added to accommodate Ursula's clothes, and a cozy sitting area had been created.

"And if you don't like the decor, we can change that," Rose added.

Ursula turned to them, smiling. "It's beautiful. Thank you. I love it."

Oliver put his arm around her and pulled her close, then looked at Quinn and Rose. "It's perfect. Thank you!"

"You're welcome," Quinn said.

Rose tugged at his shirtsleeve. "We should leave."

Quinn nodded. "We're spending the evening with Zane and Portia, so the house is all yours tonight. Blake went patrolling with Cain."

"Patrolling?"

Quinn rolled his eyes. "Don't ask. He kept on nagging us to let him go on patrol."

Rose smiled mischievously, winking at Oliver. "Quinn caved."

But her husband merely shrugged. "Can't protect him forever." Then he reached into this back pocket and pulled out an envelope. "Before I forget it, Maya gave me this for you."

Excitement made Oliver's heart beat faster. He knew what was inside: the results of Ursula's blood test. Before leaving for Washington, Ursula had provided Maya with two blood samples: one before having sex, and one after Oliver and she had enjoyed their last night in each other's arms before leaving for the East Coast.

His hand trembled when he took the envelope from Quinn's hands. When he looked up, their gazes collided. Quinn was smiling as if he knew what this letter meant. Then he and Rose turned and closed the door behind them. He listened to their footsteps as they walked downstairs.

Slowly, he released Ursula. She stared at the envelope in his hands.

"The results," she whispered.

With shaking fingers, he opened the letter and pulled out a single sheet of paper. His eyes took several seconds to focus, before he was able to read what was written in neat handwriting.

"Dear Oliver," he read aloud. *"All tests I performed on Ursula's blood samples came back with the same result."*

Oliver sensed how Ursula held her breath.

"It's confirmed: her blood is safe once she's had an orgasm." Relief poured through him. *"However, I cannot say how long her blood needs in order to return to its former potency after sex. More tests will be necessary to determine that. But for now, as long as you only drink her blood right after she has climaxed, you'll be safe. Love, Maya."*

He dropped the letter and pulled her against him. "You have to make a decision now."

She lifted her eyes. Mesmerized by what he saw in them, he stopped breathing.

"I think my decision was clear from the moment you kissed me there in the hallway the first day I stayed in this house. I was just too afraid to admit it to myself. Too scared that I could want something that had been forced on me by others for such a long time. But I'm not scared anymore."

He swallowed hard, having trouble containing the lust that coursed through his veins at the knowledge of what would happen tonight. Speech eluded him, so he did the only thing he could: he slid his mouth over hers and kissed her. Her lips yielded to him, parting for him when he licked his tongue against their seam.

There would be no holding back tonight, no trying to keep the beast in check. Finally, Ursula would be truly his.

There was no rush when he undressed her as she did the same to him. When he laid her onto the crisp sheets and pressed her body against his heated skin, a shudder went through him. How he had survived the last two weeks without touching her, he couldn't remember.

"It was torture not to make love to you while we were back east," he murmured against her lips.

She sighed. "I was hoping every night that you would climb through the window in my bedroom and stay with me." Ursula's hands caressed the sensitive skin on his nape, sending a shiver racing down his spine.

"It was too risky. I would never have been able to leave your bed before sunrise if I had done that."

"I missed you."

In response, Oliver sank his lips back on hers, while his hands roamed her body. He palmed her breasts, teasing her sensitive nipples so they turned into hard peaks. When he ripped his mouth from hers, it was only so he could suck one hard peak into his mouth while kneading her warm flesh.

Farther south, his cock, fully erect and as hard as an iron bar, pressed against her thigh, eager to connect with her body. But he knew he couldn't allow himself to drive into her so soon. He wouldn't last long enough to make her climax.

He slid down her body, spreading her legs wide on his descent and settled between them. Her fingers dug into his shoulders in anticipation: she knew what was coming.

A strangled moan left her lips the moment he blew a hot breath against her sex. A lap of his tongue followed. When he tasted the dew that had already built on her plump nether lips, his entire body went rigid.

"Fuck, baby!"

It was better than he remembered. Her scent was a mixture of sweet and tangy flavors as it spread over the back of his tongue and down his throat. His nostrils flared, and the beast in him roared.

Bite her, now! the devil inside him demanded.

With difficulty, he pushed back the overwhelming desire to taste her blood and concentrated on licking her warm flesh. He spread her wider with his fingers, exposing her clit, then pressed his tongue onto it before sucking the tiny organ into his mouth.

Under his grip, he felt her jolt, but his hands held her down so she couldn't escape him. In long and languid strokes, he continued licking her clit and exploring her moist folds, while she twisted underneath him, her moans and sighs filling the room.

Her fingernails dug deeper into his shoulders, but he welcomed the pain. Had he been human, she would have drawn blood, but his vampire skin was too tough for her fingernails to pierce it.

Oliver listened to her heartbeat and the sound of her blood as it rushed through her veins, trying to pump more oxygen to her cells. Her body heated with every second that he continued to tease her tender flesh. He'd never been so attuned to the body of another being and had no trouble reading Ursula's body and understanding what she needed from him.

Her hips moved against his mouth in an unmistakable rhythm, asking for more. He was only too happy to comply with her demands. Gently, he drove a finger into her moist slit and intensified the pressure on her clit, licking her harder and faster. When she tensed, her body half lifting off the bed, he drove a second finger into her tight sheath and pulled her clit into his mouth, pressing his lips together.

She came, panting uncontrollably, her interior muscles gripping his fingers tightly, her body shivering.

If he were less impatient, he would allow her to rest for a moment, but patience was a foreign word to him now. He couldn't wait any longer. He pulled himself up and covered her with his body. His cock lined up with her still-quivering pussy, and with one thrust he seated himself in her.

On a moan, Ursula's eyes flew open. Then her hand came up, and one finger stroked over his lips.

"Show them to me."

His fangs had already descended. Slowly, he parted his lips and allowed them to emerge while he watched Ursula's reaction. She showed no fear.

"Touch them," he demanded.

Hesitantly, her finger slid against the outer side of one fang. He growled involuntarily, the sensation of Ursula touching him sending a bolt of electricity through him.

Her eyes widened, but instead of pulling her finger back, she stroked his fang once more. "Sink them into me. I want to feel you."

Ursula tilted her head to the side, exposing her pale neck. Breathing heavily, Oliver lowered his head to her neck, feeling her tremble when his lips touched her skin.

"Easy, baby, I won't hurt you."

He licked over her skin, then scraped his fangs against the spot where her plump vein beat against his lips. The contact made his cock jerk inside her, and he pulled his hips back, withdrawing almost completely. On his next thrust into her welcoming body, he drove his fangs into her neck, piercing her vein.

Her hot blood rushed into his mouth, overwhelming his taste buds. His mouth flooded with it. When the liquid ran over the back of his tongue and down his throat, his heart pumped faster. He'd never tasted anything as amazing. She tasted rich and pure, appeasing the beast inside him. With every drop he took, he felt himself grow stronger and more invincible. This was what he'd been searching for ever since he'd become a vampire. Ursula's blood.

He drove harder into her, his cock moving faster in and out of her clenching sheath. With every thrust he felt his excitement build and drive him closer toward ecstasy until he could hold back no longer. His orgasm broke, the sensation so powerful that he felt as if his body were shattering into a thousand pieces. As it ebbed, waves originating from Ursula's body crashed against him like a giant ocean wave.

Slowly, he pulled his fangs from her neck and licked over the incisions.

When he looked at her, he noticed her eyes covered in a wet sheen. Panicked, he pulled back. "Did I hurt you?"

She shook her head and sniffed. "I've never felt anything so beautiful."

He pressed a gentle kiss on her lips. "Me neither."

Then he rolled off her and pulled her into the curve of his body, her back connecting to his front, his arms holding her to him. For a long moment neither of them spoke. Only their heavy breathing could be heard in the room.

"Do you remember when the guard mentioned the code word at that truck stop?" Ursula suddenly asked.

"He said *emperors' blood*," Oliver answered, surprised that she would bring up this particular event at a time like this.

"My mother told me that we descend from the emperors' line. We're many generations removed from it, but I think if we checked on the ancestry of the other girls who were imprisoned with me, we'd find the same. It must be the emperors' blood that has the drugging effect."

Surprised at the revelation, he pressed a kiss to her shoulder. "Then it looks like I've fallen in love with a princess."

She turned her face to gaze at him, warmth and affection radiating from her eyes. "And it looks like I've fallen in love with a vampire."

He chuckled. "It would make a great movie. *The princess and the vampire*. I can see the movie posters already."

She turned in his arms and ran her hands down his body. "How about we work on the script a little more? I think this movie needs more steamy scenes."

Oliver rolled onto his back, pulling her on top of him. "I fully agree."

Then he drew Ursula's head down to him and captured her lips. He had no intention of releasing them any time soon.

~ ~ ~

ABOUT THE AUTHOR

Tina Folsom was born in Germany and has been living in English speaking countries for over 25 years, the last 14 of them in San Francisco, where she's married to an American.

Tina has always been a bit of a globe trotter: after living in Lausanne, Switzerland, she briefly worked on a cruise ship in the Mediterranean, then lived a year in Munich, before moving to London. There, she became an accountant. But after 8 years she decided to move overseas.

In New York she studied drama at the American Academy of Dramatic Arts, then moved to Los Angeles a year later to pursue studies in screenwriting. This is also where she met her husband, who she followed to San Francisco three months after first meeting him.

In San Francisco, Tina worked as a tax accountant and even opened her own firm, then went into real estate, however, she missed writing. In 2008 she wrote her first romance and never looked back.

She's always loved vampires and decided that vampire and paranormal romance was her calling. She now has 32 novels in English and several dozens in other languages (Spanish, German, and French) and continues to write, as well as have her existing novels translated.

For more about Tina Folsom:
http://www.tinawritesromance.com
http://www.facebook.com/TinaFolsomFans
http://www.twitter.com/Tina_Folsom
You can also email her at tina@tinawritesromance.com

Made in the USA
Middletown, DE
13 September 2017